SCOTT MICHAEL POWERS

THE MURDER PLAGUE

A DYSTOPIAN NOVEL

Black Rose Writing | Texas

This is a work of fiction. Names, characters, businesses, places, events, and incidents are either the products of the author's imagination or used in a fictitious manner. Any resemblance to actual persons, living or dead, or actual events is purely coincidental.

ISBN: 978-1-68513-368-9
LIBRARY OF CONGRESS CONTROL NUMBER: 2023944366
PUBLISHED BY BLACK ROSE WRITING
www.blackrosewriting.com

Printed in the United States of America
Suggested Retail Price (SRP) $21.95

The Murder Plague is printed in Gentium Book

*As a planet-friendly publisher, Black Rose Writing does its best to eliminate unnecessary waste to reduce paper usage and energy costs, while never compromising the reading experience. As a result, the final word count vs. page count may not meet common expectations.

ACKNOWLEDGEMENTS

First, I dedicate this book to my wife Connie, my first reader, my first editor, my most-trusted advisor, my problem solver, my well of confidence, my love.

I extend deep thanks to editor Shiela Shedd for bringing exceptional wordsmithing to this work.

I also thank all who read all or parts of this story in various drafts and provided invaluable comments. They included Martha Baker, David Buzan, Christy Cooper Burnett, Carolyn Geduld, Margaret Newkirk, Donna Nold, Margaret Ponsonby, Mark Powers, Carla D. Seyler, David Smigelski, and Geoff Sugerman.

Finally, thanks to publisher Reagan Rothe at Black Rose Writing and his whole team, with a particular toast toward David King for designing a cover that scared even me.

PRAISE FOR
THE
MURDER PLAGUE

"If you thought living through the Covid pandemic was like a years-long fever dream, get ready to feel that anxiety multiplied tenfold in The Murder Plague. A setting familiar to most readers and a cast of relatable characters give this dramatic novel a disturbingly intimate feel. … The Murder Plague is a chilling bloodbath that you'll binge from the edge of your seat."
–IndiesToday

"Powers delivers the suspenseful goods in a much too possible tale of viral apocalypse, supported by science and research, and populated by fully-realized characters. Scarcely a page goes by without a keen observation, a clever use of language, and big things to think about. I loved this book!"
–Kenneth Pelham, author of *Gumshoes, Fangs, Rockets, & Spies–How Literary Genres Evolve and Change Our World*

"*The Murder Plague* is a high stakes dystopian thriller with well developed characters and heart pounding action that will keep you turning the pages. Shocking twists and turns keep you at the edge of your seat until the end. The 'what if 'in this book scared me in the best possible way! You will remember it long after you read the last page."
–Christy Cooper-Burnett, author of *Passport to Terror*

"From the very beginning, The Murder Plague conjures a world where no one is safe and even the strong may not survive. Scott Michael Powers tells a frightening and realistic story of how easily life can deteriorate with a careless act. Compelling, three-dimensional characters give substance to a world that has changed beyond recognition. I couldn't put it down. Excellent read!"
–Carla D. Seyler, author of *A Place Unmade*

"Ripped-from-the-headlines thriller goes straight for the jugular. This is a frighteningly believable story that elevates pandemic fears into a sweat-inducing reading experience."
–David Buzan, author of *In the Lair of Legends*

"*The Murder Plague* is an interesting twist on the zombie genre. ... The plague is traced from patient zero, a microbiologist working in a contaminated lab, to her contacts and to the contacts of her contacts–each with his or her own story–spelling the silent spread of the virus among the novel's fully-rounded characters."
–Carolyn Geduld, author of *The Struggle*

THE
MURDER PLAGUE

PREVIEW

The open market across the street in the former grocery store parking lot offered some cover and a few escape paths. The landscaping included a handful of mature parking lot trees, short, but thick. At a dead run, Guy Phillips knew he could get from the booths and back around the corner of the old grocery store in about fifteen seconds.

The market covered a quarter of the lot, with a few dozen tables offering everything from fresh foods to soap—anything that might bring someone a buck.

Guy viewed the vendors and the thirty or forty people—including a few who were not there to buy, but to sell anything they had—with suspicion. Several men slung rifles or shotguns across their backs. Everyone certainly was armed. So was Guy. Armed was the new normal. What he watched for was someone who was positioning himself for offense. He could not make up his mind on anyone; he ventured forward anyway, out of necessity.

Guy could feel a demanding growl in his stomach, as empty as his pantry. He needed food, and this place offered it. He crossed the desolate street.

Guy was tall and lean. And he was black in a mostly white, gentrified neighborhood. He stood out in this crowd. His height gave him a clear view of everyone else. That height advantage and his slender build, honed once through running and now maintained on Pam's elliptical, gave him agility and confidence.

Guy's messy, receding hair, already grayed at age forty, topped a hickory-dark oval face. His eyes were olive shaped, his nose reedy. His mouth could open to what everyone used to describe as a beautiful smile with a blessing of naturally straight white teeth. But here, a hospital mask covered his mouth and nose.

His weapons: a Mossberg 500 six-shot, pistol-grip shotgun strapped across his back and a Ruger.22-caliber revolver sunk heavy in his dad-jeans pocket. He had found both. The Ruger came from some young man he'd encountered in a bar early on, maybe three months ago. He had pulled the Mossberg from under the decaying corpse of some fat guy he came across just down the street from here a couple of weeks ago. Six months ago, Guy had never even touched a gun. Now he had these and a couple more back in his house.

"You've got a shotgun! I've got shells!" declared a little man, white, in his twenties with a fluff of scraggly beard leaking out all sides of his mask. He shoved a plastic grocery bag up toward Guy's face. It was full of various-sized bullets and shotgun shells.

"I'm good," Guy said. He tried to step past him.

The man stepped in front of Guy.

"Please sir. I need..." the man pleaded. He shoved the bag upward again toward guy's face. "Please. Shells?"

Guy had boxes of them at home. Gun shops still operated. Yet he always went soft for the desperate. Back in the day, he routinely handed five-dollar bills out of his car window to people with cardboard signs. With a sigh, Guy felt his shoulders slump in submission to that same old compassion.

"You got seventy millimeter?" Guy asked.

The man dug around in the bag and came out with two. Guy gave him a five-dollar bill and dropped the shells into a Publix bag he had brought along. The man's eyes glittered as he thanked Guy over and over, backing away and then vanishing into the crowd.

The melons smelled good and Guy bought one. He gathered some cucumbers, asparagus, citrus, and tomatoes, and some fish that had no doubt come from one of the countless lakes that pockmarked the region. A woman vendor displayed home-plucked, whole chickens. Guy bought one, dropping it unwrapped into the bag.

Cash still worked fine. Six months ago, cash was going obsolete, replaced by apps and smart cards nearly everywhere. Not now. Not here, anyway. Unlike most people, Guy still had a job, so he still had cash.

Much of the city government services still functioned, especially the utilities. Guy was the plant engineer for the city utilities commission's main water plant. He, as much as anyone, kept the city's water flowing. Nowadays he tried to work from home like everyone else, by computer. He ventured to the plant a couple times a week. He hated that necessity.

He stepped back from the chicken table and saw the man. Guy's heart thumped violently and his skin burst with a fresh, cool glisten.

The man was just down the row, about ten yards away, so obviously troubled that he stood out like Guy.

White, about fifty years old, unmasked, clean-cut and shaven, in a button-down shirt and dress shorts, the guy looking around as if measuring the scene. His face tensed with anger, his eyes almost disappeared.

Guy put down his bag and tried to slide his shotgun off his back.

He reached too late.

The button-down man swung around an Uzi and opened rapid fire, spinning, spraying bullets. Screams erupted. People dove and ran, overturning tables, sending wares flying onto the pavement. The rattle of the gun punctuated shrieks and howls, crashes and chaotic scrambling. Someone returned fire. Guy almost had his own gun leveled when he felt a bullet blow through his right thigh.

The impact knocked him down. The pain, crushing and burning his leg, stunned him. Guy's brain clouded. He fought for breath and clarity and looked up to see the button-down man walking away from him, changing magazines. The man resumed shooting, with short bursts toward people crouching or lying on the ground. Guy heard other guns firing, but the Uzi did not stop. He gasped for a couple of deep breaths and his head cleared. He turned to reassess.

Behind button-down, a thick Hispanic woman in her forties—it was the chicken vendor—leaped from the ground and aimed a handgun. Pop, pop, and button-down went down. Shrieking cries through hyperventilation, but looking unharmed, she stepped over someone else to move closer to button-down. She fired two more shots, and Guy saw the second bullet kick off the side of button-down's skull, splashing the pavement with blood and gray matter.

It was over.

Just a few seconds. More than a dozen people shot, including Guy. He knew some would die. Police, emergency medical services and hospitals all still operated, but they were slim-staffed, overwhelmed, cautious, and unreliable.

Guy turned inward. With both hands, he grabbed his wounded leg. God. Damn. His thigh convulsed with every beat of his fluttering heart. It was the first time he had been shot. God. Damn. Could he survive? He was sure the bullet had missed his femur, but he was afraid it had nicked his femoral artery. Blood flowed fast in throbs, and it soaked his jeans to his shoe. He tried to stand, but stumbled and fell.

"Crap," he said.

He fished his phone from a pocket. He dialed 911. It rang and rang.

Finally, "This is 911. What is your emergency?"

"Shooting," Guy said in a deep exhale. He paused, coughing a breath. "I'm shot. Ten or fifteen other people hit. I dunno. Maybe more.

"Ugh," he coughed out.

His point was illustrated by the wailing, streamed profanities, and clatter as angry survivors scrambled to pack and get away.

The dispatcher had heard it all before.

An overturned table lay near him. Guy crawled over some oranges on the ground and leaned his back into the table.

The wait was mercifully short. In less than a minute, he heard sirens. He recognized them as police sirens. He wanted to hear fire trucks and medic squads. Still, police was a good start.

Guy slowly kicked off his shoes. He undid his jeans and pulled them down. They did not slide. Blood on his leg dragged at the fabric and forced him to peel the pants. It felt as if the denim took flesh with it.

He saw the wounds and his stomach swirled and flushed bile into his mouth. The bullet had blown clean through his thigh, about six inches below his crotch. Blood pumped out both sides with every heartbeat.

Should he tie a tourniquet? With what? His pants? For the first time, Guy wished he had a belt. Funny time for it, but he recalled his father's frequent harping that Guy never wore one. He panicked briefly, unsure how to tie a tourniquet. From his pants pockets, he retrieved his wallet, keys, and pistol and dropped them into the Publix bag. He tied the pants legs around his thigh the best he could. He pulled it tight. Guy screamed the indignant call of a wounded animal rising to angry life after just surviving.

He found a chair, set it upright and sat, stretching his searing leg.

A police car pulled into the parking lot just a few feet from the wreckage and carnage. Both cops got out, yelling angrily at each other as if they were more interested in some disagreement they brought from the car. Both wore full riot gear, heavily laden with bullet-proof padding and topped with helmets. Both grasped handguns in front of their faces. Guy watched them survey the scene and then help the first victim they encountered.

The first cop kneeled.

The second cop slowly swung his sidearm until he had it positioned behind the first cop's exposed neck. He fired and the first cop buckled and collapsed.

Guy's next heartbeat smashed against his forehead and his leg like a storm wave hitting a seawall. Then another. He dropped off his chair and panic-crawled behind an overturned table. Lying on his back, he cocked his shotgun and waited as he heard the cop methodically moving down that first row, shooting everyone who cried. Guy heard some rounds sounding different from the cop's gun, but the return fire did not interrupt the rhythm of the cop's Glock.

Nearly everyone who had not been shot by the first gunman had already fled. Only those unlucky people who could not get away had remained. The maimed. The already dead. The cop systematically finished them off. Bam. His gun was loud. Bam. Bam.

Guy could not run. He was not sure he could walk; he could barely stand. All he could do was lie in wait. His hands squeezed the Mossberg's butt stock against his forearm, slathered with so much sweat he feared the gun could slip from his trembling fingers.

He also heard more sirens. A mix of emergency sounds. Who would get there first? More cops? Would they stop this guy in time? Paramedics? They would not dare get out of their units. They would probably quickly assess and drive away like hell.

Bam. Bam. Pause. Bam. Bam.

And then the cop appeared. First the gun and then the riot helmet moved over the table. He contemplated Guy for a second. For just long enough.

Guy yanked his shotgun's trigger. The blast blew the cop off his feet and away. It also blew the gun right out of Guy's hands.

Then Guy heard the Uzi firing again for about two seconds.

"Looser!" a high-pitched man's voice screamed. "Goddamn you, pig!"

Guy retrieved his pistol from his bag. He pushed himself up over the table to see a short white man with silver hair standing over the cop. The cop lay dead. Surely dead. The man turned the gun toward Guy, who was now standing on one leg and holding the tabletop for support. Guy raised his arms, holding his Ruger pointing up. He hop-skipped to stay balanced on his good leg. The man nodded. Same team.

The man with the Uzi had taken a gut shot. His yellow "Yellow Dog Tavern," sleeveless shirt was red from the belly down. His blue cargo shorts were wet. His legs were bloody. Guy marveled for the moment at how the guy had gotten up at all, how he had managed to finish off the cop, let alone how he now still stood over him like a gloating linebacker. Adrenaline, Guy supposed, as in the stories about women who picked up trucks pinning six-year-old children.

"Nice shot," Yellow Dog squeaked to Guy. He turned back to the cop. "Loser!"

Yellow Dog gave the cop another burst. The gun reached clicking, empty. Yellow Dog shook it, clicked it again, dropped it. He collapsed to his left knee, and then his right. His power to lift trucks had drained away. Victory drained from his face. He turned to Guy.

"Least we stopped him, eh?"

Yellow dog breathed wrenching, troubled gasps.

"You'll make it," Guy said.

"Bullshit."

"The paramedics will be here soon. We'll be all right."

"Bullshit."

Bullshit was right. The sirens had disappeared. Word had probably spread back through the dispatcher. Scene not secure. No one else dared come. Not for a while.

Guy took his first long look around and listened. Nothing. Nothing moved. Nobody else crawled, or even moaned. Guy's lungs involuntarily pulled a deep, filling breath, like a yawn. He released it slowly, deliberately. He looked back at the man. Yellow Dog had slumped into a fetal position, grunting.

"Huh!" he said. "Huh."

Guy grasped the table, dragged his leg and managed to hobble. He put his bag and then his shotgun over his left shoulder and headed away, with no shoes or socks, his pants still tied around his bare, bloody leg. He lurch-stepped, his bad leg's foot tappy-tapping the pavement. He crossed the rest of the parking lot and the empty street, stopping once in the middle to pull the pants knot tighter. He headed down the street. Slowly. Awkwardly. Painfully. Step, tappy-tap. Step.

His right thigh was not the worst of it now. His heart raced. His head swooned. After about a block, he sat down on a bus bench.

On his phone, he requested a ride share, plotting a route to the nearest hospital's emergency room. People still drove ride shares. In the oddest ways, parts of the economy still operated, albeit without a lot of certainty. Some people needed rides. Some people needed cash. The law of supply and demand survived like a cockroach. Guy could only hope. Darryl in a White Highlander was four minutes out.

Guy tightened the pull on his pants knot again. Then he slumped on the bus bench. He had to lie down. Damn the cruel bench manufacturer for making a bench with an armrest in the middle to prevent people—the homeless, the weary—from doing exactly that repose. And to hell with the city for buying it. Or the bus agency. Whoever. He rolled onto the sidewalk.

Guy closed his eyes. He had to close his eyes. His heart raged like an obsolete boiler about to explode. His leg screamed. And now his stomach roiled. If he'd had any food there at all, it would be vomited onto the sidewalk. Thank God he had not eaten since yesterday sometime.

An SUV pulled up beside the bench. Guy managed to open an eye. The driver was a black man in his thirties. He honked, but Guy felt mute. He could only lift an arm and barely wave.

Carefully, the driver got out, handgun first. The man was bulked like a free-weights fanatic. Through a mask, he yelled, "Hey! You Guy? You coming, my friend?" Island Creole accent. Guy rolled his head. All he could do. The driver put on latex gloves and stepped close. He relieved Guy of his shotgun. He frisked Guy. He opened the bag and lifted out Guy's pistol. He shuffled through the food. He found Guy's wallet and counted out some cash. He stuffed the bills in his shirt. He put the bag and guns on his passenger seat.

"Fare," the driver called out to Guy, as if it mattered. "And tip."

Guy was somehow okay with that charge. He had sunk to a state of agonizing immobility that left him ready to be okay with just about anything. Whatever, now, let it come.

"All right," the driver said, his voice slow and deep, as if he were plotting as he spoke. "I'm going to take care of you, my friend."

He opened the SUV's hatch. He untied Guy's pants. He put Guy's wallet and cellphone in pockets, and then he tied the pants legs back on, tighter than Guy himself had done.

Guy wanted to scream, but he did not have it in him anymore. Pain slithered like snakes in his veins, unchallenged now, conquering. The driver hoisted Guy. He rolled him into the back of the SUV and slammed the hatch.

They arrived at the hospital emergency room driveway in just a couple of minutes. The driver lifted Guy and laid him gently on the sidewalk. He scampered back into his vehicle and pulled away just as two armed hospital security officers emerged to see what was delivered.

PART 1

CHAPTER 1

DAY 8: FRIDAY, APRIL 19

On an evening nearly six months before Guy Phillips was shot, Mae Louise Vicar found herself working late, as usual.

Soon, the young microbiologist would earn two claims to infamy. The first, as the most loathsome mass-murderer in these parts since the madman Omar Mateen shot up an Orlando gay nightclub, killing forty-nine. Then, a few weeks after Mae Louise Vicar herself was dead, she would become known as the start of it all, Patient Zero of the Murder Plague, or Typhoid Mae, as the media came to call her.

But none of that horror had happened yet, that tragic future unimaginable on this beautiful spring day of routine work to be followed by partying tonight. On this day, the young woman raised by Tom and Ann Vicar of Xenia, Ohio, was a source of nothing but pride and joy shared by her parents, her friends, her colleagues, her church, and her community.

Tom and Ann's daughter was thirty years old, tall and willowy, with flowing blond hair framing a fair, triangular face with deep cobalt eyes. Mae Louise Vicar drew stares any time she wanted them; other times she dressed down to play the part of her profession: brilliant scientist.

In her mind, she was no angel, not proud at all of many of the things she had done. Small, meaningless indiscretions that stung her self-esteem.

On this day, Mae Louise Vicar—Mae to her coworkers, Mae-Lu to her friends, Mae Louise to her family, and Dr. M.L. Vicar to her publishers—tried hard and hoped harder to get her work done in time meet friends for dinner, drinks and dancing. Specifically, the plan covered dinner with Kanetha, Margaret and Danielle, and then? Who knows what after that beginning?

Mae was a microbiologist at a shiny medical research institute, the Nona Institute of Medical Investigation, NIMI, to the press. In a post-COVID world, NIMI sucked in a stack of federal National Institutes of Health research grants into viral engineering. Money for the taking. The NIMI campus overflowed with state-of-the-art equipment and a bounty of bright young researchers, Mae included.

Mae worked in a small but critical lab halfway up NIMI's eight floors of tiered granite and glass, in an awkwardly underdeveloped office park local leaders had dubbed Medical City, rising from a vista of vacant, former pastureland on the city's outskirts.

Mae worked with a small team trying to identify genetic characteristics of highly contagious strains of deadly viruses, tinkering with their DNA. They sought ways of turning off the infectious nature by adjusting how the microbes interacted with receptors in human cells. Mae labored with a benign but particularly vicious form of a virus, a relative of both German measles and demyelinating encephalomyelitis.

Her task today: cataloging data she and her supervisor Dr. Crosby—Tim, though he asked everyone to call him Dr. Crosby—had drawn out in the lab last week. This stage involved desk work. Mostly, she performed mathematical analysis, working with tables of thousands of data. Sorting, querying, quantifying, seeking outliers, means, outliers of means, and running regressions. It was also her work yesterday. And the day before. All week, in fact. Who knew lab work could be so painfully tedious?

She smiled at that thought and pushed hair out of her eyes. She was good at this work. This drudgery was her thing. But she was tired, and she was beginning to fear there might be little chance she'd be finished on time tonight, as Dr. Crosby, Tim, she grinned, had demanded.

Her cell phone rang. She knew it would be Kanetha. She looked. Yep. It was Kanetha.

"Darling! Wait until you see this little teal dress I'll be wearing tonight. Smokin'!"

Kanetha Wilson played the leader of their little ring. Mae-Lu was her project. Tonight's gathering was Kanetha's party, and Mae knew she would put up a fight.

"Hey, Kanetha… I don't think I'm going to make it."

"Don't tell me that, girl! This is my goodbye thing. I'm in charge and I say—"

"I know. I just—"

"No, you do not know," snapped Kanetha, who could elevate psychological intimidation to a profession. "I'm leaving Sunday for two weeks. I need this, and I need you to be there. For me."

"I get that, but I—"

"It's for you too, girl. Look. You blew us off last time. You think you can spend all your time working? You're wrong, girl. You need to have a little fun. And I need my Mae-Lu time."

"But Doctor Cros—"

"Hold it right there, girlfriend. That boss of yours is abusing you. Look around, girl. Anyone else still there? Hmmm? I did not think so. He knows he can push you because you let him push you. You got to stand up for yourself. It's Friday night! Besides, I need you sitting next to me so that I look that much better. Understand? And don't wear that short number with the flowers; it looks too good on you. Just wear your LBD."

The phone died, and with it Mae's resolve to complete her work. It was true that Kanetha was leaving for two weeks, but that absence was hardly long enough to demand a goodbye party. And yet

Kanetha knew how to push the one button that always tilted Mae: guilt. Just like Dr. Crosby did. Be there for me. I need you there, she'd said.

Mae stretched her neck, leaning her head over the back of her chair. She took a long look at the ceiling lights. This commitment to duty was not what Mae wanted; it never was about what Mae wanted. What did Mae want? To party? Dance? Maybe meet some guy? Not particularly; she could live with or without it. To complete her report then? There'd just be another after that cycle. It all was an endless progression. Then what was it she wanted? Would it always be about doing what she was told by Dr. Crosby? By Kanetha? She sighed and leaned back toward her computer screen. The data swam by, unconcerned. She'd lost this battle. She saved and booted down.

• • •

To get to the nightclub in the heart of the city's tourist district, she had to park in one of Universal Orlando Resort's enormous garages, and then follow a series of escalators and moving sidewalks for what seemed like a mile. At eight on a Friday night, the scene thickened with crowds. Exhausted tourists dragging tired kids wearing "Thing 1" and "Thing 2" tee shirts, headed out, while the city's resident partiers headed in. Outdoors, the resort played bone-breaking rock music at full blast over an artfully hidden sound system.

Even after years of wearing high heels, she still did not like them, but she had finally got pretty good at walking in them. Clop, clop, clop. She stood tall enough already, and the heels put her up to six feet. Her body was well-gymed, her hair fell loose, dropping flared golden locks just over her shoulders. Her features, already fairly pronounced, especially her high cheekbones, popped thanks to blood-red lipstick, dark mascara just a dab of rouge. She looked like a young Lauren Bacall.

She picked her black dress, because that is what Kanetha told her to wear. Mae really had no idea what to do, other than what Kanetha said.

The effect worked. Men turned heads as she passed. Clop, clop, clop.

Kanetha and the other girls waited in front of the second entrance along nightclub row. Kanetha, as usual, looked deadly, with her tawny skin, shoulder-length, red-highlighted hair pulled into a mix of box braids and curls, and that stunning teal dress she mentioned, which dropped diagonally from her left shoulder and again from her right hip. Margaret, pale-skinned, and as tall as Mae but with short, walnut hair, looked more business-like in a white dress with a high neckline and black sleeves. Danielle, with almost umber skin, was shorter by several inches, and wore a yellow sheath that fell straight from her shoulders to her thighs. Her heels made her big butt stick out. Kanetha surely would tell her that point, if she had not already.

They greeted each other with cheek kisses.

A line fifteen or twenty partiers deep snaked from the door. It did not matter for them. Margaret worked at the resort as a planning executive; she always hustled them straight in. That sway did not necessarily mean a table immediately, but Margaret and her friends never stood on the plaza waiting to get into a club. Not there.

Margaret's verve pushed Mae's guilt button just a little. She wondered if Margaret bent rules by throwing her influence around for their benefit, and if she might get into trouble if ever reported. But maybe that push is just the way things worked, and Mae did not mind the special treatment. She was just worried about her friend's well-being.

They pushed through. Some young man with the silliest attempt at a thin beard protested with a "Hey!" and Margaret responded with, "Chill, dude." Kanetha blew the guy a kiss.

"He's kinda cute," she said to Danielle.

Danielle hardly ever spoke. She nodded and then ducked through the door, just ahead of Mae.

Partiers already crowded the place. Margaret found a table on the back patio and immediately summoned a server. They had eaten there often enough to know the menu and their favorites.

Their drinks arrived swiftly and Margaret, being Margaret, raised a toast.

"To the children of Malawi, may they get this new care center, all that Kanetha can teach, and may they survive her bitchy sense of humor."

They clinked glasses.

"And may they be easier to deal with than you three princesses," Kanetha replied.

Volunteer work, with an international aid organization called His Children, linked the four friends. It cemented their friendships and gave them plenty to talk about. Danielle and Kanetha had known each other for years; they had joined the organization together. Margaret's corporate volunteer services office had steered her to His Children, and Mae had arrived through her church.

They volunteered a few weekends a year raising money or gathering goods—food, medical supplies, education supplies, clothing. Each of them also spent two weeks every other year traveling overseas to help build, teach and organize. They worked to create schools, medical clinics, day care centers, and sometimes simple shelters. A network of churches fueled the effort.

Food and drinks came and went, and the evening heated up. The table Margaret had grabbed was next to an outdoor dance floor. The house reggae band cooked, and the four women were the center of attention Kanetha wanted. Early on, Mae knew that she and Kanetha would end the night calling for an Uber ride, again, so neither of them showed much caution.

Shortly before midnight, Mae danced with some guy from California named Ben, who was in town for an internet advertising sales conference at one of the conference hotels. Kanetha sat at their table, hooting at her. Mae heard, gave Kanetha a cat-like smile, and put her palms on Ben's chest. She shimmied her rear, dropping into a crouch. He reached down and lifted her back up by her arms. His arms were strong; his lift not just effortless but in time with the music. She let their hands rise above her and she used that axis as a pivot point to pirouette... fully in her zone.

Mae imagined spending the night with this guy. Never about her, huh? Well, why not? What could they say if she had her little moment? Kanetha would tell her it was her idea all along, that Mae-Lu needed a night of wild abandon. She needed a little something. Who was Mae to disagree with that logic? When she had gotten up from the table a few minutes earlier, Mae had felt the alcohol rush, but now she was feeling something else. An awakened energy, a longing. She looked back again toward her friends and stuck out her tongue. It lasted a millisecond before Mae realized she was acting drunk and withdrew it. She turned back to Ben; his eyes and closed-mouth smile were warm as the heat rising within her. She gave him a light kiss, and he slid his hands along her sides.

Kanetha whooped. When Mae looked back at her friend, Kanetha took a picture with her cell phone. Danielle was dancing too, saw, and giggled into her hand. Mae pulled away and spun around again, her arms twirling at length.

On the backswing, her left hand popped a middle-aged woman hard in the face.

Mae did not notice, but the woman's husband did. He reached out and grabbed Mae's arm, stopping her spin. She stumbled and twisted her ankle, losing a shoe. The husband held onto Mae's arm, trying to keep her from falling, but it only made matters worse. She fell on her hip hard as the man tried to steady her, and he wound up getting tangled in her frantic limbs. He fell too, right on top of her.

When the guy regained his feet, Ben was in his face. The husband pointed to his wife, who was dabbing blood from her lip with her hand, weeping and looking horrified, playing the drama queen.

"She hit my wife!"

"It was an accident!" Ben said.

"I'm sooooo sorry," Mae wailed from the floor.

The man held Mae's wrist, as if he would help her up, but as she tried to rise she yanked her hand loose, stumbled backwards a couple of steps, and fell into a waiter carrying a full tray of fresh drinks.

As Mae rolled, Ben gave the husband a shove to walk past him to get to Mae. The guy tackled him and they went down.

Back at the table, Kanetha and Danielle were up, screaming. Margaret sank onto the table, hiding her face in her hands.

"I'm soooo sorry," Mae said to the waiter, who was squatting, gathering broken glass around him. She picked up an empty Red Label bottle next to her, examined it, finished the third left in the bottle, and then set it on his tray on the floor.

"I'm really, really sorry," she said to the woman who still was dabbing her lip with her palm, smearing her lipstick all over her chin.

Mae thought that whimper was funny and laughed her little girl giggle.

The woman gave Mae the finger. Suddenly, Mae was no longer sorry. She offered a finger back.

Ben struggled out of the man's hold, flipped, and was on him. The dance floor cleared around them. Two bouncers pushed through. Ben had the husband rolled and pinned. He punched the guy's face just as the bouncers reached them. One grabbed each of Ben's shoulders and pulled him off.

Ben was a medium-sized man, but he had big shoulders and arms. He shrugged them off with a trained move, and the bouncer's hands flew from his arms. Ben put up his hands, palms out. No more trouble here. Yet the other guy, still on the floor, grabbed Ben around the ankles and tried to tackle from there. Ben stepped out of it and one bouncer grabbed the husband, yanking him to his feet.

"You need to come with us," ordered the bleached bouncer, big enough to back up his command.

Mae was up now, holding her shoes in her hands, careful to step, because there was broken glass on the floor. She felt her ankle give way just a little.

"Let's get out of here," Ben said.

He grabbed her arm and headed for the door. A bouncer followed. So did Kanetha, Danielle and Margaret, but they were on the other side of a crowd.

Ben and Mae got to the front walk outside just as they saw the Universal security officers approaching. They turned and ducked the other way.

"Are you alright?" Ben asked.

"I twisted my ankle, but it's getting better as I walk," she said.

"Pricks," he said.

She looked him in the face, hard and close.

"You're a wrestler." It was not a question.

"Did it show?"

"Yeah, but that's not it. It's your ears," she giggled. "You've got wrestler's ears. I dated a wrestler in college."

He put his hands over his ears. They were swollen, puffy, deformed.

"I love them. They're a man's ears," she said, emphasizing man. She pulled his left hand off his ear and kissed his lobe. She felt that kiss surge through her like an electric shock.

They circled the resort's lagoon and then took a ferry along the canal, back to his hotel. They sat at the edge and he put his arm around her. The moon was out. It was nearly full. The noise of the entertainment district drifted off behind them. It felt to Mae as if they could be on a canal in Venice, though she had never been there. She kissed his right ear this time, and he turned and took her into a full kiss. She closed her eyes, and for a moment, she was afloat in another world.

In his room, Ben pulled off his shirt, revealing broad arms, a full rack of shoulders, and a muscular chest. Mae responded by sliding out of her dress as quickly as she could, then reaching around and dropping her bra. Mae always undersold herself. She worked out hard and ran hard, and she offered him an hourglass body with strong hips and taut legs. He wrapped his arms around her thin waist and lifted. She wrapped her legs around his waist, lifting her breasts to his mouth where his lips and he gave her nipples all the attention she could want. He carried her over and placed her on the bed.

Ben was a physical lover with an athlete's strength and stamina. She smiled and tossed her hair in a fun, flirtatious motion. She dropped her head backward, closed her eyes and imagined they were somewhere else, somewhere far, far away, in a place where there was only them, in a time where there was nothing else. They were on a desert island. No. They were in a small cottage on the outskirts of Paris.

When Mae made love, it was always in her own imagined paradise.

This man might call her tomorrow, but she would not answer. He would leave tomorrow, or perhaps Sunday, like the millions of others who came to her town every year. That disregard was all right with her. She preferred that there be no tomorrow to worry about. And she figured it had to be all right with him, too.

Kanetha was right. She needed this release.

Sleep came, but only briefly. Shortly, she awoke next to this stranger, and the elusive fantasy she had been living faded with the night. She could picture it, but she could not summon it back. The old guilt knife pricked at her, and she knew she would lie there awake a while. It had nothing to do with Ben, or any man. Her thoughts drifted away from her Paris cottage, back into her day life. Part of it was the alcohol, the bright glow of a fresh intoxication taking a darker turn now in her disoriented brain. But her guilt framework? That shadow was well-established.

She had promised Dr. Crosby she would finish that data analysis this week, yet she did not. She could have. It would only have taken a couple more hours, but she did not.

Mae tossed. She turned. She tried to convince herself that she worked hard enough and shouldn't hold herself to some unreasonably high standard. But this remorse was not about how hard or how efficiently she worked. Dr. Crosby was counting on reviewing the results for a planning meeting, and now he could not. Counting on her...but no. Even that coming moment was not the source of her growing unease. What bothered her, simply, was she had promised something, could have delivered on it, but she did not. And for what? For this indiscretion? She was ashamed.

• • •

Silly Mae.

If she had possessed any idea how hard Tim Crosby had screwed her—and not in a good way—she would have realized her concern was beyond petty.

Because while Mae fretted over her broken word, Dr. Crosby was at a conference in Chicago, partying well, sleeping well, and being paid well.

Before he left, he had slept well all week at home in bed with his wife. He had all last week too; in fact, Mae and her lab work never entered his mind once the clock struck five.

He had even slept well at home the night he had accidentally broken the seal on one of their latest genetically engineered virus strains and had said nothing to her or anyone else.

Broke it outside the cleanroom. Never reported it; never acknowledged it in any way.

Oh, he had resealed the damned tube, but did not decontaminate the area. Ignored protocol. Defied safety. Left the lab, closed the door, and rushed away, half-intending to come back later in his clean suit to decontaminate, but then finding it was too late. Maybe he would do it tomorrow, if he had the chance.

Mae had entered behind him to do a little late-night task. She had set herself to work at the exact spot he had been working with the should-have-been-sealed sample. The vial sat in the rack before her that day. It had been compromised. The whole damned room was now compromised. He was compromised. She was compromised.

The world was compromised, but no one could know that terror. And all Dr. Crosby could do at the point when he saw Mae in there was pretend it had never happened. Self-preservation required Dr. Crosby to conclude at that moment there was absurdly low risk of infection compared with the likely prospect that he might get caught and summarily fired for his flagrant and reckless violation of safety protocol.

And he had other plans. He had Chicago.

The stuff was benign. Surely. Surely.

(All the data up to that point said so.)

Though this series of virus units were contagious through airborne exposure, there was very little chance that he or Mae or anyone else could have gotten infected just by sitting near (or in this case, the same place) where the vial was opened.

Thousand-to-one anyone was infected; another thousand-to-one it would matter. Dr. Crosby figured good living would reward him that day with at least that short-odds victory.

He kept his mouth shut and waited until Mae was done, and everyone had cleared out. Then he slipped back into the room and decontaminated everything.

It was Mae's unlucky day. Eventually, that day would be identified as Day 1.

The virus already was affecting her in ways no one could have imagined and would in ways no one dared fear.

On this eighth day, she was highly infectious. She had just infected Ben Wester from Los Angeles, her friends, and who knows how many other people on the crowded sidewalks of a tourist resort, the crowded nightclub and the dance floor.

To think she was worried about disappointing Dr. Crosby on Monday morning when he learned she had not worked late Friday to finish crunching the data he wanted. Mae tossed in bed again and stared at this man, this stranger, breathing slowly and deeply beside her. She hated herself right now.

She glanced at a clock. It was 1:51 a.m. Not that anybody was counting yet, but it was now Day 9.

In a crowded conference hotel in downtown Chicago, Dr. Tim Crosby slept peacefully.

CHAPTER 2

DAY 15: FRIDAY, APRIL 26

Mae Louise Vicar had been in a pissy mood for several days and it was only getting worse. It was not her fault. Everything was going wrong. Everyone was acting stupid.

For starters, her research partner and boss, Dr. Crosby, was pulling rank, pushing her to do more than her share of the grunt work on the data analysis. Her neighbors let their dog bark incessantly last night, and when she pounded on their apartment door and complained, the man called her a bitch. He actually drew her into a shouting match right there in the hallway. When her internet went down on Wednesday, the phone tech somewhere on the other side of the planet was an absolute idiot, and Mae just had to scream at him. Everyone else, everywhere she went, was rude or inconsiderate or a real pain in the ass. No one was doing what they should. It was as if the entire world had taken an asshole pill. Every driver, it seemed, was going out of their way, cutting her off in traffic. The grocery store clerk worked the line in front of her so slowly it had to be deliberate. What was wrong with these people?

No planetary misalignments. No full moon. The weather was pleasant and steady.

And then came this morning's call from Kanetha. The African village she was in had no phone service, no cell phone, no Internet.

But her team had a satellite phone link and each team member got call rights. Kanetha called her girl Mae-Lu today. The news was not good.

Mae was expecting the call, waiting by her computer, when the alert popped up and Kanetha's face appeared.

"Hey girl! How's it going?" Mae asked.

"We're screwed, sweetie. The equipment never arrived. We've got piles of wood and bricks, but we can't level the area without a Bobcat, and we can't build anything without the cement mixer."

"What happened?"

"That piece of ratshit Bernden happened. That's what happened. He was supposed to transfer the sponsor money to the contractor, but it never arrived."

"Why not?"

"He says there were international banking issues. Bullshit."

"Bullshit!" Mae agreed. Then she looked Kanetha in the eye and repeated it louder, expressing anger that suddenly swelled like a bubble and popped inside her. She felt anger surge through her arteries. "Bullshit! He's done this before!"

"So we're stuck."

They stared at each other through the computer screens. Kanetha rubbed her forehead.

"How are the kids?" Mae asked.

"Great. Great. They're great."

That was the beauty of video conferencing. Mae could see the lie as easily as if they were sitting together on a couch.

"Tell me the truth, Kanetha."

"Geez, shit, Mae-Lu. Times have been tough here. There's a drought. Right? Things are shit, you know? And what little crops they've been able to salvage, the damn district authorities have raided. Half the people are gone, Mae-Lu. Almost all the men, some of the women, they've gone off to make money."

"Who's watching the kids?"

Kanetha shook her head.

"How's Carlos?"

Carlos was not exactly the boy's given name. Kanetha and Mae had never been sure how to pronounce his name, and no one had ever written it down before they had, so they wrote Carlos, called him Carlos, so Carlos it was. It was something close, anyway. He was a precocious ten-year-old that Kanetha had discovered on her previous trip, and passed along to Mae to watch over when she went last October. The boy was an impossible flirt, always hitting on one of them in the sweetest imaginable way, with big, bright eyes he could roll like billiard balls. The kid had a rare heart for anywhere in the world. He was always the first to offer to help, first to show sympathy and give support, first to share his food with others. It was not just his way of getting attention, though he enjoyed anyone's attention. Carlos lived to help people. He would give the shirt off his back. Literally. He only had one shirt at a time. Mae brought him an Orlando Magic jersey, and he took off the shirt Kanetha had given to him months earlier and presented that shirt to another boy.

Kanetha looked away from the screen.

"How's Carlos, Kanetha?"

Kanetha looked down. Mae's face tightened. She squeezed her hands into fists.

"Goddamn it, Kanetha! How's our kid?"

"He was gone when I got here," Kanetha replied softly. She looked around as if someone were watching. She moved her face tight into the screen. "I don't know the full story. They say he got sick. He... Shit, Mae-Lu. You know Carlos. He was probably giving his food to other kids. He got sick. He died."

Kanetha looked away. She looked back at the screen. "It happens. It happens here all the time," she said. "Shit happens, baby. Kids like Carlos die. All the damn time. Get over it."

"Don't tell me to get over it!" Mae screamed. "Okay, this really sucks of you, Kanetha. How dare you tell me Carlos died; there's no possible way. How dare you! You lie! That is a sick joke, Kanetha. Take it back!"

Kanetha's eyes were glazed and her cheek jerked as she fought off a sob.

"I gotta go, girl. Love you. Bye."

Kanetha's hand moved to the screen, and her image dropped away.

Mae's scream began as a low growl, then rolled up her throat and out of her open mouth. All her muscles tensed. She wanted to hit something. She picked up a table lamp and threw it onto the floor, smashing the glass body and the bulb and crushing the shade. She put her face in her hands and waited for the tears. They did not come. They were not coming. She pounded the table with a fist. Once, twice, the third time hard, rocking it.

She grabbed her keys and headed out. She strode down the corridor from her apartment to the elevator as if in a hurry. The elevator took forever to arrive. When it finally opened, those two goddamn kids from somewhere upstairs, both just a little older than Carlos, each with more shirts than they would ever need. Shirts from Park Avenue boutiques, not from a box from an aid organization. Enough shirts for that whole goddamned village! They ran past her, laughing. She stepped into the elevator and saw that the boys had pushed all the floor buttons. The building had eleven floors. Mae lived on eight.

She kicked the door open as it tried to close and saw the boys look over their shoulders at the noise of her kick.

"Assholes!" she shouted.

The shorter one flipped her the finger and the skinny, dark-haired boy ravished with zits laughed like a spoiled brat.

She almost went after them. Instead, Mae pounded on the door close button. Finally, the elevator began to move and Mae became aware, alone in the car, that she was taking quick, deep breaths. The elevator dropped to seven, to six, to five, to four, and each time the door opened, she could feel anger simmering within her. At three, she got out. That floor was the parking garage level. She saw the boys walking toward the back exit of the garage. They had taken the stairs down. They were smoking.

"Hey!" she yelled at them.

"Piss off, bitch!" the short kid yelled back with a voice that was breaking. Then he and his friend disappeared through the stairwell door.

Mae's Explorer squealed tires as she backed out. Inside the garage, the sound reverberated like a rubber scream.

Out on the street, the stoplights were like the elevator buttons. Every. Damn. One. Of. Them. Red. Mae gripped the steering wheel hard. She was frustrated enough to kill it. To kill something.

Damn it, she thought.

Damn it.

Mae's fury felt electric. The world was moving entirely too slowly for her mood. Everything was entirely too quiet. Mae turned on the radio and found a heavy-metal station. She never much liked metal music, but right now she needed something that matched her rage. She cranked it up.

Not enough. She turned it all the way. The windows of the SUV vibrated, yet still it was not enough.

She entered a school zone and slowed to twenty miles per hour, irked at yet another delay. She could feel the car's energy dissipate through her foot. Her leg shook with anticipation.

Mae passed an elementary school on her left and watched as the children made their way into a little landscaped field next to the parking lot, where they were congregating. This district was a pleasant neighborhood, and those kids had it easy. Damn them, she thought. Not one of them ever would go without a meal. Not one of them would ever see their fathers go off to work on some remote pipeline for months at a time to earn less money than these kids got for Christmas presents. Not one of them would ever see their mothers go off to the cities to prostitute themselves so the family could have a little money to get through the next few days. Not one of them would give a shirt off his back. Not one of them would starve himself to death so that some little sister could have something to eat.

Nope. These kids just made people late for work, flipped off their neighbors, called them bitches and smoked cigarettes. Damn them all.

Damn them, she thought as she drove past. Clearing the opposite school zone line, she gunned the Explorer and felt the power of the big V-6 roar through her body as the vehicle jumped from twenty to forty miles per hour.

Adrenaline and norepinephrine flooded Mae's body, clanging alarms. Her heart pushed hard. Her muscles thickened with extra blood. Her joints cocked like a sprinter's, waiting for the gun. Her breaths came full and quick. Her brain sucked in oxygen until her thoughts stampeded, tripping over each other unfinished.

Her second level of chemical messaging fired. Dopamine surged her brain's frontal cortex, demanding action, seeking overwhelming pleasure, a seemingly improbable outcome, given her anger.

Where was the serotonin? Had there been a supervisor at her helm, she would have shouted desperate calls for the chemical that serves as the brain's emotional thermostat. That valve was closed. Without it, misdirected yet unchallenged rage pulsated through Mae.

She had never felt more keenly perceptive.

She opened the windows so the radio would play outside. Now people on the street were rocking. Yeah, baby.

Her mind flipped again to those pretty little shit stains playing in the schoolyard. How dare they? She could just kill them all. She could turn this Explorer around, drive over the sidewalk, and hunt them down as easily as running over a paper cup on the road. Nothing in her brain protested this idea. Her rage-fueled mind was popping too much to let dissenting thoughts appear long enough to be considered.

She needed to make a statement. She needed action. Now.

She was a block past now, but she could feel the decision being made. Now or never. The kids would go inside in a few minutes. Decision has been made, she told herself.

Damn it all.

Mae made a screeching U-turn at the next intersection, hoping she was not too late. Stopping no longer was an option. She drove back toward the school, slow enough to not draw attention. She fought to manage the pent-up energy waiting in her throttle leg. She entered the school zone and slowed to twenty.

There was an opening about forty feet wide between a fence at her end of the schoolyard and a cluster of trees. Beyond the trees there was another twenty-five yards of grass before a low wall lining a parking lot. The kids were entering the yard, but they were not yet heading toward the building. This undertaking was before-school social time. Billie-likes-Suzie-but-Suzie-likes-Johnny garbage. Dozens of children milled.

Mae plotted her course.

She gunned the SUV. It hopped the curb as if it were a speed bump.

If there were little screams, Mae did not hear them over the brain-crunching music coming from seven speakers.

She had two little girls in her sights just past the curb, and she mowed them down like weeds. She felt the bumps as the big Michelins rolled over their bodies and the bouncing excited her. She turned the wheel slightly to the right and plowed through a crowd of four or five children; she was not counting. They just stood there, naively in shock, like they were waiting their turn. And Mae had given it to them. She turned to the left, not quick enough, and banged the right passenger door and rear quarter panel against a live oak tree, but redirected her course.

She felt the tree collision in her head, and that smack pissed her off.

She chased two boys running with flailing arms. One went under the grill and the other came over the hood. She saw his expression of sheer horror and agony as his little face smashed into her windshield, cracking it right under the rear-view mirror.

Mae turned to the right, and the broken body rolled over the hood and fell. A group of children huddled in frozen terror near the parking lot wall, and she drove straight at them. Some kids got over the wall, but two or three were not so quick. She braked just before she hit them and the wall, so that she hit them hard enough to squish them, but not hard enough to set off the airbag or smash the wall behind them.

And then she threw the Explorer into reverse and backed up quick and hard. She ran over something, probably a child she never saw. The thump, thump of her tires made her laugh hysterically.

Mae's little girl laugh, a high-pitched giggle, could not be heard over the radio, but it felt good.

Now she saw trouble and focused on it.

The city assigned a police officer to every school. He was at the wrong place when Mae had started her rampage at the opposite end of the school. But he was here now, running from the parking lot with his service revolver out and pointed at her.

Go on. Bring it, Mae thought.

She threw the vehicle back into drive and turned toward him. She floored it and the SUV threw up sod. It lurched toward the officer and sped up. Mae screamed giggles like someone on a wild amusement park ride.

Officer Tyler Sizemore, it would be reported later, had graduated from the academy just four months earlier. He aimed. He waited a beat. Two beats.

Mae drove, picking up speed. She screamed like a warrior attacking from a foxhole.

He fired.

•   •   •

Two bullets exploded her windshield, one blew through Mae Louse Vicar's neck, smashing her spine. She slumped against the wheel. Her foot flopped from the gas pedal. The vehicle coasted, turned, and then butted hard against the wall she had hit earlier, punching down a section of concrete debris. It stopped there.

Behind her, broken, bleeding and dead children lay all over the grass. Adults from seemingly everywhere converged, running towards the carnage. Inside the SUV, the radio station switched to a payday loan agency's commercial, offering quick and easy cash for anyone, at one hundred and ten decibels. Outside the Explorer, moans and shrieks and cries turned the schoolyard into the heart of Hell.

Mae heard none of it. Officer Sizemore's bullet had turned off her heart, her neurotransmitter and hormone flows, her brain, everything. Her rage went out with a pop, like an old-fashioned lightbulb. She was at peace, a lightless, senseless peace. Her body slumped, held in place by her shoulder belt. Her head tilted over the belt, her glassy-eyed stare aligned with the radio. A bloody airbag sagged into her lap.

Five children were dead at the scene and two more would die in hospitals over the weekend. Six others were injured. Four of them would never fully recover.

Their names, their pictures, and the interviews with their sobbing mothers and vengeful fathers haunted the nation. The dead included the sisters Hannah and Samantha Kellogg, ages seven and eight; Octavio Diaz, nine; Marisa Coleman, six; David Pinar, seven; Caleb Lindley, nine; and Jordan Moore, seven.

Their family's losses became the community's, the city's, and the nation's.

Orlando had endured such pain before, on that June morning at the Pulse nightclub. The city had suffered far more horror in that first atrocity. Still, this tragedy was no easier.

Every senseless massacre hits distanced people as if they were personally involved. This one, with these precious, innocent little babies, caused reciprocal agony everywhere. It seemed, for the many, many people touched by the carnage, that the next few days passed only because time, the apathetic constant, had to continue.

A wrenching memorial service at Colonial Baptist Church, where the Kellogg and Diaz families attended, was broadcast live. Malory Kellogg broke the nation's heart with a poignant eulogy to her daughters, keying on fine details like Samantha's curious insistence on wearing only one sock. Her emotional speech made the girls seem both personal and universal, turning them into everyone's daughters. She also spoke, ominously and presciently, of a hole opening up in the world, draining away joy and all that is good. Next, Little Octavio's uncle, Julian Diaz, spoke with fire and brimstone anger, an anger so heartfelt and passionate that it aroused the nation.

"Why? Why? Why!?" he demanded repeatedly. The church responded with silence. No answer emerged. Not yet.

During a hymn, David Pinar's mother Maria had to be carried from the church, hysterical and completely inconsolable, on national TV. The scene played over and over, all over the world.

Orlando was a city that understood unity in tough times. From the site of the Pulse nightclub to the downtown performing arts center to the university's fountain, vigils drew tens of thousands. Once again. People with absolutely no connection to the victims gathered and prayed, and sang, and wept, and hugged, because gathering and praying and singing and weeping and hugging were things they could do. And they all needed to do something.

At the scene of the crime, a spontaneous memorial shrine gathered under the tree Mae had scraped. Flowers, crosses, signs, toys, stuffed bears, hand-drawn cards, pictures and letters quickly took over the lawn. A photograph of that memorial, centered on the pictures, ran on the cover of Time Magazine, fronted by the headline: "Why? Why? Why?"

That mystery was the question on everyone's mind in those subsequent days. It became the mantra of the lost.

As with nearly all previous mass murders, the question trialed America.

Unlike with most, there were no guns to blame this time. Unlike with many, certainly unlike with Pulse—where a gay-hating, ISIS-pledging monster espoused multiple answers to that question—there was no obvious answer drawn from Mae Louise Vicar. She did not fit any usual profiles. First, she was clean. Her system revealed no drugs or alcohol. No evidence appeared that she used drugs, even by prescription, or abused alcohol. She was, by all accounts, apolitical, well-liked, responsible, level-headed and stable. No men trouble. Or women trouble. Mae Louise Vicar was religious, but mainstream; involved and dedicated, but not overwhelmed. She had expressed no previous interest in violence. Her police record comprised two speeding tickets, both a few years old. She had never even shown much interest in video games.

That did not stop police, the media, and every psychologist and criminologist who had fifteen minutes available for a live interview from offering theories based on little bits here and there. Her supervisor at work, a Dr. Tim Crosby, and a handful of others who knew her offered that she had been erratic and moody during her last few days. Very troubled, very troubling, very unlike the Mae Louise they knew, Crosby told NBC's Today Show. Mostly baseless reports circulated that she had exhibited signs of delusions, maybe even paranoia. Rumors arose she lived a secret, double life. No one really knew anything about it, which only made it more suspicious. Her social media accounts were mined for every glitch in character expression. False speculations went unchallenged and became the foundations for deeper false speculations.

A computer animation that more easily fit society's need quickly replaced Mae Louise Vicar's life story.

Her parents went into hiding.

Her priest offered incomprehensible wisdom and guidance.

The medical institute provided no comment.

Authorities at His Children issued a statement decrying the tragedy and offering prayers for all. They said nothing about Mae Louise, except privately to the police.

Mae's neighbors stopped answering their doors and phones. Margaret Seitzer suddenly barely even knew her. Danielle Jones, as always, kept to herself.

All the world responded with shock, anguish, and anger toward Mae Louise Vicar.

All the world, that is, except for Kanetha Wilson.

Kanetha reacted with shock, anguish, and anger for Mae Louise Vicar.

"That's not my girl!" Kanetha said to anyone and everyone. "That's not my Mae-Lu."

CHAPTER 3

DAY 19: TUESDAY, APRIL 30

Kanetha came back as soon as she could. It took a day for news to reach her, and three days to get home from Malawi.

There was only one person who might understand what she was feeling, only one person who would ever consider what she had to say when she was in a state like this bewilderment: her father, Devon "Pops" Wilson.

Pops had aged well beyond his 60 years, a survivor with scars that arose from inner wounds. His round, blotchy face reminded her of oil-stained, sun-cracked, ruddy-brown leather seats. His teeth wore the stains of a lifetime of the nicotine and caffeine that had kept his motor running day in and out.

Kanetha sprawled on a couch that still smelled of dog hair even though Pops' latest German shepherd had passed months ago. She held a can of beer as if it were a lifeline. Her father had his recliner. He sat like a therapist, hand to chin, ankles crossed. Of all the jobs he had ever held, psychologist was one he had never been trained or paid for but was the one he had always been best at.

Pops had never met Mae-Louise Vicar. His daughter, though, that puzzle was his specialty. She had bucked his advice for many years, then one day he just seemed wise to her, without ever having changed.

"Lord almighty, Kanetha! If you make too much of a stink about this, they'll make a laughingstock out of you. Hell, they might even put the blame on your shoulders. People out there that don't give a damn about truth; they believe what they want to believe. It's sport to attack people who say otherwise. They can be darned vicious."

"You think I give a shit, Pops?"

"Watch your mouth, girl."

"I mean it."

"This is my home. You leave that talk outside."

"Someone's got to speak up for Mae-Lu."

"She killed all those babies! Don't matter what anybody says."

"Yes, she did. But she was not in her right head, you know?"

Pops nodded. Kanetha's mood instantly sweetened.

"You taught me never to give up on someone you love, Pops. Never," Kanetha offered.

"Your ma was not easy. Maybe if I'd ...."

"I know."

Kanetha wiped her palms on her legs as if the stink of memory had soiled her hands.

Pops lit a cigarette. He examined it. He took a drag, placed it in the ashtray beside him, and then wiped his own hands on his knees.

"Remember when we took you to Disney World when you were about five?" he asked her.

"How could I forget? The one time my parents take me to Disney World, Mom gets arrested, and we get kicked out."

"You were very young."

"Not that young. I remember her screaming and trying to hit police officers. When your mom gets taken to the street and cuffed in the middle of the Happiest Place on Earth, it tends to stick with you. You know what? It was just like her, though. Thanks for reminding me."

"Well, it started out as an act of joy."

"Please," Kanetha said.

"Do you remember her dancing, or just the fighting?"

"I," Kanetha said. She focused on the air above her father's head, trying to form an answer from the fog of memory. It was no use. Nothing there. "What are you talking about?"

"It was a hot day. Crowded as all get-out. Lot of stimulation. Too much. Too much for her. I should have seen that. Her head was running about a hundred miles an hour, like it did sometimes. Oh, yes. But getting around Disney was like: just hurry up and wait. Hurry up and wait. It was building up in her. I could see that. So, yes, I should have done something. But, well, you know.

"Anyways, we got caught in these thick crowds waiting for the parade to come along. But it's not coming. Nothing happening. Nothing in sight. People just waiting."

Pops paused for suspense and a drag of nicotine.

"You and I, any ordinary person, what we see is a crowd waiting for a parade. What your ma saw was a crowd waiting for something. She said something like, 'I gotta cheer these people up.' Next thing, she stepped over the rope and started into her old dance routine, right there in the middle of Main Street. Oh, she was loving it."

"I don't remember that," Kanetha said.

Her father was grinning.

Kanetha felt conned. "She did not," she said. "You're making that up."

Pops laughed, hearty, from the diaphragm. He took another drag on the cigarette.

"She danced... gotta be a full two minutes, unmolested. Her whole routine. Maybe twice through. Who knows? Twice. You know, your ma used to love to dance for people. Good, too. And there she was, by God. Just out there by herself, doing her thing. At first, people did not know what to think. They were embarrassed for her. But after a minute or so, everyone was watching. These two big Disney dudes finally show up and politely try to wave her to stop. She would not. They asked her straight up. She just kept dancing around them. One of those guys grabbed her shoulder, maybe harder than he meant. That's when she took her first swing and hit him. Nobody ever grabbed your mother. Not without getting poked.

"Suddenly, quick as you can say Mickey Mouse, there's armed deputies there, too. It took a bunch of them of them to get her down, cuffed, off the street, gone," Pops said.

"That part I remember."

"So you said."

"So, now you're telling me she got arrested for dancing?" Kanetha asked.

"Nah. She got arrested for hitting cops. But she hit cops because they would not let her dance."

"All I remember was her fighting with those guys."

Kanetha searched Pop's eyes. He still had not fully recovered from his laughing spell. Or was that mirth?

"You're making up the dancing part," she challenged.

"Am I? Who's gonna say so? Who's gonna call me a liar on this?"

"You're making it up. I'll call Aunt Jackie. She'll know," Kanetha said.

"She was not there. It was just you and me and her. I remember. You don't. And she's dead. There's no YouTube video. Too long ago for that nonsense. I say she danced, she danced." He shrugged.

"She did not though. Did she?" Kanetha said. "Why are you lying to me?"

"You're about the only person in the whole world who would care at this point. Do you believe me? Do you believe me if I tell you it's the truth?" Pops asked. He crushed out his cigarette. "The truth is important. Your mother danced on Main Street Disney. It was an act of joy. Anyone who says different is wrong and needs to be set straight.

"Hard to know what the truth is about what your friend did, either," Pops added. "But all that means is, no one who really, truly wants to know the truth has looked for it hard enough yet. No one ever will. Except someone who cares.

"A friend, maybe," Pops added.

"Pops."

"It ain't going to be easy. But you never liked easy, did you?" Pops said. "Lord, Kanetha, it's always you against the world. Always has been. Why's it always you against the world, daughter?"

"Cause I'm always right and the world's always wrong," Kanetha said.

"You'd think the world'd learn by now."

"It will, Pops."

•   •   •

The media loved having someone, anyone, to talk about what happened, so Kanetha Wilson quickly became a star.

She spoke to no one, not even her father, of her last conversation with Mae-Lu. That was no one's damned business, and she had concluded it was pointless; potential fuel for the ugly theories already spreading like skunk musk wherever her friend was mentioned. But she spoke out.

"That's not my Mae-Lu!" Kanetha said over and over. "No. You listen. Mae-Lu was not like that. She was one of the best people I know. She loved children. She would never do something like this. Don't you say there was 'something' about her. Nothing. Nothing! There's something very wrong here. These pieces do not fit together."

Quickly, Kanetha began spinning her own theory that her friend, the brilliant microbiologist, must have been infected by something at the institute that drove her mad. The theory won no traction anywhere and drained credibility. Still, Kanetha was the only one who spoke up for Mae, and that resolve made her a popular with media and others.

She became known in the media as "Mae Louise Vicar's friend." And she had never imagined how many celebrities would want to talk with her. The calls from TV, radio, newspapers, magazines and blogs came in from places stretching from London to Perth. Kanetha took them all. She conducted dozens of interviews with newspapers she never bothered to read afterwards, even though they all were online. Good Morning America flew her to New York to appear on the show.

The only times Kanetha lost her temper came when journalists and talking heads made compulsory comparisons with Pulse's shooter. "The two should never be spoken of in the same sentence," she repeatedly declared. "How dare you!"

Then came the time Kanetha flew to Atlanta to appear on a CNN talk show.

By then she was practiced in defending her friend from all sorts of assertions, but this host was openly hostile, not just about Mae-Lu, but about Kanetha's own motives. She pushed and pushed her until Kanetha gave up any pretense of civility. She sucked in a breath. She listened to her own heartbeat pound in her ears. It was strong, and that familiar pulse was reassuring. She lowered her chin to be eye-to-eye with the camera.

"Kiss my ass, bitch," she said. "You don't know me. And you obviously don't know anything about my Mae-Lu."

That eruption brought a smirk and a smile from the host, showing she had just won, and so she broke for a commercial. That arrogance was it. Kanetha ripped off her mic and stormed out, shouting what she really thought as she cleared the studio.

It was the last big interview Kanetha consented, though she gave a couple more quickie telephone interviews to newspapers.

Hate flooded Kanetha through social media and every other communication she could not avoid. She answered many. She received threats. She answered those messages too, when she could.

"Go screw yourself, you pathetic coward," she would reply.

CHAPTER 4

DAY 28: THURSDAY, MAY 9

In her first week home, Kanetha's only talk with the police was a disappointingly shallow interview she gave a young Orlando detective. Kanetha was almost offended at how unimportant the detective made her feel with his routine questions, and at his disinterest in her answers. He was going through motions. He was checking a box. Of course, Kanetha thought. The obvious murderer was dead, so this case needed little now. It would be closed, and Mae-Lu would go into the official files as a monster who at least had the good manners to get herself killed in the act, thereby tying a neat goddamned bow on everything. That narrative pissed off Kanetha. When the detective excused himself, she swore at him on his way out.

The good news, she allowed herself, was that he did not seem terribly interested in Kanetha's vague lies when he asked her about the last time she had spoken with Mae-Lu.

But still. Why the hell was he not terribly interested? Huh?

It turned out, however, that the young detective had just been feeling her out, setting a baseline. His was a prelude interview.

A few days after Kanetha returned from Atlanta, she drove into a parking space in front of her apartment building—in a sprawling development called Lake Holland Manner—and immediately spotted a man sitting in a car, waiting for her, two spaces away.

She had come to be cautious and had developed a good eye for trouble, what with all the angry threats she had received. She could tell in a glance that this guy was not trouble in the violent sense. Her second thought was that he was a cop. She was not a bit surprised when he climbed out of his sedan in synch with her exiting her car. He flopped open a badge as if she was expecting him.

His name was Det. Lt. Marty Francisco. He was medium build, middle-aged, with uncombed black hair and slightly brownish skin, pockmarked on his paunchy cheeks and nose by a lifelong bout with rosacea acne. He wore a yellow and black tropical shirt covered by a light brown jacket.

He wanted to come up to her apartment to talk. Kanetha led the way, saying little, feeling a little busted. Once inside her first-floor apartment, though, she took her big chair, waved him to a couch in front of the window, and immediately toughened up. I can handle that bitch in Atlanta. I can certainly handle you, she thought.

The detective allowed a moment of silence to build ease.

"I want to talk to you about the last time you spoke with Mae Louse," he said.

"I've been over this," she answered.

"I know. You told Detective Price you called Mae Louise from the airport before you left for Africa and teased her about a one-night stand. You said she was embarrassed but in good spirits. You said the call was mostly about your trip."

"That's right."

Another pause.

"You know, Miss Wilson, those international calls are very easy to trace. Naturally, we looked at Miss Vicar's computer account. She spoke to someone in Malawi on a His Children line for about ten minutes, about twenty minutes before she killed all those kids. His Children tells us that was your call."

For just a moment, Kanetha felt the sizzle of panic along her nerve paths. She said nothing. She wondered if she needed a lawyer. She crossed her legs. She crossed her arms. She sank back into her chair. She shut down. The detective did not seem to care. He went on.

"What I want to know, what I intend to find out, is what you told her that set her off?"

"I set her off? I set her off?" Kanetha said. She thought about it for a moment. "Why?"

"Why what?"

"She's dead. She did it. Case closed. Right? Nothin' I can add changes any of that. Right?"

Another pause. Damn, Kanetha thought, recognizing his strategy. He's good at these silences. She almost blurted out something, anything, just to fill the silence, but she controlled herself.

"I don't give a shit about the who. I don't give a shit about the what," Marty said. "I give a shit about the why. This case. I don't have a why yet."

He got up. He walked toward her kitchen. Another moment of silence ticked away as he kept his back to her.

"This case," he said finally, "will not close until I say so. And it will not close until I know why a young woman who had everything going for her and was, by most accounts, decent, went postal.

"This case cannot close until we know something that will prevent this from ever happening again."

"Look into those germs she was studying," Kanetha said.

"Yes, I know your theory. You know we have. We've spoken to her supervisor and co-workers over at the institute. Nothing there. They call your ideas stupid, ill-informed science fiction."

"It's got to be true."

"What did you tell her?"

Okay. Kanetha came loose and leaned forward. She felt her heart quicken for a counterattack. She leaned toward him.

"I told her things weren't going so well in Malawi. Okay? I told her we weren't going to be able to build anything. I told her an adorable little boy we both came to know and love had died."

"And she was upset?"

"Sure, she was pissed. Anybody would be. You would be. But she did not get so pissed off that she'd kill someone."

"So you brought her bad news, and she got pissed off," Marty said.

Another silence. Kanetha crossed her legs and folded her arms again. She had just said that concession. She would not dignify his rhetoric by repeating it.

"And then she went out and killed a bunch of innocent children," Marty said.

"Crazy, huh?" Kanetha said.

"I did not say that."

"No. No, you tell me. You tell me. When was the last time you got bad news and went out and killed someone? Huh? You're a cop. You've got a gun. You can kill someone anytime you feel like it. When was the last time you got bad news and killed someone?

"When? Huh?" she finished.

Another unnerving silence.

"There's a missing piece here. You know there is. It was those goddamned germs. I'm telling you," Kanetha said, this time sounding as if she was pleading for him to follow her just a little here; follow her to the truth.

Marty sat down again. He leaned toward her like a friend, offering comfort.

"You're grasping at straws, Miss Wilson."

"Yeah, well."

"I would too, if I were you. You're right. It's crazy. It makes no sense to me. And you're right. There is something missing. You and I may be the only two people in the world who aren't writing this off as some crazy bitch goes psycho, and that's that. We're on the same side, you know."

"Screw you," Kanetha said.

But after he left, that night, late that night, when she curled into a fetal position in her bed, Kanetha asked herself the same question everyone else was asking.

Why? Why? Why?

And then, like other people, Kanetha Wilson broke down crying, for the first time. Alone in the dark, she sobbed violently. Until now, it had all been righteous indignation. Now it was becoming grief, spurred by not knowing.

·   ·   ·

The answer would come one day. But by then Mae Louise Vicar would be as old news as May baseball scores in September.

The missing piece Kanetha spoke of, and which Marty knew (or hoped) existed, was locked in Mae's brain.

Luckily, Officer Sizemore had missed when he had shot at Mae.

He had aimed for her head, which was the broadest, tallest target he could see through her windshield.

Fortunately, Officer Sizemore missed vertically, instead of horizontally. One of his bullets hit her in the neck, severing her spinal cord completely. The effect was what he had wanted. She died instantly.

The unintended bonus was that her pretty little head was completely spared, providing the county's medical examiner all she needed to open a new lead.

That lead would provide Kanetha Wilson, Det. Lt. Martin Francisco, and a micro-neurologist named Dr. Michael D. Andrusek the evidence they needed to eventually answer the question: Why? Their conclusion made none of them happy.

CHAPTER 5

DAY 29: FRIDAY, MAY 10

Mike Andrusek never quite fit in. Anywhere. Anytime. It was his life's curse. In high school, growing up on Texas' working-class coastline, in Point Comfort, the young Mike was too smart for his fellow students, who were mostly the sons and daughters of chemical plant roughnecks, rice farmers, and shrimpers. And he was too acerbic for even the most caring of teachers to mentor.

In college back East, at medical school, his residency, and then adding a doctorate in microbiology, he was too "Texas hick," the microbiology student who drove a battered, old Ford F-150 pickup, hunted in his spare time, and made it a point to bait his more polished, liberal-minded fellows.

He also had grown up big, the son of a Texas A&M offensive tackle with too little ambition for himself after football, but too much ambition for his son. Mike got some of his father's size and all of his father's stored-up drive. So Mike never hesitated to intimidate people who tried to dismiss him, and he usually did so for his own private amusement. Mike loved to amuse himself.

He found some of his own kind at the Centers for Disease Control and Prevention in Atlanta working on applied micro-neurology, but that gig did not last. Mike was nobody's yes man. He was impatient with protocols that took long enough on their own because of the science, and then took far longer because of the politics and bureaucracy that distinguished the CDC as a government science center renowned for delay.

Atlanta also gave him his single, great, ill-fated fling at romance: a brief marriage to a flaming socialite who taught him he could be better off without her.

After ten years at the CDC, he checked out and headed for the big money and frontier-spirit of the new medical sciences research center, NIMI.

No one at the CDC threw Mike Andrusek a going-away party.

Here, his brilliance for projecting and demonstrating molecular interactions between viruses and neurological functions filled a research vacuum at the institute simply because the institute was still new enough to not yet have filled its britches. The institute professed a marvelous "bring it on" attitude that welcomed almost any specialty with the potential for groundbreaking research, especially if it attracted money. Dr. Mike Andrusek still had those CDC connections and knew how that bureaucracy worked, so he won a couple of big grants and established his own fiefdom. He had his own lab, a couple of lab assistants, and a supervisor that neither fully understood nor cared about what he was doing. Everyone left him alone. And he got it done.

The sweet spot, as far as he was concerned.

He had met the young Dr. Mae Louise Vicar once or twice, but could not say he actually knew her. Like everyone else, though, he thought about her a lot lately.

What a shame. What a goddamn shame. How the hell could someone go off like that eruption? Despite his intimacy with the workings of the brain, Mike did not have any better answers than anyone else.

He had arranged to work a late shift lately because he felt he peaked in the evenings. It also gave him opportunities to get some fishing in during the morning, and the fishing was very good around here at this time of the year. The area was splashed with hundreds of lakes and was within a short drive of some of the best coastal fishing Florida offered, in the Mosquito and Indian River lagoons and offshore from Cape Canaveral.

On this day, shortly after noon, he parked his pickup—yes; it was a new one, fully loaded with 6.2 liters of V8 muscle—in a far corner of the lot and made his way into the lobby.

Mike stood six-feet-two and weighed well over two hundred pounds. With his brown ponytail, ragged mustache and typically under-shaven face, he curried that dangerous-Texan look, and it worked for him. Even here, people who did not know him initially both underestimated and feared him, just enough.

The institute's main building lobby atrium was high-ceilinged and bright, filled with glass, chrome, and long, stringy, colorful tapestries vaguely suggestive of cellular structures.

A pretty young black woman occupied the officers at the security desk. Mike almost flashed his badge and passed her by, but her angry impatience made him curious. So he stood back and watched.

"I have to see him!" she said.

"Dr. Crosby does not want to see you," replied the guard, a paunchy white man in his fifties, with meticulously cropped short hair and a finely trimmed gray goatee. "He's very busy today. You'll need to make an appointment."

"I've tried," she said, folding her arms, settling in for a standoff. "He won't return my calls."

Now Mike recognized her.

She was that friend of Dr. Vicar's who had been on all the TV news shows, not just the local shows. A celebrity. This confrontation could be interesting.

"I'm sorry miss, you'll have to leave," the goateed guard said.

"No! I'm not leaving until Dr. Crosby comes down to see me."

A celebrity troublemaker. What fun! Now Mike was hooked. If there'd been a chair there, he'd have taken it.

Two more security guards had joined the fracas. Any of them could carry this woman out, and together they created what looked somewhat like an excessive show of force. But this woman was not shrinking.

A security guard with silver bars on his shoulder stepped to the fore. "Miss, listen. Dr. Crosby and the institute are not commenting on—"

"No, you listen. Mae-Lu was my friend. You can't just—She could not do what she did."

"Please miss, you'll have to leave."

"She was working with engineered viruses. I know that. She must have been infected by one. Don't you get it? You might all be at risk!"

"Miss, please come with me." The lieutenant, white and plain, about forty years old, grasped her elbow. Big mistake. Kanetha thrashed her elbow away. She was ready for a fight, however irrational that act would be. So were they. The three guards took positions in a triangle, two steps away and blocking her. Mike did not want to see this end with them carrying her across the lobby, or worse. He stepped forward.

"Perhaps I can help," Mike said.

He did not know why. It was the rebel in him, wanting just a tiny opportunity to take down The Man by siding with this woman when she was clearly trespassing into a building and an area where she was not wanted.

"Dr. Andrusek, we have a situation," the lieutenant responded. "Please step back, sir."

"Hold on. Young lady?" Mike offered a hand toward her and pointed his other toward the reception waiting area filled with couches, chairs, and coffee tables littered with old Travel & Leisure magazines and painfully boring promotional glossies produced by, for, and about the Institute.

Kanetha stepped through her cage of security guards toward Mike then stepped past him and strode full pace to the sitting area.

She took a chair. He sat on the couch next to her. Two TV monitors faced the sitting area, one tuned to CNN and the other to CNBC.

"I'm Dr. Mike Andrusek. I doubt there's anything I can do for you, but do tell me, what's up?"

"If you can't help me, why are you wasting my time?"

He smiled. He looked back at the security guards, who were talking.

"To piss them off."

Kanetha smiled. She crossed her legs and leaned into him.

"Dr. Andrusek, is there any chance...?"

"What's your name?"

"Kanetha. Kanetha Wilson. I'm Mae-Louis—"

"I know who you are. I just did not remember your name. Kanetha. What do you do?"

"I'm a human resources officer at Kellerman Dairy. What difference does it make?"

"None at all. What brings you here to visit us today, Miss Wilson?"

"Dr. Anderson—"

"Andrusek. Call me Mike."

"Do you know anything about viruses?"

"Some."

"Is it possible that Mae-Lu was working on something that infected her and caused her to go crazy and kill those kids?"

This argument was desperation. Desperation was a flip side of paranoia. Hope driven by ignorance. He did not know what he could say to her that would ease her mind.

"Kanetha."

"Don't patronize me. Just—" she said, holding him off with her right palm, "answer my goddamn question. All right?"

"Theoretically, maybe. But the controls here—"

"Jeez. So it is possible."

"No."

"You just said it was."

"Safety controls here are stringent. They're state-of-the art. I can't imagine a situation that would have allowed an experienced scientist like Dr. Vicar to contaminate herself."

"You can't imagine? You can't imagine! Can you imagine her going batshit crazy and killing all those kids? Because I can't!"

Mike sighed and contemplated his next response. He looked at her again, but Kanetha was no longer paying attention to him. She had turned her attention to the TV hanging from the glassy column behind him.

"Kanetha?"

She was transfixed, so he turned to look.

CNN was broadcasting a helicopter shot of a big-box store building, surrounded by a parking lot filled with emergency vehicles. The TVs were muted, but the crawler on the screen announced, "… confirm twenty-four dead, including the alleged gunman. Repeat. A mass shooting in a Des Moines, Iowa, Walmart. Police confirm twenty-four dead, including the alleged gunman…"

"Jesus," Mike said.

He turned back to Kanetha. She was covering her mouth with a hand, catching little breaths, like hiccups.

"Kanetha," he offered.

"I gotta go," she managed, wiping her eyes. "Sorry."

"Here, wait," he said. He fished out his wallet and withdrew a business card. He jotted a phone number on it. "Here's my cell. Call me. We can finish this conversation."

She took the card, saying nothing else, and stormed out of the building. And with that episode over, Mike made his way to work, smirking mildly at the security guard on his way past.

He monitored the news all afternoon, and his thoughts ping-ponged between Des Moines and his encounter with Kanetha Wilson.

Can you imagine her going bat-shit crazy and killing all those kids? Because I can't!

It was the point she had been making everywhere, from cable TV news channels to local radio shows. Until now, he had tuned her out, like everyone else had done.

But it now dawned on Mike: she might well have a point.

What were the odds? It was easy to assume Kanetha was overselling her friend's innocence, but all the other reports supported her. What were the odds that she had been infected with something that affected her brain? Which was the longer shot?

Mike got almost no work done that evening.

The news out of Des Moines was horrible. A man whom police still were not identifying walked into a Walmart store with guns in a backpack. He approached crowded checkout lines, pulled out two guns, and opened fire. He knew what he was doing. He killed methodically. The final death toll had thankfully gone down by one during the day, stopping at twenty-two innocent victims. Two cops assigned to the store engaged him and got him. His was the twenty-third death. Only six people were wounded, which apparently meant he was an excellent shot.

When Mike got home that night, he followed his routine. It was past 11 p.m., so there was not much point in doing anything else. He took his basset hound, Stranger, for a walk through the lakeside woods behind his building. Back inside, he pulled the twisty out of his hair. He changed into gym shorts and a tee shirt. He opened a beer. He curled up on the couch with Stranger. Instead of channel surfing, as usual, he turned to a TV news network and overdosed on Iowa.

By then, police had identified the shooter, a sixty-year-old barber. Like the massacre two weeks earlier, the man had no obvious reasons for going, as Kanetha had put it, batshit crazy. The dead included six children, eleven women and five men. Two of the victims were store employees. The Walmart was in a black neighborhood and the shooter and most of the victims were black.

There already were personal stories emerging, and Mike felt it was a little like the way it had been the week before, when Mae Vicar attacked those kids right here. He had not felt such a personal tug at his emotions by previous mass murders, not until Mae's. But after Mae's, he had changed. Already this one in Iowa was having some of that effect. Was he softening? Did Mae's rampage open a new sympathy vein in him? Did Kanetha's visit?

The news felt personal. That feeling just was not right.

The dog liked Mike to massage his neck, under and around the collar. Stranger was appreciative and squirmed. It made Mike feel good, too.

"It's okay, Stranger," he assured him. "It's okay."

CHAPTER 6

DAY 30: SATURDAY, MAY 11

If Mae Louise Vicar had gotten to know Ben Wester much, she probably would not have liked him, and she certainly would not have slept with him. He was a man of little genuine compassion. He had grown deeply disappointed with people. He believed the world was populated by winners and losers, or rather, winners and whiners. And he would be damned if he was going to lose. Or whine. He knew how to blame others. He knew how to steal credit.

Ben could turn on the charm anytime he wished, and he did so for one reason, because it worked for him. It got him laid, or it got him paid. Bingo. But he could not sustain it long enough to develop a relationship or even any real friends. It made him a great salesman. It made him a lousy employee. This internet advertising sales job was his fifth in four years, maybe his tenth in twelve years. He always made the money he needed, but soon afterwards, his anti-social side would eventually outweigh his charm and things would sour.

Things were turning ugly lately at 21st Century Breakthrough. Ben knew exactly why. It was not the sales staff's fault. It certainly was not his fault. The fools who ran the company had no clue how to monetize their services; they were constantly revising rate charts and services. That left clients confused, and they were bailing.

Latest case in point, Inland Empire Raceworld, Ben's biggest account.

Tonight at Raceworld was "Crash Mageddon," a night of demolition derbies and figure-eight racing of school buses and tractor-trailers. It was a night when scores of area home-garage enthusiasts threw away months of hard work for chances at modest prizes and glory drawn from sizeable crowds of fans, over packed into cheap grandstands to cheer the crunch of machine versus machine. Ben had been here a couple of times before at the track owner's invitation. Truthfully, it was a lot of fun.

Tonight would not be fun. Ben was in no mood for fun. He was flat-out peeved. His boss had made it clear the loss of the Raceworld account was Ben's fault and that Ben was now at risk of being fired if he could not get it back. By text message, of all things. Now Ben was fired up.

When he arrived at the track, a figure-eight race with cars was going on. The track lights flooded the area so that, in the dark of the night, the surrounding mountains completely disappeared. At one end of the track, a clump of tall palm trees waved like flagpoles. They were possibly the only vegetation, as the rest of the complex was all rock-hard crusted sand, concrete and asphalt.

Ben came in through the employee entrance, telling the guard he was there for a meeting with the owner, Al Fugiere.

This night, the crowd was thick. The grandstands were full, the lines at the beer and hotdog stands were long. Despite numerous signs and frequent public address warnings, clusters of fans clung here and there to track fences. In open areas near a couple of turns, savvy fans had brought their own chairs, essentially tailgating. It was a cool night, borderline cold, so most people wore jackets.

The track administration box was set high, stacked on top of the main concession stand, giving it a clear 360 view through windows on all sides. Ben climbed the metal stairs at the back. He could see Fugiere through one window. He knocked. He saw Fugiere turn to see him through the rear window. But a guy Ben knew only as Kirby answered the door. Kirby's wide body was covered with tattoos, including his face. He had no hair, not even on his sculpted arms, which hung from a sleeveless jacket. Kirby recognized Ben.

"I've got to speak to Al," Ben said.

"He's not here."

"I can see him, Kirby."

"He doesn't want to see you."

"Goddamn it, Kirby, let me in. I just want two minutes with him."

"Go away before you get hurt."

Ben felt his blood surge. His forehead warmed. His shoulders rose with a big breath. He put his hand in his coat pocket. The Glock was there.

Kirby eyed him with cold calculation and slid his own jacket back to reveal a holstered pistol of his own.

"Don't mess with me, Wester. Get the hell out of here before I have you carried out."

Ben hesitated. He felt a bolt of adrenaline whip through. He could have shot Kirby then and there. He should have blasted him out of the doorway, stepped over him and filled the entire little office full of lead. Taken out the other Kirbys first, then pressed his gun's barrel into Fugiere's eye and made him cry. But he did not. He just turned and walked down the stairs.

As he did so, more chemical neurotransmitters began fueling his brain like kerosene.

As he pressed through the crowd, Ben's steps slowed, dragged by deep humiliation, frustration, anger, and self-loathing. His vision narrowed, crowded by tumbling thoughts that distracted him from any focus. Ben bumped into some guy carrying four beers and the beers all spilled, some on Ben, some on the guy.

"What the hell?" the guy screamed at Ben.

Focus came quickly. Ben felt as if his entire life were concentrating on this one moment, this scene with a tubby, red-bearded asshole with beer on his Luke Bryan tee shirt. This cretin. This moron is like all morons.

"To hell with you," Ben said.

The guy shoved Ben.

Ben reached into his coat pocket. He felt the grip. He felt the trigger. He felt his simmering rage finally explode. He felt it flow through that arm, through that hand, gorging that trigger finger.

He shot the guy. Twice. The man fell amid a fusillade of screams. Ben turned and shot the woman closest to him, who was howling annoyingly. Then he shot another screaming little bitch. Pandemonium erupted as the grandstand there began emptying. People jumped off the sides and off the back, pushed, fell down.

Ben's heart was pounding. His breaths came like a locomotive, yet he felt empowered, strong. His body was firing in go mode.

Ben saw a man in the back row of the grandstands level his own gun at him, but Ben got a sight on him quickly, and, bang, bang, you're dead. The man fell backwards off from the riser.

The roar of the engines made the gunshot sounds a local spectacle only, and much of the crowd at the racetrack remained transfixed by the action on the track. But here, at this end of this side of the crowd, the area was emptying quickly.

With everyone running away from Ben, space opened around him. He slipped behind a light pole and surveyed quickly. The tall light standards threw as many shadows as they did light, giving the entire area a ghostly feel of brightness amid holes of darkness. In the shadow, Ben made out another man who had brought his own gun. He was crouched behind the riser. He stepped out into the light and shot at Ben, but missed. Ben shot back and did not miss. The man's head exploded in a puff of red mist illuminated by the floodlights.

Ben spun. Another cowboy who had brought his toys to the racetrack was aiming at Ben from his right. Ben rolled as the cowboy's bullets sank into the wooden light standard. A third shot passed by, and Ben heard a shriek as some woman behind him took the bullet for him. Ben returned fire and hit the man in the shoulder. Then he raced over to deliver a kill shot to the squirming little turd. He grabbed the cowboy's revolver.

Now Ben fired with both guns into the backs of panicked fans as they thickened to a stop, trying to force through the gate in a cluster of bodies.

Ben spun quickly to see more trouble. Kirby and two other badasses were running down the stairs, armed. They saw him spin and stopped to aim. Ben rolled behind a trash can and the trio, wide open, fired at him. The bullets hit the can. He returned fire and hit Kirby, but the big man did not fall. Ben took close aim and fired again, and this time popped Kirby in the chest. He collapsed straight backwards onto the stairs. The other two were trapped between him and the doorway above. They shot at him. He shot at them. He had cover. They did not. The Glock's clip was empty now, so Ben switched the cowboy's revolver to his right hand.

Ben had spent many Saturday mornings at the shooting range.

This altercation was what he had always trained for.

Always, in that basement shooting range, the vision was never of shooting a burglar, but of an open-air shootout. It was never about surviving a home invasion but surviving armed anarchy. This scene was his fantasy, playing out under the light standards of the inland empire. This struggle was what he wanted. Ben found every fantasy, every anger, every insult coming together. He felt rage pulsing through his wrist into his hand.

He got them both on the stairs.

The race continued, the drivers unaware of what was happening behind him. Yet panic was spreading in waves throughout the track's spectators. The public address announcer, aware something was amiss, called for people to leave immediately. Most already were.

Ben pushed a fresh clip into his Glock.

On his left, Ben saw two fans headed his way, away from the rush. He surveyed all directions and saw a third man crouching behind the corner of the concession stand, as if ready to attack. Ben ran at him. That man fired once, missed, and then turned and ran like hell away, holding his gun. He looked over his shoulder to see if Ben was following. Ben squeezed off three rounds with quick pulls and hit him in the back. The man went down.

Never look back.

That exchange left the two to his left. Ben turned and did not see them anywhere. Did they run off? Did they advance? The shadows gave the now mostly empty area a Neverland quality. The screaming was deafening. He stood still in the open, in the light, challenging them to take their best shots and reveal their positions.

Most of the crowd had pushed safely away. The jam at the gate had eased.

Where were the cops? Fugiere always hired several off-duty sheriff's deputies to run security, but none had appeared yet. His conclusion was they were having trouble getting into the grandstands area because of the rioting crush headed out.

The race had halted finally. Drivers were running for the opposite side of the track. Ben walked back to the concession stand and looked over the counter. Two young women were lying in terror on the floor, not even looking up, not even aware, as far as he could tell, that he was standing there looking down at them. Aw, to hell with it, he thought.

He shot them both.

One of the last remaining heroes announced himself. Ben felt the guy's bullet rip through his left shoulder. He collapsed, dropping the revolver. His shoulder burned as if a cattle brand had been pushed into it. For a moment, he almost gave up to the pain. But his eyes cleared, and he saw the two men running low to the ground toward him.

He moved the Glock toward them and fired. They dove, and Ben did not think he hit either of them. He skipped bullets in front of them, kicking dust up from hard-packed dirt. They fired back, and who knows where their bullets went? Ben got up and ran toward the fence. Still lying down, they followed his run with more missed shots. He aimed at the closest man, still on the ground, and fired two shots. The man's face exploded. His body lurched and then settled. The other man got up and ran away.

The second clip must be nearly empty, Ben thought. He could not reload again. The angry pain in his left shoulder clouded any of Ben's attempts to move his left arm. What to do? He could try to climb the stairs again and find Fugiere, but that quest seemed hardly worth the effort at this point. Ben contemplated his next move while a sheriff's deputy finally worked his way to a corner of the grandstand.

"Freeze!" he announced.

Ben swiveled, and the deputy let loose with four shots.

"Ha! I got him!" the deputy cried out to no one.

Ben's knees gave way first, and he twisted as he fell. His face smashed nose-first against the blacktop.

•   •   •

By now, the area was largely cleared. Other deputies arrived, methodically checking for other shooters. One deputy kicked Ben over onto his back and then kicked away the gun. The terror was over, but a long night lay ahead.

The Raceworld massacre came early enough in the night to make the late news as breathless, breaking-bulletins in the Pacific and Mountain Time Zone markets, but far too late to be broadcast to most people farther east that night, unless they were up and watching the late-late night news channels.

People out East had to awaken the next day to wall-to-wall coverage on their favorite morning shows.

For many, the first thought would be of desperate, though delusional, relief.

After all, as everyone knows, these things always happen in threes. Orlando, Des Moines, and Fontana, California: that was three. The danger was past.

Whew. Thank God it was not here.

Celebrity deaths, plane crashes, assassinations, natural disasters, mass murders, personal bad luck; it matters little that they can come just as easily in ones or twos or fours or fives. Three completes the accepted standard of a natural cycle.

Orlando, Des Moines, now Fontana. For the moment, Ben Wester had provided a sense of perverse closure to the minds of millions of people. All over America the next morning, people would eat their Wheaties, watch their TVs, and think it was over.

Once again, Kanetha Wilson found herself in a lonely minority of dissension.

CHAPTER 7

DAY 31: SUNDAY, MAY 12

Mike's cell phone lay on a charger on his bedstand. The phone rang, playing the tune of Waylon Jennings' "Luckenbach, Texas." Mike looked at the clock. It was six-twelve a.m. He had planned no fishing this morning and had no interest in getting up early. Sunday was his day of rest, just as the Lord had commanded. He grabbed the phone and did not recognize the incoming number, so he touched the "Decline" button and rolled over.

Stranger lay on the floor beside him, completely unmoved.

Moments later, there it was again, Waylon wailin'.

Mike punched the "Accept" button.

"Who is this?"

"It's Kanetha. Kanetha Wilson. We met Friday at the Institute."

"Kanetha? Jesus. It's, it's... what's up?"

"Have you seen the news? There's been another one."

Mike had not seen the news. He had shot pool until late last night, won some money, came home alone and crashed. That collapse was what? Five hours ago? Four?

"There's been another massacre, Mike. Only this time—"

"Kanetha..."

"Only this time—"

"Kanetha..."

"Damn it, Mike, shut up and let me finish! It was a guy Mae-Lu slept with three weeks ago!"

Silence followed as Mike's half-hung over, half still-asleep brain tried to process. The words punched through. It was as if they pulled up the shades on him. He was wide awake now and sat up.

"Come again?"

"Mike," she pleaded. She sounded out of breath. "This guy out in California shot up a racetrack last night. He killed twelve people and then the cops killed him. They've released the guy's name and picture. Ben Wester. I swear to God! We met him here in Orlando three weeks ago and he had sex with Mae-Lu that night. Same guy. I swear."

"Are you sure?"

Kanetha paused for just a second or two, as if she were catching her breath.

"I didn't ever catch his last name when he was here, but the guy's first name was definitely Ben. And he was from L.A. And he had these elephant ears. I'd recognize him anywhere. I swear to God, it's the same guy."

Mike was sitting up in bed now. Stranger lifted his head. The dog knew something was wrong. So did Mike. Coincidence? A hundred-sixty million to one. Much greater odds than some sort of lab accident over in microbiology.

"Mike?"

"Meet me for coffee, now." He gave her directions and hung up.

He flipped on the news and there it was. Thirteen dead, including the gunman, and nine wounded at some racetrack in Fontana, Calif. The gunman just started shooting people. Some shot back. He shot them. And then a sheriff's deputy got him, police said. In the riotous stampede of panicked fans, nineteen more people were injured. The dead suspect's name was Ben Wester. He worked for an Internet marketing agency and lived alone. His photograph showed him to be an attractive man, except for the left ear turned slightly toward the camera. It looked like cauliflower, puffed out.

On initial blush, this man looked to fit mass-murder profiles far more easily than the man in Des Moines or Mae Louise Vicar. The talking heads were running with that news, almost as if it validated some desperately needed connection to the known real world. Wester had a criminal record, including assault. He owned many guns. Early indications suggested he might have been a sociopath. This scenario made sense, so it all made a little sense.

Mike did not bother to shower. He cleaned himself up, got dressed, fed Stranger and left.

Kanetha was waiting when he arrived at the coffee shop, wearing a wide-brimmed hat and large sunglasses. Several customers already were there, and the baristas were entirely too hard at work for any sensible human being at seven-fifteen a.m. on a Sunday morning. Kanetha was sitting against a window, but took only a nod from Mike and waited. He ordered a black Pike Place blend with a few ice cubes dropped in to cool it. He then motioned for Kanetha to follow. They went out to the outdoor seating where they could be alone for the moment. The brick patio was surrounded by four-foot-high shrubs. Rattan chairs surrounded seven black metal tables, all empty.

Mike dragged out a chair at a table in the back corner, a measure of isolation within isolation. Kanetha took it; he sat across.

She spooned the cream foam off the top of her white chocolate mocha and then withdrew her phone. She rolled through pictures and handed it to Mike.

"This is the guy."

He stared at a picture of Mae Louise Vicar dancing with a man in a crowded bar. She had his hands on the man's chest. The man's face was turned almost directly into Kanetha's phone, his head angled slightly to his right to stare at Mae. His ear was mottled. He expanded the image with his thumb and forefinger for a close-up. The focus was a hair fuzzy, but the impact was clear.

"And this," Kanetha said, reaching for her phone and taking it back.

"Is the," she said, rolling through pictures.

"Guy who," she said, settling on one.

"Shot all those people last night."

She handed the phone back to Mike.

She had pulled up the Associated Press picture of the Fontana suspect, Ben Wester. It was the same photograph Mike had seen on TV earlier that morning. Same face. Same ear. He rolled back through the pictures to the dancing photo. Then rolled back to the AP picture.

Clearly the same guy.

"Now, do you believe me?"

Mike knew how to turn on his calm, analytical voice. He used that tone now.

"Kanetha, this is provocative, but we will need much more evidence before we can start assuming that this is a pathogen. Have you contacted the police about this?"

"You said 'we.'"

"Have you called the police?"

"You said 'we,' so you're in."

"Kanetha."

"Screw the police. You know what they think of Mae-Lu. They think I'm a nut. I'm done with them."

"But the police in California—"

"Can figure it out on their own."

"Kanetha, stop. Think for a minute. If you're right, and I'm not saying you're not anymore, if you're right, the ramifications for public health are stupefying."

"Right," Kanetha said slowly and softly, a touch of visible sarcasm emphasized as her head dipped so that she looked at him from tilted-up eyes. "Mae-Lu got a virus that caused her to become a psychotic killer. And it's spreading. I get it. This is COVID with collateral victims. Not good."

"COVID spoiled the country against believing in risks measured by probabilities. No one wants to go through that again. It's not as if—"

"It is spreading!" she screamed, her fists raised and shaking to make that point.

"So, what do you want from me?"

"Find out what the hell it is!"

•   •   •

Dr. Tim Crosby lived in a well-manicured country club neighborhood. Well-manicured, but not gated, so Mike could park in front of his house. It looked like every other house on the street: beige, new, stone facade, two stories dominated by a two-and-a-half car garage that seemed to hide most of the residence from the street view. His yard was thick, green St. Augustine, well-fertilized and watered. His driveway was clean and empty, except for a bagged newspaper at the bottom. The upshot from that detail: he had not yet emerged to go anywhere this morning.

Mike rang the doorbell. A teenage girl answered, and without saying a word, went to fetch her father.

Dr. Crosby was less eager. He swung the door open and saw Mike standing on the stoop and Kanetha standing a few strides behind him on the walk. He recognized them both. His face said he deciphered trouble: everything dropped. He was a lean, long-distance runner type, with a long, narrow face, topped with dark-brown hair trimmed and touched-up by an expensive barber. He had stylishly small glasses, bony cheeks and thin lips. Mike pegged him as dressed for golf.

"What do you want, Dr. Andrusek?"

"We want to talk to you."

"It's Sunday morning. I'm with my family. We're going to church in a little bit. For crying out loud, talk to me tomorrow."

"Now, Crosby."

Mike turned on the intimidation with his stance, one foot forward, shoulders leaning in, neck stretched. Tim's eyes darted from Mike's body, which seemed poised to step into the doorway, to Kanetha with her folded arms of disgust a few feet behind.

"What's this all about?"

"Have you seen the news?"

"Yeah."

"Did you know that guy in California was here in Orlando three weeks ago and had a one-night stand with Mae Vicar? Three weeks ago."

"I think you're crazy."

"It's true," Kanetha said.

"I know she's crazy," Dr. Crosby said, waving a scolding finger at Kanetha.

"We need to talk," Mike said.

"Tomorrow. At work," Dr. Crosby said. He tried to close the door, but Mike pushed his boot into the opening. "Damn it, Andrusek. I'm with my family."

"Then you probably don't want them to hear us," Mike said.

"Leave now, or I'm calling the police," Dr. Crosby said.

"Please do," Kanetha said, stepping up behind Mike. "I've got some new evidence I want to share with them."

This time, Tim's stare went from Kanetha to Mike.

"Cancel your tee time, Crosby," Mike said. "I want to see your lab."

• • •

Dr. Crosby drove his silver Lexus. Mike and Kanetha followed in his truck.

Dr. Crosby was silent and fuming as he led them through the parking lot and across the lobby to the elevators. Kanetha took note that the weekend security guard was not one of the grizzlies she had encountered on her last visit. She was disappointed. She wanted to show off that she was back, with the guy she wanted, and by invitation. An opportunity lost.

The elevator door closed. The silence ended.

"Andrusek, you're way the hell out of line," Dr. Crosby said.

"This is serious, Crosby."

"Where do you get off accusing me of contaminating my lab with a dangerous pathogen?"

"What? Your words, not mine. We just want to know what Dr. Vicar was working with."

"Nothing worth canceling my golf game."

Kanetha spoke up. "Mae-Lu goes crazy. Then the guy she slept with goes crazy. What the fuck are the odds, Dr. Crosby?"

"How do you know it was the same guy?"

Smirking, she shoved her cell phone into his face. "It's him."

Blood drained from Dr. Crosby's face, then colored it back up.

The elevator door opened.

"If you're suggesting Dr. Vicar was exposed to something that caused her to go crazy, then she exposed someone else, then why wasn't I exposed? Why weren't you?" Dr. Crosby said to Kanetha as they stepped into the corridor.

She did not like that question.

"Were you exposed?"

"I would have no idea," Dr. Crosby said. "I worked closely with her. Every day. What sort of incubation period do you think we're talking about?"

"Wester was exposed to Dr. Vicar three weeks ago; last night he went postal," Mike offered. "So let's say three weeks is the window."

"How do you know she was exposed to it here?"

"We don't. We don't even know what it is yet, or if it is. We're only acting on a hunch, Crosby."

"A hunch. You're going to pay for this, Andrusek."

They entered the lab. Lab tables. Equipment ranging from microscopes to washing-machine sized analyzers, computers.

Refrigerators, some marked "no food." The door closed behind them. Dr. Crosby folded his arms.

"What was she working on, Crosby?"

"It's hard to say."

Mike got in his face. "Stop jerking us around, Crosby. This is a long shot, but if it's real, holy shit. You were working with her. Every day, you said. What was she working on?"

Dr. Crosby nodded. He went through a secured door into an adjacent room, sharing windows with this one. In there, he opened a refrigerator and withdrew a rack of test-tubes. He brought it back through the door and set it down on a lab table.

"That."

Which one?

There were dozens of tubes in the rack.

"All of them."

Mike thought that response was too easy. He figured Crosby knew the route, he just needed to be poked to follow it. He put his hand behind the rack and pushed it down the table until it was in front of Tim.

"Which one, Crosby?"

He did not answer right away. He was lost in the rack before him. He reached down, lifted one, examined the label, put it back. He examined a second. Then a third. When he lifted a fourth, he rolled it a little in his fingers.

"If I had to guess, I'd start with this one."

Kanetha's phone chimed, announcing a text message.

She stepped behind the two scientists to read.

Her knees buckled. Mike noticed and reacted with a lurch. He caught her by the arms.

"Kanetha, are you alright?"

She was still reading and still standing. Mike walked her to a chair and sat her down. She was still reading.

"What's wrong?"

"The village. In Malawi, where I was working. Where Mae-Lu and I had worked. I was there two weeks ago, for a week."

She looked up from her cell phone. Mike and Dr. Crosby were both listening intently.

"There was," she said. She wiped tears. "An..." she looked back at her phone's screen. "an incident there. I, it, they..."

"Kanetha?"

She looked up at them with soaked, dark eyes.

"They're dead. They're all dead."

CHAPTER 8

DAY 32: MONDAY, MAY 13

Kanetha Wilson was a prisoner of quarantine now.

More important to her, she was a captive of grief and self-loathing anger. The Malawi massacre had barely made the news last night and this morning. No one attributed it to anything else except the inexplicable—to Americans, anyway—pattern of factional violence that rocked so many African countries on a regular and complex basis. A gunman wiped out a remote village. That atrocity merited three or four paragraphs in the international news briefs collection of most American newspapers. The New York Times ran a bigger story. But even the Times had no reason to draw any connections from Africa to what had happened in the United States the past couple of weeks.

Kanetha did, though, immediately. And so did Drs. Andrusek and Crosby.

Mike and Crosby had declared a quarantine lock-down for the entire fourth floor, where Crosby's lab was located, until they could figure out what to do next.

Kanetha had nothing to do while the two microbiologists worked. She swam in guilt, self-recrimination and despair.

The floor had a breakroom with couches, chairs, tables, and vending machines. Mike put her in there and told her to get some rest, but she could not rest. Her heart beat double-time. He gave her a laptop to occupy herself, but she could spend only moments at a time sitting. Nor could she eat, though she bought and drank coffee. Occasionally, Mike would appear, but he had no news to report for her.

Sometimes, the darkest thought would emerge and stop Kanetha's pounding heart. She might yet go mad herself. So might the doctors.

She was sure she was at least a carrier. Nothing she could have done about it, even if she had known. That concession did not help.

She had brought death to all those people she had worked so hard to help. She loved them. She did not know who was killed. She did not know who did the shootings. Her mind ran a PowerPoint show of their faces, and she knew. She knew each of them was shot dead. Without actually producing tears, she cried for them individually. She would bring up a face, a name, and flail herself with sorrow.

Then there was herself. Her self. How long before the disease corrupted her mind and turned her into an uncontrollable killer like her girl? She was deeply suspicious of the natural anger and apprehension she felt now. She fretted that it, the virus, might already affect her. She had no homicidal impulses (except possibly toward Dr. Crosby, but that response seemed natural), yet she wondered if that ambivalence is what Mae-Lu had felt until the very last moment before rage.

Was it just a matter of time before Kanetha became a raging mess? Like Mae-Lu? Or...like her own mother.

Kanetha's memories of her mother were mixed. During the good times, Yvonne Wilson was a dynamo of just-do-it and had instilled in her only child a goal-oriented work ethic, a sense of priorities, and an urgency to address the top priorities without diversion. She was a woman brimming with lectures, full of lessons. But by the time Kanetha was ten, those lessons always came with heart-breaking caveats: Do as I say, not as I do.

Don't be like me.

Among other adults, Yvonne Wilson was the Queen of Social, always in charge, adding energy and direction to any gathering. She had three older, married sisters. Kanetha's aunts, uncles and cousins visited frequently, and even a young Kanetha marveled at how her mother was the organizer, the glue, the life of a party. Kanetha learned that control from her mother.

Occasionally, gatherings large or small ended with episodes of uncontrollable anger, and Kanetha wondered now whether her mother's sisters came over to humor her, to watch over her, or out of some desperate hope to make a difference. If Yvonne Wilson melted down, though, they left quickly.

Her mother was bipolar. Kanetha did not know it then, would not have known what the word meant, had she ever heard it. Her father, who was a rock, never spoke of the condition to his daughter, but he surely knew it. Pops Wilson handled his wife with the love, patience, and the strength of a parent containing a toddler throwing a tantrum. But she wore him down. At any rate, he was often gone, working two and sometimes even three jobs, missing dinners, evenings and weekends when his wife was most prone to episodes. Kanetha did not know this reality, but it occurred to her later: her mother was incapable of working. The same rage fests that their family absorbed at home were instant firing offenses in the workplace. Kanetha's mother became unemployable, leading her father to work more and more.

So, Kanetha, even in grade school, became a parent figure. Strong. Capable. Modeling herself after her father.

Once or twice a month Yvonne Wilson would melt down before her daughter's eyes, in mere seconds. Kanetha could predict an episode, seeing it first in her mother's eyes, then hearing it in her mother's suddenly disturbing, sharp, survival tone of voice. It might happen at dinner when she discovered a fork had come out of the dishwasher with hardened grime stuck between the prongs. It might come when she was paying the bills and realized she could not. Or it could come within a phone call.

Yvonne Wilson would say something like, "I am so sick and tired of this." Then she would swear.

Kanetha would cringe in defense, and then watch her mother pick up her plate full of food and smash the dish into the side of the table. Or she would hurl a full glass at the wall. Or she would kick over a chair.

"It's alright, mom," Kanetha would say.

Yvonne Wilson always would catch herself before she could hurt her daughter. She would storm off to the bedroom where the rage would continue, safely away from her baby. Kanetha would clean up the mess and wait. The holes in the walls were rarely fixed. They multiplied.

Sometimes the yelling and thumps of thrown objects would continue for a half-hour or more, but usually not much longer. When the yelling stopped, Kanetha knew it was time to go visit her mother in the bedroom. She would find her lying in bed, crying. Kanetha would cuddle up next to her and put an arm over her.

"It's alright, Mom."

"Oh baby," her mother would reply through tears. "I am so sorry. I am so sorry."

Kanetha handled it well until she entered her early teens. That era was when her mother began self-medicating with street drugs. It was not too long before Yvonne Wilson occasionally disappeared for a night or longer.

One hot September night, when Kanetha was thirteen, her mother got into an argument with her sister on the phone. It was just like scores of other rages. Yvonne smashed the receiver down on the phone. She swore at her oldest sister. She pushed over a table. She stormed off to her room, yelling and kicking doors and walls.

Kanetha picked up the table and put the receiver on the hook and waited.

And then came the gunshot, followed by silence.

Kanetha froze with terror. She called her Aunt Jackie. Her aunt called 911 and Pop's work. Jackie, the police and paramedics all arrived about the same time, just minutes later. They went into the bedroom while Kanetha sat frozen on the couch.

Kanetha was not sure whether to cry in despair or feel great relief when Aunt Jackie came back and hugged her and told her it was over. She did neither. She just watched the comings and goings of first responders. Pops got home after his wife's body was loaded away, already gone, and he sat down and balled. Kanetha, still tearless, sat beside him and hugged her father close as he bucked with sobs.

Eventually, Kanetha consoled herself that her mother had done the right thing. It was a terrible conclusion, but Kanetha knew, too well, her mother's pain. It would not stop on its own. Her mother never wanted to see doctors; Yvonne Wilson no doubt was afraid they would tell her the truth.

Kanetha knew that if she ever fell under the power of this disease and entered an uncontrollable rage, she, too, could kill herself. She was certain she would not follow Mae-Lu's path. Sitting at a small table in a break room, in a medical research building that was far from her world, Kanetha made herself that promise. Still, she feared she might not keep it.

•　•　•

Mike called his colleagues at the CDC in Atlanta but had a difficult time convincing them that anything was amiss. They concurred with his quarantine and promised to have someone call him today.

Meanwhile, Mike and Crosby got to work studying the virus sample that Crosby had identified. Mike drew blood from each of them and they set out to see if they could detect the virus in any of their samples.

It was not a simple task. Looking for an individual virus in a blood sample was like looking for a single disparate amoeba in a bucket of ocean water. It would not declare itself soon, if it was there at all.

Around three a.m. Mike came into the break room to get a cup of coffee. He had nothing new to report. But Kanetha was finally ready to ask the question that had haunted her since Sunday morning.

"Mike, am I next?"

"I don't think so. You were exposed twenty-five days ago and show no symptoms. The cases we've got so far all erupted within about twelve to eighteen days of exposure. You may be the best example we have of someone who is not affected, immune, maybe. That's very important, crucial, maybe. How are you feeling?"

"I'm pissed off."

He smiled. He was weary. "You should be. But do you feel like killing anyone?"

"Maybe Dr. Crosby," she said.

"Me too." The smile grew, then vanished. "He's still not saying shit about what happened, but I think he knows... something. Outwardly, he's in denial that we've been exposed to anything that might be infectious or dangerous. He's pissed off, too. He's bitching that he's stuck here against his will. What about me? You want to kill me?"

"No."

"You probably will eventually, but not because of the disease. I can be a real prick when I need to be. And I think this is one of those times."

Kanetha laughed.

"You'll be alright."

They had four incidents in two weeks, and three of them were clearly connected. Mae Louise Vicar had slept with Ben Wester. Vicar had a full-blown outbreak and so did Wester. Wilson had been with Mae-Lu, then traveled immediately to Malawi, where a gunman slaughtered a village. In each case, the massacres occurred a couple weeks after contact with Patient Zero, suggesting that an infection took that long to trigger a full-blown rage.

There was no obvious connection to Des Moines, however. The shooter, Howard Morris, as far as media reports had shown, had not been out of Des Moines, and certainly had not been to Orlando. Perhaps, Dr. Crosby suggested, it was an unrelated incident. A coincidence. Your garden-variety mass murder. "God knows there are enough of them nowadays," he had said. The odds did not rule it out. Mike was doubtful, since the media also reported that Morris was rather like Mae, with little or no history that would suggest a psychopathic, homicidal rampage. If anyone might have been an isolated killer, Wester fit the bill, and maybe whomever it was who killed all those people in Malawi.

Mike had been trying to find detailed information on the Malawi incident, but he was clearly frustrated.' No firm casualty counts had been reported.

Dr. Mae Louise Vicar's lab notes had quickly confirmed Crosby's "maybe." For several days a week or more prior to her visit to the nightclub, she had been focusing specifically on Virus Strain K12Q, the one that Crosby had selected from the tray.

Crosby had spent most of his time running an analysis on the suspect virus. Mike found that preference very suspicious, but had not yet confronted him about it. Crosby knew something. A lot more than he had given. Mike just hoped that knowledge and Crosby's reputation as a top-rank lab rat would take them wherever they needed to go.

When Mike returned to the lab, Crosby was on the phone.

"Your turn," he said, holding the receiver out. "It's Lowe."

Dr. Katherine Lowe was president and CEO of the Institute. She was known for being impossibly disconnected from the army of scientists working beneath her. When she communicated with someone, it was important. This call, of course, was important. Mike had been expecting it.

"I just spoke with Dr. Crosby. I'm ending this now," she said.

"Hear me out," Mike said, knowing he was wasting his breath. When she spoke, the mission of those individuals who worked for her was to listen. When she made a decision, the purpose of those people beneath her was to concur. Or at least to shut up. "This is real."

"Dr. Andrusek. It seems to me you have no reason to believe anyone has been exposed to anything. You have no reason to believe the three of you are infected with anything. People will be showing up for work there in about four hours. And they will show up for work."

"Katherine," Mike said. Everyone else called her Dr. Lowe. He had a history of calling her Katherine to her face, though, and right now, she needed shaking. "The epidemiological evidence is strong and convincing."

"If your hypothesis is correct, Dr. Crosby, this young lady has been walking around infectious for several weeks. It's hard to imagine quarantining her now would have any impact."

"Let's at least wait for the CDC team to get here and make an assessment. They'll be here this afternoon. One day," Mike pleaded.

"They're not coming," she said.

"Excuse me?"

"I just got off the phone with Dr. Taro. He agrees with me that there is precious little reason to believe we've had an exposure, let alone an outbreak. And the external data is unconvincingly thin. He wants us to monitor and report. I'm putting you in charge of that."

"Katherine. We've got three mass-murders, three...."

"Do you have any idea how common this is?" she snapped, interrupting him with a distinct bite of contempt. "Just this past week there was a bombing in India that killed sixteen people. In the United States alone there were six cases in which at least three people were killed. That's typical. In Kobe there was a bombing. In Hong Kong, there was a six-person shooting. There were other mass shootings in Sao Paulo, Nairobi and outside Budapest. That's one week."

"How do you know all that?"

"The CDC tracks all of this. The people there are not stupid, as you should know."

"Katherine, this is different. We've got three mass murderers who all can be traced back to contact with a single woman, Kanetha Wilson."

Mike was sorry as soon as he said it. The implication had arrived in his mind for the first time: Kanetha indeed was a link to three different mass murderers.

"There are other considerations, Dr. Andrusek. All you have is a hypothesis. A dangerous hypothesis. Have you thought this through? The backlash from COVID set epidemiological precautions back a generation. We have to be very, very careful now.

"This city, this state, is very vulnerable. And it's still very divided. This becomes political the moment someone says anything aloud in public," she continued. "Half the political leadership will want to shut us down entirely for the risk, and the other half of the political leadership will want to shut us down immediately for the stupidity. Either way, they win votes."

"Good! Fine! Shut it down!" Mike screamed into the phone. "The consequences will be catastrophic worldwide if we don't. We get millions of visitors from England, Europe, Brazil, Canada, Japan—not to mention every state. If people here are infected, they'll get infected and take it home. We've got to shut it down!"

"COVID taught us the perils of overreactions. Our economy was virtually wrecked because someone said 'shut it down.' A lot of brilliant careers were destroyed when people got angry about that."

"Damn it, Katherine."

"Good morning, Dr. Andrusek."

The phone went dead. Mike slammed the receiver down. Was this irk a spark of rage? He could feel his whole body tingling with anger.

Crosby already was booting down his computer.

"I'll send you a report on what I've found tomorrow," he said, standing up.

Mike shoved him against the wall and placed his forearm on Crosby's sternum. Crosby shook his head as if he were shaking it off.

"Keep your hands off me, Andrusek. You're already on thin ice around here."

"What do you know, Crosby?"

"Get out of my way."

"So help me—You were too sure of that sample. What do you know!"

Crosby stared down Mike as if to say, Try it. Hit me.

Mike figured Crosby was the kind of guy who took kick-boxing classes on the weekend and thought that training made him tough. Mike actually had been in fights and had won enough, and lost enough, that he was ready and willing to use his size to sway an opponent. Eventually, little cardio rats like Crosby always backed down.

Crosby slipped out from under Mike's arm, stepped around him, gave him one last glance, pulled open the door and left.

"You think you're leaving?" Kanetha shrieked from outside the door. She had caught Crosby in the corridor.

"I'm done. This is bullshit."

Kanetha closed in on him as Mike entered the corridor.

"Oh, no you're not," she said. "You're going to fix this thing."

"There's nothing to fix."

"I don't know what you did. And I don't know what you can do about it. But you. You! You sure as shit know. You're going to fix this because something is crazy-ass wrong. And you know what it is. You're going to fix it or else."

"Or else what? Are you threatening me?"

"Hell yes, I am. I promise you this, Dr. Crosby. If I come down with a full-blown case of whatever this shit is, I'm coming after you first and I will make it hurt. Oh, yes, I will."

The three of them traded silent glances. Mike's accompanied a smirk.

"You're scared, Dr. Crosby. And you know what? You should be," Kanetha said. "That's because you know it's true. You know it's true! Goddamn you for pretending you don't!"

"I don't know anything!" he shouted.

"Well. You know this. You'll be back. People are dying and it's getting worse. And from what I can understand from Dr. Andrusek, this could get crazy out of hand. Now you'll turn around and you'll get back in there, and you'll fix it. Or I swear to God, I'll go bat-shit crazy on you and I will kill you. I know where you live and I do have a gun. And I do know how to use it."

"I'll be back," Crosby said, pressing the last word, making it sound as if he had simply been misunderstood, and had planned all along to return.

"Good. because I might not even wait to get sick. I might just do it because you deserve it, you lying sack of shit."

"I'll be back in the morning. I need... I need some sleep. I'm tired, alright? And I need some time to think this through."

Kanetha nodded. "You go get some sleep. Then you come back and You. Fix. This!"

Crosby strolled away. He punched the elevator button. A few seconds later, he banged on it. After a few seconds more, he headed for the stairwell door and disappeared.

"You and me," Mike said, waving his hand at Kanetha. "We're gonna make a helluva good team."

"I don't know what I can do to help."

"You scare people. That's a valuable talent."

Kanetha smiled.

"Remind me to introduce you to our CEO."

CHAPTER 9

DAY 34: WEDNESDAY, MAY 15

The notion that bad things come in threes lasted four days. This day was the day that America came to the shocking realization that had already haunted Kanetha Wilson. Something was wrong. Something was ghastly wrong.

First, in Huntsville, Alabama, a man dressed in fatigues and weighted down with several guns and ammunition magazines parked his truck in front of the entrance of the auto-parts plant where he worked and ventured forth shooting everybody he encountered, starting with the security guards near the entrance. The scene began late morning and lasted hours as police swarmed but could not get to him right away. No early reports even estimated a death toll because the scene was active for so long that authorities could not get to all the bodies right away. Eventually, the man died in a volley of police bullets.

While this violence still was going on, a stock trader in New York City killed himself and took six people with him when he triggered an improvised explosive device that he carried in a bag onto a crowded subway car during the lunchtime rush.

Out in Los Angeles, Southern California suffered its second mass murder in a less than a week when a young, heavily tattooed Mexican-American man (who would later be called a suspected gang-banger) did some banging in a fashionable restaurant. The hostess questioned him at the entrance, as if she had wanted to deny him entry. She died first. Nine people at the closest tables were shot and five died. The man escaped and eluded a manhunt, though by nightfall they had found his body and those of three more people along his trail.

Also that night came Orlando's second time around as the city that had suffered so much to become the poster child of pain, took it again.

Veronica Van Zandt harbored secrets, many secrets. She kept most of them in her phone and backed them up into the cloud. Names. Addresses. Locations. Preferences. Attitudes. Secret pleasures. Peculiarities. Sizes. Durations. Payment histories. All secret. All meticulously catalogued and sorted. She even kept information her clients did not realize she had collected and would rather she not have. Real names, wives' names. Children. Business and political associates. Birthdays. Anniversaries. Special honors. Employers. Churches. Car makes, models and license plate numbers. Veronica loved the Internet. She loved Facebook, Twitter and LinkedIn, for all they could tell her.

What social media did not tell her, Veronica found through her friend Emely Sanchez, a private investigator, who helped her fill in all the gaps in her database. Emely also had full access to Veronica's cloud database and could update it remotely from her little walk-up office in a Puerto Rican neighborhood on the city's East Side.

Today's successful, independent call girl relied on her database, the new Little Black Book, as much as any veteran luxury car salesman. Research and organization were important. Every bit of information added to the comforting illusion of familiarity and intimacy. It kept Veronica ready, which kept her clients coming back. Occasionally, Emely followed Veronica, shooting intimate photographs of her with some of her high-status clients, filing those images away in the database. It all added to her security and protection, keeping Veronica safe from her own clients.

Or so she thought.

Veronica's client list was impressive, hundreds of names long, though among them there were just a few dozen regulars, duly noted. Dozens more were occasional, someone she might do business with once or twice a year, or from whom she might receive a referral. Veronica's list also was impressive because of who was on it. She had a chamber of commerce president, a city councilman, police officials, several lawyers, a couple of judges, bankers and captains of industry. She, like every call girl worth her Viktor&Rolf, had professional athletes and big-name entertainers; the city was crawling with them.

Veronica was easy, but she was not cheap. She was statuesque, fit and blond, although she could be red-headed or brunette, if the client preferred. She had fine-tuned a natural cover-girl beauty that made marketing herself an effortless task. She was the girl next door, only perfect. She could stroll down Winter Park's trendy Park Avenue shopping district and be mistaken for a daughter of civic royalty. Strangers opened doors for her. Literally, and in her business.

One of the more forgettable people on Veronica's list was a successful insurance agent by the name of Todd Cook. She had seen Todd about a week after his birthday, every year for the past four years.

It would horrify Todd Cook to learn what Veronica's database could say about him. He was thirty-five, married with two daughters. His wife's name was Iris. He sold business liability insurance, and his boss's name was Sanford Barnes. He voted Republican, attended the First Baptist Church of Orlando, and drove a silver BMW 328i sedan with the license plate COVERU. It was one of those "Choose Life" specialty plates offered by Florida. He had a small dick, liked foreplay, enjoyed role-playing sex games, and always paid cash.

What she did not know about Todd Cook was that, for his birthday this year, he and Iris partied the night away at City Walk.

It had been an eventful night. He and Iris got into a shoving match with another couple at a bar, and he got into a bit of a fight. Security threw them out and advised them that the only reason they were not pegged as trespassers, banned from ever coming back, was because it appeared that the other man was the aggressor, and that man got away.

Todd spent the next few days obsessing about the woman he had grabbed in the bar. Luscious was the word that came to his mind. He fantasized about her the rest of the evening. He thought about her for the next several days. His fantasy and memory melded and her features changed, so he never recognized Mae Louise Vicar's picture when she made the news.

In his mind, at least in his slightly altered memory, she drew a stunning resemblance to the woman he knew only as Veronica. Nothing, nothing could have made Mae Louise Vicar sexier to Todd Cook than his mental association with Veronica Van Zandt.

He made an appointment to see Veronica the following Thursday night, at a hotel in the Walt Disney World tourist corridor. In the hotel bar, they began the night by acting out scenes he had fantasized for them. They both had come with other "dates," though they did not actually have any accomplices to act out those parts. That scene was a little awkward to play out, but Veronica went along. She chose a random, well-built man to cling to momentarily, and on the dance floor, her makeshift date bumped Todd and he shoved the man back. The man stormed off. But in the melee, Todd's and Veronica's eyes met; they knew they were going to wind up with one another. In Todd's fantasy, his wife had come along but had wandered off to meet friends. To end her role altogether, she had left with them, leaving him by himself at the club. He headed for the elevator. Veronica followed him a minute later. He reached his room upstairs. She showed up behind him to apologize for her date's beastly behavior. She stood with her feet and knees together. Her arms stretched down and her hands folded into each other. She rolled wide, innocent eyes.

"Sorry," she said. "My date is a kind of a jerk."

"Don't worry about it," Todd replied.

She moved in close and whispered into his ear.

"Anyway," she said. "It's you I want to fuck."

And he led her into the hotel room and obliged.

Five hundred bucks is five hundred bucks, Veronica always concluded.

She was as careful as she could be about hygiene and protection, but there was only so much she could protect against.

A week later, Veronica hit a rough patch. She argued with her landlord. She argued by phone with her brother in Nashville. Her clients started showing up late and ugly. Everyone playing the asshole. Everything that could go the wrong way went the wrong way. Veronica was getting very unhappy about her career choice and lifestyle. Very unhappy.

On this night, her client was Jed Clinton. That was not his real name. She knew his real name, Stephen Bligh. He was a famous lawyer who was in the news all the time, usually protecting high-profile murderers. It's not as if he could get away with going incognito, even if Veronica did not have Emely to research real identities. Jed Clinton, as she called him, was a little unpredictable, full of himself, often snotty to her. On a good night, he could be an asshole.

This night he was crossing the line. She had come to his lakefront home in a posh neighborhood just south of downtown. The house was old and big, three stories, with a little servants' bungalow out back that was bigger than the house in which she grew up. He had no servants, so the bungalow was reserved for out-of-town guests, and that's where they met.

She turned the doorknob and let herself in without knocking. He was sitting in an overstuffed leather easy chair, facing the door, wearing a maroon velour bathrobe, tied closed, and matching slippers.

He was fifty years old, heavy but in a muscular way. His hair was way too brown for his age, but he paid a good barber to keep it looking fine and trim. His face looked experienced, not aged, with a ski-slope nose and fleshy lips.

She eased the door closed behind her, set her purse on a chair, then turned to pose for him as if she were modeling these clothes.

She wore a slinky, glittery silver, sleeveless party dress. The short skirt and the four-inch, strappy sandals displayed legs that looked as if they came off a Barbie doll. Normally, Jed loved this look. But he waved at her in annoyance.

"Someone sees you dressed like that. They'll think you're a hooker," he said. "What's the matter with you?"

No one called Veronica a hooker. That disparage was one of her buttons. She did not walk streets; she had moved up from that life more than a decade ago. Normally with a client, she could fight through her irritation and respond with grace, but she was not feeling normal tonight. She felt her lungs expand with a fighting breath, but she held it. When she exhaled, she felt the anger focus her eyes.

"This is Celine," she snapped. "What's the matter with you?" The dress was a knock-off, but he could not possibly know that. Was he calling her out on it?

Jed got up with a stumble. He was drunk. That's what was the matter with him. She hated drunk clients.

"Did anyone see you come in?"

"No."

"Because, shit, I swear, I don't need the neighbors talking."

"No one saw me. Look, maybe we should start over."

"Maybe we should just get this over with. Come on, I've been horny all day. Get in bed."

He might as well have screamed it. She felt herself shaking with anger. She turned and folded her arms.

"What's the hell's the matter, Jed?"

"What's the matter with you? Come on."

He pushed open the door to the master bedroom. A king-sized bed filled it almost wall to wall.

"Get in," he said.

"You're drunk. You're treating me like a whore."

"You are a whore."

She slapped him, hard.

Jed slapped her back much harder, knocking her onto the bed. She bounced back toward him and he grabbed her by the shoulders and shoved her down. She kicked at his crotch, but missed his nuts. He slapped her again. Her vision tunneled. She could barely see where he was.

"Bitch. Get the fuck out of here. You think I'm going to pay you tonight?"

"Don't call me again."

She stood and bumped into him as she passed. He shoved her and this time she swung with a fist, missing. He swung back with a fist and knocked her hard on the side of the head. She spilled past him onto the hardwood floor, on her hands and knees. He reached for her again and she scrambled away. He lunged. She dove. She reached for her purse as he grabbed her legs. He pulled her toward him. She opened her purse. He got his hands on her waist and flipped her over. She yanked out her Sig Sauer nine-millimeter—a special edition Hello Kitty pistol, the adorable logo, complete with a big pink bow, on the grip—shoved it into Jed's face and pulled the trigger. He lurched backward, then rocked back toward her. She fired again. This time, his head jerked to the left, and he fell in a heap.

His blood splattered her face, chest, and dress. She could feel the warm wetness. She wiped her face with her empty hand and saw the blood on her hand.

Hell, she thought, I just killed Stephen Bligh.

The bastard. The blood-sucking pig.

Good.

She struggled to get her legs out from under his torso. Furious, she fired again, just to watch his lifeless head jerk. And again. It felt good.

Good.

Veronica knew it was over. Cops hated this guy, but his law firm contracted with the best private detectives in the county, ruthless and devious detectives, and they would find her before the police had their first clue. Suddenly, there was nothing left.

All those bastards...and there were plenty of them. She knew them now for what they were. Blood-sucking pigs.

Veronica went to the bathroom to clean herself up a bit. Then she gathered her things, turned off the lights, let herself out, and strolled to her Mustang convertible. It was dark blue but looked black in the night. The top was down. Inside, she asked Siri to direct her to another client's address and reloaded her gun.

Veronica was screwed, and she was going to end all of those men who had screwed her. Or as many as she could.

First stop was a house a couple of miles away, a two-story with a pair of BMWs in the driveway. It was luck of the draw that the closest house was the home of Todd Cook.

A woman answered the door and looked Veronica over carefully, as if she were a threat. She was, after all, dressed like a very expensive whore. Imagine that, thought Veronica.

"Is Todd home?" Veronica asked.

"May I ask who you are and what you want?"

"Todd is a low-life scum pig who cheats on you with prostitutes," Veronica said. "I'm his favorite."

"How dare you!" the woman replied. "How—How dare you come to this house, my home, and—"

"Your husband paid me to fuck him two weeks ago. And your name would be Iris. Your anniversary is March 19. And you have two daughters. Look, I don't have a lot of time. I have something very important to tell Todd. Please get him. It's something he needs to know."

Iris glowered.

"Todd?" Iris called.

"Todd!" she screamed.

A moment later, Todd himself came around the door. He caught his wife's fearful face and then glanced up to see Veronica.

"What?" he demanded. "What are you doing here?"

"You're a philandering pig," Veronica said. "Say hello', Kitty."

She shot him in the chest.

Iris screamed.

Todd put his hands over his heart and looked up again at Veronica.

She fired again and this time Todd collapsed. Iris went down too, in horror, covering her husband's body. Veronica turned and ran to her car. She drove off fast, then leveled out to the speed limit. She had never felt so invigorated. This rush was so much better than sex.

At the second house she visited, no one was home.

The third house was in a gated community. Fortunately, Veronica's database knew the code.

She punched the number into the keypad, and the seven-foot-tall, black steel gate slowly rolled away, opening the lane. She slipped the Mustang through as soon as there was just enough space.

This time her client answered the door himself.

"You philandering pig," she announced, loud enough that someone in the kitchen should be able to hear her. Then she fired. Bang. Bang. Bang. Three shots.

She ran for her car, laughing, hoping the neighbors would glance through their blinds to see the blood-soaked hooker running from the murder scene.

Veronica got to nine houses and killed six clients, not including Stephen Bligh, before the police and the Society of Philandering Pigs finally got lucky. The housewife in house nine, in another gated community, got a call out to 911 before Veronica even got her car in gear. The dispatch went out before she had reached the end of that block.

•   •   •

Police officer Jamie Ruiz was patrolling around the corner from that neighborhood. When she arrived at the exit gate, he was already waiting for her, a half block away, in the shadows, with his lights off.

Veronica came through the exit gate, and Officer Ruiz floored his throttle. The patrol car blasted down the street and blocked the turn-out from the neighborhood exit to the street. Veronica hit the brakes, and the Mustang stopped on a dime. The gate had slowly closed behind her. In the moment before Veronica could calculate an escape route through the narrow openings between trees, utility poles, and the patrol car, Officer Ruiz got out and pointed his gun over the roof.

"Police! Get your hands up! Get your hands up!" he screamed.

Veronica raised her hands behind the wheel. The officer scooted around his car, double-fisting his gun and keeping it aimed at her. Once he was close to her front wheel, Veronica reached a hand down and lifted Hello Kitty from her lap. The officer saw this move, leaped forward and fired, hitting Veronica squarely in the chest.

Veronica Van Zandt fell dead on her car horn, which blasted until Officer Ruiz reached in and pushed her body back into the seat.

CHAPTER 10

DAY 43: FRIDAY, MAY 24

For the next few days, all anyone anywhere in the country, all over the world, was thinking was this question:

What the hell is going on?

A dominant early theory based on social psychology formed and caught momentum quickly. In the simplest terms, this onslaught was a pattern of copycats. The initial rash had triggered a pent-up, psychopathic response, an impulse in those individuals who were harboring a similar urge to kill. If someone had daydreamed of committing mass murder, this moment felt like the right time to make it happen.

It was the thing to do now. Veronica and her fellow killers in Los Angeles, Mobile, and New York had erupted on a Tuesday. On Wednesday there was another incident, in Daytona Beach. No mass murders occurred on Thursday, but there were two on Friday, two more on Saturday and two more on Sunday, including one during a church service. A new theory emerged in some quarters, that the devil himself was emerging and the End of Days was in motion. A prominent mega-church pastor outside Houston called upon Christians everywhere to praise the Lord and await the Rapture.

Kanetha Wilson and Mike Andrusek knew better. So, now, did Tim Crosby and the CDC. Even Katherine Lowe, the Institute's president, was fully on board with exploring the theory that they had some sort of infectious, rage-inflicting virus spreading rapidly and killing by the dozen. They also were convinced that it had likely started at the Institute, because they could trace too many threads back to Mae Louise Vicar. Not all, but several. Enough.

Yet they were not yet ready to announce anything. What could they say? We think we know what it is, but we do not know what to do about it. That proclamation would surely make the panic worse. This news was a horrible secret kept on a need-to-know basis for the time being.

Some people knew. Quite a few, in fact. The Institute dedicated ten researchers and lab assistants in various specialties to work the virus. The CDC had that many people at work in Atlanta, plus teams of epidemiologists traveling city to city to check on outbreaks. Other research centers throughout the country were engaged, splicing and dicing samples, infecting mice and monkeys, running simulations and amassing data on the virus Drs. Tim Crosby and Mae Louise Vicar had created. Mike had pulled in a few friends and colleagues from various hospitals and universities around the country, too. The research effort geared toward big; sadly, massive was needed. And in these early days and weeks, Mike, with Kanetha's help, would always push for more. But for now, big was turning up data. Big was more than encouraging.

Simply reading his email took Mike hours each day.

Kanetha quit her job at the dairy and Katherine agreed to hire her as Mike's special assistant, even though she had no lab experience, training, or any scientific knowledge. The last time she had looked into a microscope, she said, was in high school biology class. But Mike found enough for her to do to keep her useful. And he knew the most important thing she could do was be there. He needed her drive. And he needed to keep an eye on her.

Why was she not erupting? Or Crosby, who had certainly also been exposed? Or himself? And what about the others?

•   •   •

The CDC epidemiology team was all over Orlando. Margaret Seitzer and Danielle Jones had been interviewed, poked and prodded, along with a never-ending web of other contacts of both Mae and Kanetha.

It did not take too long for the CDC investigators to figure out that one of Veronica's victims, Todd Cook, was in that bar the night Mae Louise Vicar and Ben Wester hooked up, and that he had fought with both of them. That pulled the thread straight from Mae to Veronica.

Police still were mostly clueless about the CDC investigation. They were aware of it, mainly because they ran into CDC investigators everywhere. But the center had only told law enforcement what it needed to know.

Orlando Police had Veronica's cell phone, for all the good it was doing. Emely Sanchez had carefully coded in a self-destruct worm. When the police data forensics lab tried to get at the data, it disappeared, along with its encrypted links to the cloud. The cops figured they could eventually recover it. But Emely would have had two words for them if she had known they were trying.

Good luck.

As it happened, though, Emely did not digitally destroy everything Veronica compiled. The detectives eventually discovered that Veronica had regularly transferred money to her monthly. It was not one of those leads that Francisco thought was worth much in what was essentially an open-and-shut murder case with a dead perpetrator. But still.

Orlando homicide Det. Lt. Marty Francisco stashed the lead in a pocket.

And one day he would be glad he did.

He already knew Emely. They had crossed paths before, and Marty knew she was both smart and careful. Veronica had hired wisely. Emely Sanchez was formidable and seemed to have an impressive list of truly sleazy clients. But it was a testament to her abilities that almost all of them stayed out of jail. Marty was looking forward to dealing with her, but not just yet. He had more pressing matters. Serial mass murders were tough to top as a priority.

The CDC team also quickly established a link from the Daytona Beach murderer, a drifter and odd-jobs man, a large man named Sam Echols, who walked into a gamers store, shouted, "You like violence? I'll show you violence!" then pulled out a hunting knife and stabbed a seventeen-year-old boy in the throat. In seconds, he had slashed and stabbed four others.

He had attended Kanetha's church two weeks earlier.

●　　●　　●

Katherine Lowe indeed had put Mike in charge of the project, though Dr. Crosby was running his lab fairly independently, out of spite. Every now and then, Mike would dispatch Kanetha to intimidate Crosby. It always worked. If Crosby showed any lack of motivation or commitment (and truthfully, it was rare), Kanetha kept him at his highest resolve.

Mike slept most nights in his office. So did Kanetha. Crosby insisted on clocking out and driving home to his wife and two daughters every night. It was a short drive.

Mae Louise Vicar's schoolyard massacre finally became yesterday's news. So, little attention was paid to the autopsy report finally released by the Medical Examiner of Orange and Osceola counties, except for the basics of the executive summary. And they were hardly revealing.

Mae Louise Vicar died of injuries attributed to a bullet wound to her neck. It shattered the body of the c-2 bone of her cervical vertebra which then made a seventy percent sheer of the spinal cord at that location, as well as a rupture of the anterior spinal artery, resulting in loss of function in all organs below the brain and significant blood loss. Fragments ruptured the exterior jugular vein just below the C-6 cervical vertebra, an injury that would have killed her if the bullet had not already done so.

In short, Mae Louise's cause of death was news to no one; the local press did not even report on it right away.

Yet, buried in the full autopsy report file were deeper details about the physiology of Mae Louise Vicar, backed by a separate consulting report that the medical examiner had sought from a neurology pathologist at Johns Hopkins University, Dr. Peter Betsakos. It delved into anomalies the medical examiner had noted while making a routine assessment of Mae's brain.

Dr. Mike Andrusek had a copy of the autopsy report within an hour of its release. Betsakos described some inflammation in the brain, particularly of the amygdala lobes. In short, the regions of her brain that regulated emotions such as depression and rage were swollen. They were not cancerous. They were gorged, stressed.

Andrusek manically sent emails to Betsakos, to his contacts at the CDC, and to colleagues around the country. Betsakos sent him more data backing his report and more detailed analysis. By lunch, Mike was convinced Kanetha Wilson had been right all along.

Something, likely Virus Strain K12Q, appeared to have attacked a region of her brain that controlled or triggered rage.

The questions now were how and why, and what could be done?

Mike wanted to go public. Now. This crisis needed the complete attention of the world's scientific community. But the CDC and Katherine Lowe still were not ready. They had access to plenty of dead killers now and they wanted confirmation, more data and more analysis beyond Mike's "This is it!" hunch. Additional autopsy studies were quickly and quietly sought in a dozen cases where the killers were lying on morgue slabs. Above all, the CDC wanted to avoid the international panic that would come from the theory that an infectious disease was causing all these mass murders.

Mike was beside himself with fury. This moment was one of those times when care and protocol and political and social concerns needed to go to hell.

Sending protocol and political and social concerns to Hell was one of his specialties.

As covertly as he could, he polled his friends from Los Angeles to Boston on whether they would support him if he went public, and on their thoughts about how best to do so. Their responses were less than consensus. But Mike was not looking for democracy. He was simply trying to identify his allies and enemies.

Around two p.m., he awoke Kanetha, who was sleeping on one of rollaway beds Mike had set up in his office. He pulled open the blinds, flooding the room with the afternoon's direct sun.

"What the hell?" she said.

"Fuck 'em, Kanetha," Mike said. "It's time we went public."

"About time."

"I need you to go back to your apartment, now. Call every one of your contacts with the media. Set up a five-p.m. press conference. Tell them you've got very important new information on the Mae Louise Vicar massacre. Don't use my name. Don't mention the Institute or the virus, don't speak to the theories. I don't want anyone to get suspicious about my involvement and try to shut us down. Do you have any national contacts?"

"Sure."

"Make sure you get them interested. We'll have to set up a dial-in conference so national media can tune in from afar. I'll set that up with a location while you're driving home."

"Now?"

"We need to make the six o'clock news. Go."

She got up, and with no wasted effort, gathered her shoes and her purse.

"And Kanetha?"

She turned to him.

"We're going to own this thing. The good and the bad. By tonight, we're going to be isolated and vilified. We're going to be disavowed. We're going to get shit on by everyone, and that's just those who don't believe us. Those who do..."

"Nothing new for me," she said.

Mike did just as he said. At two-thirty, when Kanetha called him back from her apartment, he had a location set up with a streaming video and dial-in number available for any reporters who could not make it to the show. He wrote up a press advisory statement with the number and a brief description of an important announcement in the Mae Louise Vicar case, for her to forward to all her contacts.

Kanetha had the advisory distributed by three forty-five, and between then and four-fifteen, she was on the phone constantly with the local TV stations, the Orlando Sentinel, the Tampa Bay Times, the AP, Reuters, and a few out-of-town reporters. At four-thirty, she headed downtown.

Mike got out of the office unnoticed and with no one interfering. On his drive over, however, his cell phone went off repeatedly with calls and texts. They were not from Kanetha, so he ignored them all. He knew who they were. Word of Kanetha's press conference had bounced back from the curious media to the police, and then to Katherine, the CDC, and others. Now they all were trying to find out what the hell was going on, and if Mike was at all involved.

They were about to find out.

• • •

The city's best grande dame downtown hotel had managed, with an hour's notice, to arrange a meeting room with a whiteboard, a podium, a sound system, video and audio feeds, a table with a teleconference telephone and a few chairs for reporters. When Mike—wearing his suit, charcoal and striped, for the first time in months—arrived, Kanetha was already there, as were four TV crews, a couple of other reporters and still photographers. Two of them already had their cameras set up on tripods and a third was stretching his tripod's legs. Mike had advised her to avoid any contact with anyone, even though most of the journalists in the room knew her and wanted to talk with her. She had waved them away.

There was one other distinction for both Kanetha and Mike. They wore masks. That apparel was not entirely unusual since the COVID crisis, but people noticed. Mike was sure it made an impression.

The hotel provided an events coordinator who was checking the teleconference connections. Mike approached her first and introduced himself. She saw the mask and stepped back from him. He nodded.

"The livestream is up; you've got four reporters on the phone so far. I've done a mic check and a white balance. Anything else you need?

"No, thanks."

She took a chair in the corner.

Mike's appearance had focused the curiosity of some journalists in the room. They did not know who he was. One of them, a young, tall Latina who identified herself as from the Orlando Sentinel, sought him out. Mike begged off. Annoyed at his non-response, she pressed, at least for his name and title.

"In a minute," he said. "We'll answer all your questions in a minute."

The minute passed.

Kanetha stepped behind the lectern when Mike turned to sketch a rough outline map of the United States on the whiteboard. He wrote names into various locales, including Vicar, Wilson, and Echols over Florida. He drew a rough outline of the west coast of Africa. He did not know where Malawi was, or the name of the killer there, so he just drew an X.

Mike pushed the whiteboard out a little so everyone in the room could see it. When he looked up, he saw others had entered the room and were standing against the back wall, including Dr. Adrian Bradford, the local team leader for the CDC.

Mike joined Kanetha at the podium, which was covered with microphones and digital recorders. The in-person press gathering had increased to five cameras—three of the TV stations had sent only cameras, not reporters—and seven or eight miscellaneous reporters, including several from independent news services and blogs.

At the moment before they began, complete silence fell upon the room.

"Most of you know me," Kanetha said, breaking the silence. "My name is Kanetha Wilson. As you know, I've been advocating for answers to the inexplicable actions and death of my good friend, Mae Louise Vicar. Finally, I believe we have some of those answers. With me today is Dr. Michael Andrusek, director of the nano-neurology lab and leader of a special task force investigating these deaths at the Nona Institute here in Orlando.

Mike leaned forward and said, "May I ask who we have here? First, on the phone?"

The voices came all at once at first, then sorted themselves out, revealing reporters from the Washington Post, Los Angeles Times and the Miami Herald, as well as several online media. A talk show hostess from a cable TV news network, Karen Quinn, cut through them all. The abrasive victims' rights advocate had grilled Kanetha mercilessly in person on her show weeks ago and had trash-talked her on at least two shows subsequently.

"Thank you all for coming," Kanetha said. "Dr. Andrusek will begin. Dr. Andrusek?"

She stepped aside, and he stepped to the microphones. He had never actually participated in a press conference. He was not sure how to proceed. Yet he had given plenty of lectures and was comfortable commanding a room of skeptical minds. This time, he had prepared no remarks. He just dove in.

"Thank you," he said, leaning forward. He spoke the following words slowly and crisply, so that not one word might be misheard. "We are announcing today our theory that, with regard to this rash of mass murders, we appear to be dealing with an outbreak of a genetically altered, infectious virus that causes profound neurological changes, turning ordinary people such as Mae Louise Vicar into angry, hate-filled, killing monsters."

He might as well have announced his theory that the sun would never again rise. Shock or ridicule spread across the faces of everyone in the room except the four men against the back wall. No one said a word, but their bodies and faces shouted.

After assessing the reactions for a moment, which added more weight to the announcement, Mike continued.

"During early April, Dr. Mae Louise Vicar was working on a genetically altered version of a highly contagious germ associated, in various forms, with a variety of human and animal diseases, including encephalitis. Dr. Vicar's work was noble and important; she was seeking ways to turn off the infectious characteristics of such viruses.

"We believe this lab-created virus infected her."

Mike turned around and wrote the date "April 11" under Mae's name on the whiteboard.

"On April 20, Dr. Vicar went out partying with her friends, including our good friend Kanetha Wilson here. They went to City Walk and partied in a nightclub."

Mike drew a line between Vicar and Wilson on the board and wrote the date underneath.

"That night she also had intimate relations with a man she met in the bar. We now know his name was Ben Wester."

He drew a line from Florida to Los Angeles, touching Wester. Audible gasps came from the journalists. He wrote the date "April 20" underneath.

"The following day, Kanetha Wilson traveled to Malawi, Africa, where she worked as a missionary with the organization His Children."

Mike drew another line and wrote the date "April 21" under it.

"On April 27, Mae Louise Vicar went on an inexplicable rampage, killing seven children."

He wrote "April 27" under Mae's name.

"On May 6, Miss Wilson's church had a community barbecue lunch. Miss Wilson, who had just returned from Africa, participated, as she always does, in serving food. Among those who attended was a man named Sam Echols. We're assuming Miss Wilson served Mr. Echols, but we don't know for sure."

He drew a line from Kanetha's name to Echols and wrote the date "May 6" underneath.

"On May 13, Ben Wester shot up a racetrack in California."

He wrote "May 13" under "Wester."

"On May 15, a still-unidentified gunman opened fire in a small village in Malawi, killing between twenty and thirty people, mostly women and children. It was the very same village in which Miss Wilson had been working as a missionary two weeks earlier."

He wrote "May 15" under "Malawi."

"On May 19, Sam Echols walked into a game store in Daytona Beach and killed four people before police shot him."

Mike wrote "May 19" under Echols' name and looked over the room. That's really all he had, except for the autopsy report. But it was plenty. The same faces that had looked bemused a few minutes earlier now looked stunned.

"We assume that, as research continues, more and more connections will be found between these people, and that all of them will eventually link back to Mae Louise Vicar and her lab," Mike said. "As we speak, scientists, epidemiologists, medical researchers, microbiologists and others all around the country, including at the Center for Disease Control in Atlanta, are working on this."

"Why are you announcing this here and now?" asked the Orlando Sentinel reporter. "Why isn't this being released in a big press conference in Washington or Atlanta?"

"Yes, well," he said, "as I said, this is only a theory. There is strong disagreement, in certain channels, of when it would have been appropriate to release this to the public. Most of those in high places think it's premature. There's not enough data. And by the way, there certainly is not enough data. We need more to have any true degree of certainty. Their fear is that going public with this theory may cause panic."

"Why are you doing it then?" the reporter demanded.

"I disagree. I strongly disagree. I think we need to let the world know what might possibly be going on. We need to marshal every available research resource on this right now. We need to focus our law-enforcement and medical examiner efforts. We need to figure this out and stop it before..."

He paused.

"Before we have a world-wide pandemic."

There was some laughter from somewhere in the back of the room. Mike did not see from whom. But pandemics, for some, were a joke.

"Pandemic?" asked one of the TV reporters. "Like COVID? Do you think that's possible?"

"Look," Mike said. "I hope we're wrong. I hope we're wrong because if we're right, then yes, this is already spreading fast. Vicar. Wilson. Wester. Echols. Malawi. Around three weeks between those. That's fast. And if all these other cases are connected, pardon my French, but holy shit!"

"Kanetha," someone shouted. "What is your take on this?"

"I've been saying all along that Mae-Lu couldn't have done this. I agree with what Dr. Andrusek says. This makes sense to me."

"What is the CDC doing about this?" someone asked.

"Why don't you ask them? That's Dr. Adrian Bradford from the CDC in the back, with the purple tie."

Bradford saw everyone stare at him. He turned, opened the door, and left the room. One reporter ran after him, then a few seconds later returned, shrugging his shoulders at his compatriots.

"How does this virus affect people?" someone else asked.

"We don't know yet, but we have a clue. Today, the Medical Examiner's office released the full autopsy report on Mae Louse Vicar. Some of you might already have it. Let me draw your attention to the addendum letter attached from Dr. Pete Betsakos of Johns Hopkins. I spoke to Dr. Betsakos today. He'll be releasing a statement to the press later. His report found abnormal swelling in Dr. Vicar's brain, in an area known as the amygdala. That is a part of the brain known to have some influence on powerful emotions, including rage and anger.

"Here. I have copies of the medical examiner's report and Dr. Betsakos' report. Miss? Could you pass these out to everyone?" Mike asked, handing a stack of paper to the hotel's coordinator. He handed her a second stack. "And here's a list of other scientists who have agreed to talk about this. Not all of them entirely agree with our theory, but they're all familiar enough with it, and they're all actively working on it. So if you call enough of them, you'll get more than one assessment of this theory. I hope you do."

He paused again.

"We don't yet have any reason to connect the virus to her abnormal amygdala, except..." Mike held his hands out, palm up, "except that Dr. Betsakos stated that the swelling appears to be new and rapid. That leads only to a hypothesis that the virus has caused it. And then to a hypothesis that the swelling might be linked to these rampages.

"Despite remaining unproven, this evidence builds a theory worth pursuing with all haste."

"Do the police believe any of this? Isn't this just another attempt to divert attention from real, tragic criminal acts?" came a woman's voice from the telephone speaker. Kanetha recognized the voice. Everyone recognized the voice. It was Karen Quinn, the caustic TV talk-show hostess who had called Mae-Lu "pretty evil."

Kanetha leaned into the microphone. Mike saw her and stepped away, yielding it to her.

"Those of you in the room here, some of you might know Lt. Francisco, there in the back of the room. He's the lead detective in the Mae-Lu case," she said.

Francisco waved. "We have no comment," he said. "We're here to learn, like everyone else."

"Kanetha, aren't you just trying once again to deny your friend's responsibility for killing seven precious little children?" Quinn asked. "She brought terror and pain and death not just to them but to their families. To families everywhere. You can't make it go away by blaming some random virus."

Kanetha held her ground. "Karen, I pray for those families. But that was not Mae-Lu. I've been telling you, that's not Mae-Lu. She was a beautiful human being. I think we now know she was a victim, too."

"A victim?" Quinn replied. "Pullleaze. She was a monster! Who is this quack you've dragged out to waste our time with this ridiculous theory?"

"Look him up, bitch," Kanetha snapped.

Reporters' questions then came all at once, in a Babel-like overload.

"How fast can this spread?" a TV reporter shouted through.

"We don't know yet," Mike said. "There appears to be an incubation period of about a week to ten days and then an infectious period, and then with some people, and I stress only some people, a full-blown outbreak of psychotic symptoms two to three weeks after the initial infection."

That consideration reminded some reporters in the room of Wilson's presence on the whiteboard, in the room, and of her presence in previous interviews.

"What about Kanetha?' someone asked.

"Yeah, is she infected? She's spreading it?"

"Miss Wilson apparently was infected. She seems to be the link to outbreaks here, and here," Mike said, pointing to Daytona and Africa. "But it has been thirty-four days since her contact, and she has shown absolutely no symptoms. We have not been able to isolate the virus in her blood yet, or in anyone's, for that matter.

"Yet there is this. Miss Wilson represents our greatest hope: that this disease only affects a small percentage of people who are exposed. We don't know why."

"We've been in contact with her," said the Sentinel reporter. "Does that mean we might be infected? Does that mean we might turn into mass murderers?"

Mike sighed. He looked around at faces that now were terrified. He looked at Kanetha. She leaned in and he yielded again.

"Sure, it's possible," Kanetha said. "Any of you might have it. And any of you might get sick from it. That's the whole point we're trying to make here, OK? This is fucking scary."

·   ·   ·

It did not take long. Three hours after the press conference broke up, in a studio in Atlanta, Karen Quinn (she of the pixie blond hairdo, holier-than-thou blue eyes and shrill attack style) argued angrily with her producer and with a flunky who could not secure Andrusek or Wilson for tonight's show. They also could secure no one from the CDC, which was "no-commenting" Andrusek's shocking statements. Her staff had gotten her a couple of low-level scientists and a couple of psychologists, and she was furious at their incompetence.

She cornered the producer and his assistant in the back of the control room.

The producer was a dumpy-looking, veteran crime reporter who had become a producer for an Atlanta TV station and then moved on to Quinn's show at the cable network. Balding, short and plump, Stuart Roth was a brilliantly hardworking, aggressive producer. The flunky was a twenty-three-year-old kid, fresh out of college at Georgia Southern, named Tanya Reed.

Quinn screamed at the flunky, bringing her to tears in front of half the crew. Her producer grabbed her by the arm to lead her away, but Quinn turned her anger on him. Roth screamed back.

She stood stock-still and screamed. Shaking clenched fists, Quinn stood there, rooted, and let it all out. She stomped her feet.

"Ayyyyhargh!"

She stormed into her office and came back with her hand behind her back.

"I've had it!" she yelled at the producer.

Everyone just stood and stared. They had witnessed her tantrums before, but never anything at this level. They were terrified, but they did not know that this time she would do more than just yell at everyone, and maybe fire one or two of them. They gave her space and waited. No one wanted to face her. Standing in the middle of the room, Quinn swung her arm around. She had a Beretta handgun in her fist. She fired. Roth caught the first slug in his shoulder and spun, then dove. Quinn spun herself and began firing at everyone. The gun had a thirteen-round magazine, and once she had emptied it, she had hit four crew members plus the producer. Two of the crew members would die.

The rest, including Reed, ran. Someone pulled the fire alarm, and it blasted through the building.

Quinn stormed back into her office and reloaded. She came out and saw that everyone had left. She kicked a trashcan. She fired several rounds randomly into walls and equipment. A camera sparked briefly and let off a disappointing little puff of smoke. Quinn looked around in frustration, turned, and returned to her office. She stretched into her big, salsa-red, Old Hickory desk chair as if it were her bed and cried. Deep sobs came. She examined her gun, still hot, still wreaking of gunpowder smoke. She sniffed it, savoring the sharp sulfur. She caressed her cheek with it and absorbed its heat. She ran it over her lips and marveled at its hardness. She licked it and tasted its power. She placed the barrel in her mouth and blew off the back of her own skull.

CHAPTER 11

DAY 44: SATURDAY, MAY 25

Somehow, Mike knew this morning would be the last chance, at least for a while, that he and Stranger would have to go fishing together. So fishing they went. He needed to get away for a few hours. He knew just where to go.

They headed west to Mosquito Lagoon, just inside the Atlantic Ocean coastline and close to where rockets launch from Kennedy Space Center. Stranger jumped out, tail wagging, and gave a gloriously deep "woof." Mike grabbed his rod and gear from the back of the truck and followed Stranger to their favorite spot, about fifty yards from the bridge. Other fishermen were about, but like magnets facing each other, they naturally repelled one another to respectful distances apart.

Mike pulled on his wading boots and tied a top-water Sammy lure. He sloshed out into the shallows a few yards and let her go.

The sun was just rising behind him, giving the mostly clear but tannic shallow water a golden tint. Tenuous fog plumes rose from the lagoon, graying the far-away opposite bank.

Stranger sniffed around behind him in the sand, then dared to wander ankle-deep into the wash of the lagoon.

This stretch of inland waterway was America's redfish capital, and that was what Mike was here for. The saltwater lagoon also boasted sea trout, drum, tarpon and even the occasional flounder. Mike would be happy with any of them, but here, redfish were king. They were big, weighing up to twenty pounds or more, and they were ferocious fighters. Setting a redfish promised a shoulder-aching contest.

They were not the best-tasting fish, rather bland. But blackened or smothered with lemon-pepper, they justified the effort.

Redfish splashed their tails, giving away their locations, so Mike kept a keen eye out for activity. He also had to keep an eye out for gators. A large flock of white egrets, scores of them, maybe hundreds, fed in the shallows another fifty yards north, strutting around on Tinker-Toy legs. They were good indicators of gator activity, so Mike kept an eye on them, too.

Hard as he tried, Mike could not completely clear his mind. Hell, he had just announced to the world that his institute had unleashed a new virus that turned people into raving monsters.

Worse, it was true. He was sure of that conclusion now. What did that reality portend? Mike was up half the night dealing with the demon answers to that question. It haunted him until he came up with the idea of fishing. Then he dropped off quickly and got a good three hours' sleep before the alarm went off.

The night before, his phone had never stopped ringing and the email and texts poured in. Some were helpful, and Mike was grateful that more than a few of his colleagues around the country were with him. A few even had some good ideas, and he high-fived the air whenever someone promised to dive in to help. But others were highly critical, repeating the tired old "You're a rash fool, not a scientist" theme, which had partly defined his reputation in Atlanta.

The Institute's president, Katherine Lowe, was furious. She wanted to and surely would have fired him for going rogue and naming the institute in the press conference. But the same controversy that infuriated her also gave him solid job security, at least for the moment. She did not want to be the one who fired the scientist who had brought the world's attention to a potentially devastating problem, at least not while there was a chance he was right. And she knew he was.

She yelled at him on the phone for ten minutes, anyway.

Kanetha called three times, the last call coming around one-thirty a.m. She was having a rough time too, but was having a more difficult time dealing with it. She attracted the crazies somehow, especially after someone posted her cell phone number online. She was tough, tough enough that she never backed down. She actually took every call she could, screamed her bits at them and then hung up. But even the toughest can take only so much battering.

As he dropped another cast, Mike's cell phone vibrated in his shirt pocket. Mike had promised himself that he would take no calls this morning and had even contemplated turning off his cell phone. But he could not bring himself to do it, not with the gravity of what had gone down. He glanced at the number and realized this call was one he had to take.

It was his father, back in Texas.

"Whateryadoin?"

That greeting was his father's standard hello by phone. Mike was never sure how to answer that question. His father always judged even the simplest response. Fortunately, fishing seemed as sure a bet as anything to appease the old man.

"Fishing, Dad."

"Fishing? On a day like this?"

"What are you talking about? Mike said, seeking normalcy. "It's beautiful here."

"I just saw you on Fox this morning."

"Oh."

"So you think there might be an epidemic of some disease that makes people go postal?"

"Yeah, that's about right."

"And you said it's going to spread and get real bad."

"Yeah."

"And you're fishing?"

"Dad, I've been in the lab for weeks solid. I need a break. The world's not going to end while I take a few hours off."

"The world's going to end?"

"I did not say that, Dad."

"That's the way it came off on the news. Boy, they're making you look like a fool."

"I'm not a fool, Dad. This is for real."

There was a pause, during which Mike suddenly felt a powerful, protective love for his parents well up. For the first time in his life, he had to tell them what to do. For the first time, he had to command his father.

"Dad, it might be a good idea for you and Mom to go stay with Uncle Lee and Aunt Annie out at the ranch for a while."

"You're serious?"

"Yeah, Dad. Just hunker down for a while, see how things go."

"You're serious?"

"As a heart attack. What else you got to do?"

Uncle Lee had always been the family kook, and now that role seemed like a good thing. He had a little ranch—a modest "spread" in Texas terminology—outside of Cuero. He had a few cattle and Aunt Annie had a few chickens and a vegetable garden. Decades there had led him to believe the country was about one race riot away from the second Civil War. Back in the nineties, he had joined the survivalist movement. After "survivalists" got a bad name when some of them went around blowing up federal buildings, ranting like Klan members and threatening presidents, they simply became "preparers," which sounded practical, like devout Mormons. Then they went back to blowing things up, ranting and threatening, but with some measure of social respect.

Uncle Lee was prepared. He expanded an old storm shelter, tunneling a connection back to the house, carving out and furnishing a deeper saferoom. He plumbed in well water and septic connections and ran electricity from the house. He stocked a storage room with food and supplies. He erected a windmill connected to storage batteries, a system capable of providing a fairly steady supply of about fifty amps to the shelter. Tunnels led to four pop-up battlements outside each corner of the house, hidden by rock piles and not accessible from above ground. They provided excellent watch-and-shoot vantage points. He had underground tanks installed and filled with gasoline and kerosene. He set up pop-up tire cutters across the long gravel drive to the house. Uncle Lee also converted all his savings, and all the money he could set aside since, into Krugerrands. "Bullets and bullion," he advised a young Mike. "When shit hits the fan, you're gonna wanna be stocked with bullets and bullion."

Who was kooky now?

This chaos was exactly the world Uncle Lee and his kind had always dreamed about. Anarchy, where only the well-armed and well-prepared would survive. The grand moment at which pseudo intelligence, formal education, and willing participation in an economy and a culture that demanded "modern thinking" no longer amounted to a damn. This emergency was the revolution in which those with guns, guts, and glory would finally, finally, take over this country. He would be a pig in shit then, king of his domain. Who would have thought Uncle Lee was right all along?

Aunt Annie had a nice collection of porcelain dolls, a cardboard box stashed close by, just in case.

"The shit might hit the fan, Dad," Mike said.

"And you went fishing."

"Didn't you always say, 'I'd rather be fishing'?"

"Your mom wants to talk to you."

There was a pause while Mike's father walked through the house looking for her. That was the old man's way of ending a conversation. Not "goodbye." Not "take care." Not "I love you." Pass the phone.

Mike steadied himself.

"Dear?" she said softly. "How are you?"

"Fine, Mom. How are you?"

"We're so worried about you out there. The news, oh my! They make it all sound so serious!"

"It is serious, Mom."

"Well, I'm sure you'll figure it out, dear. Have you heard from Stephanie lately?"

Stephanie was Mike's ex-wife, someone who blazed in and out of his life in less than two years while he lived in Atlanta. They'd married six months after meeting, and the very next day Mike knew he had made a mistake. Like Mike, Stephanie was a driven and independent soul. That drive led to constant arguing about everything from where to live to what to eat. The sex and the similar personalities had been the draw. But it turned out to be just an ill-advised partnership between two people who both wanted to do their own thing. Their divorce was quick and simple, and both said good riddance. That end came three years ago now, and Mike had not spoken to her more than a couple of times in the past year.

The problem was that his mother had fallen in love with Stephanie from the start. They remained in contact. They were Facebook friends and chatted there often.

There was a piece of that world with Stephanie that Mike just never understood, yet his mother did. It was where she had him helpless.

"No, Mom."

"Well, you might be interested to know she's getting married again."

Out of the blue, the most unexpected thing happened: Mike's heart lurched.

Please, world, end now, Mike thought.

But he said, "Really, who to?"

"His name is William something. I can't remember. Just a minute. I'll look it up. I have my iPad right here."

"Don't bother, Mom. I don't care. I told Dad you two should go stay with Uncle Lee and Aunt Annie for a while."

'What on earth for?"

"This disease, Mom. It's pretty bad. I want to make sure you two are safe."

"Well, I'm sure we'll be just fine here. The condo association just hired a new security firm this year, and they've got twenty-four-hour patrols now."

"Mom, please, just go stay with Uncle Lee for a while. I think he'll explain it to you better than I can."

Mike contemplated calling Uncle Lee and getting him to appeal to his sister. By now, it probably already was crossing the kook's paranoid mind. Maybe later. Mike decided that getting his parents to the ranch was a project that must be completed, but for now, he would leave it to his father.

His reel started spinning. He tucked the phone between his shoulder and ear and gave a yank to set the hook. The fish yanked back, and he almost dropped the phone.

"Listen, I gotta go now, Mom. Love you, bye!"

He freed a hand from the pole, closed the call, and slipped the phone into a pocket.

The fish pulled to the left, then back again, and the line loosened. He reeled some in and the fish snapped again, this time breaking the line.

It figured. He always used 30-pound test, but a good move by a good fish could break even that line. He reeled it back in, sloshed back to shore, and sat down. Stranger came over to him immediately and licked his arm.

There was no escape from this thing, Mike concluded, not even here.

CHAPTER 12

DAY 45: SUNDAY, MAY 26

The medical examiner also released something else: Mae Louise Vicar's body. No one was coming for her. Her parents could not be reached. No one. A pauper's funeral was arranged. Police Det. Lt. Marty Francisco called Kanetha Wilson because he knew she might be the only person who would be interested.

She contacted Mae-Lu's Episcopalian church. Kanetha badgered the rector into serving the funeral. But he would not come himself. He assigned his most junior associate priest, a Father Richard Biddle.

Kanetha quickly tasked a funeral home to plan a graveside service at an old cemetery—old by Florida standards—in a pocket of rural, tucked into a back corner of suburban sprawl east of Orlando. To get there, Kanetha drove through a bustling area. The street passed through dense suburban apartment complexes for a couple of blocks and then it returned to its original state, a country road. After passing by a couple of semi-rural clusters of houses, she happened onto a cemetery she had never known existed.

This spot was a nice place. Kanetha was pleased. Mae-Lu would be pleased. She found the spot near the back of the cemetery, within view of a chain-link fence and a trailer park beyond. A cluster of trees stood between the grave and the chain-link, offering some shielding. Kanetha was relieved.

Mae-Lu already was there, in a plain, closed casket, displayed next to an open grave, along with two attendants. The priest was late.

Kanetha wore her only appropriate black dress. Like her, the two attendants also were black, and dressed in black. After a few minutes, a red Toyota pulled up, and the priest got out. He dipped into the backseat and emerged with a white cotton sheet. He spread it over the coffin and introduced himself.

The priest was younger than Kanetha, a plain man with an abundance of energy, Anglo in every feature, prematurely balding with a bushy brown mustache and round, wire-rim glasses hanging onto a long, thin, boney nose. He looked nervous and uncertain.

He approached Kanetha with a solemn hurry, as if all this chore was a deeply troubling affair that must be dispensed with, quickly.

"Is anyone else coming?"

"I doubt it," she said.

He nodded to the others.

The sky was appropriately cloudy. The wind picked up, rattling the trees.

Father Biddle opened with scripture from Luke, describing the crucifixion scene.

"One of the criminals who were hanged railed against him, saying, 'Are you not the Christ? Save yourself, and us!' But the other rebuked him, saying, 'Do you not fear God, since you are under the same sentence of condemnation? And we indeed justly, for we are receiving the due reward for our deeds. But this man has done nothing wrong.' And he said, 'Jesus, remember me, when you come into your Kingdom.' And He said to him, 'Truly, I say to you, today you will be with me in Paradise.'"

He looked around as if there were a crowd to scan. Kanetha felt as if he was simply avoiding making eye contact with her.

"We may never know why this young woman did the despicable acts she did, why she caused so much pain for so many, for no reason we can know. But God knows. The Lord will judge her in His full awareness. Let us pray for her soul."

Kanetha bowed, but kept her eyes upward on the priest.

"Heavenly Father, through your wisdom and mercy, grant your love to the soul of this woman who has passed from this earthly realm. Grant to her your mercy, through your Holy judgment. Grant to her your justice, but also your grace, so that she may be judged by all the good in her soul and the evil that we have witnessed. Grant to her rest, everlasting peace and the Love of being with You and your son, Jesus Christ our savior. We ask you this Father in the name of your Son, Jesus Christ, and we further ask that you bestow the same justice, grace and peace upon us all. Amen."

Finally, Father Biddle looked at Kanetha.

"Would you like to say anything about our sister, Mae Louise Vicar?"

She had not intended to speak, but she realized that if she did not, this funeral was going to last less than five minutes. And that kind of quick memorial just was not right. She looked around.

"Father, I have a question," Kanetha asked.

"Yes, my child."

Kanetha was almost amused by that salutation, considering she estimated she was a good five years older than the priest. She pressed on anyway.

"Do you think Mae-Lu went to Heaven?"

He took an uncomfortable moment to respond, as if was hoping she might withdraw the question. She did not.

"The Lord is merciful, but he also is righteous. It is His decision, not ours to know."

"Because it was not her fault, you know. It was the disease."

He did not reply. The news had certainly gotten around after the press conference. It was the talk of the world. The CDC and authorities still were silent in response, so the debate was over whether Andrusek was a kook or whether everyone must live in sheer terror. For many, it was a straightforward choice.

"Well then, God knows," she said. "And she's there."

Now the priest looked irritated, as if the woman simply did not get it. He gave her a condescending smirk, as if he considered her too insolent to address. He tried to stare her down, but she would not avert her eyes from his. He blinked first and stammered.

"What, what she did," he said.

"What she did? What she did?" Kanetha's voice raised to a yell.

"Please, child," he said. "There is such a thing as evil. Th-there can be no greater manifestation of evil than killing innocent children."

"She did nothing. My girl Mae-Lu did nothing! It was the disease that ate her brain. You know that, don't you? You said you did. And I know that. Hell, father, the whole damned world knows it."

She could not look at him. She turned to the attendants, who had retreated a few yards away.

"The Mae-Lu I know was not evil. She was an angel! Mae-Lu was someone who cared about everyone, even the suffering peoples of far-away places that most Americans never give a single thought to. Ever. The Mae-Lu I know dedicated her life to ending suffering and pain."

"Our, our Heavenly Fa-Father wi-will judge her in His wisdom," the priest stammered. "He-he will take that into account. He also will ta-take into account all the, all the su-suffering she has brought to this world. To-to us all."

"She did not do this to us. God did this to her!"

"Child," the priest interrupted. "Do not take your anger out on the Lord."

"Why not? If God creates all creatures, then surely this, this plague! This, this murder plague, was his idea. He did this to her. He did this to one of the best people I have ever known! I loved this woman."

"Your fr-fr-friend had a choice and sh-sh-sh-she chose evil. Regardless of who put th-th-those thoughts into her head, the Lord gives us free will to ch-cm- to choose. And she destroyed those precious lives."

"She did not!"

"She ki-killed innocent people! She brought pain and misery t-t-t—to us all!"

"You think she had a choice?"

"I don't think you c-c-can ignore what she became. I don't think G-G-God can. Will."

Kanetha was crying now. "Mae-Lu, I," she gasped. "This is bullshit."

"Miss Wilson!"

"You! You were put through this so that the rest of us could understand something. Something! I know you're waiting for us in Heaven regardless of what this piece-of-shit priest thinks!"

"Miss Wilson, stop!" he commanded.

She did. She looked him deeply in the eyes.

"You—you must acknowledge the e-evil she brought to this world. You must! Th-th-those families lost everything. Those innocent children suffered and died needlessly."

"Go to Hell, father. Go to Hell! And you won't see Mae-Lu there. Oh, no! You won't see Mae-Lu there. May God have mercy on your soul."

She turned and strode away. She kept walking, twenty-five yards, fifty, and as she walked, she could hear the priest behind her finishing the service without her.

"The Lord is my shepherd," he said. "I shall not want."

She crossed the drive and wandered toward the middle of the cemetery, toward a brick and limestone mausoleum as big as a house. The structure was four high walls, open at each corner and covered by one roof. Underneath were rows of cremation crypts, with stone walkways between them. In the center was a small, covered courtyard with stone bench memorials.

Kanetha sat on one and sobbed.

After a few minutes, she realized she was not alone. Another man had crept up on her from behind. She turned with a gasp.

It was that damned detective, Lt. Francisco. He stood a few paces away, wearing a cheap brown suit.

She laughed through a sob. "What the hell do you want?"

Marty stepped forward. "I missed the funeral," he said. "It must have been quick."

"Why? What do you care?"

"It's what we do," Marty replied. He sat on the other bench and looked at her. "We homicide detectives go to a lot of funerals, to see, to listen, to learn."

"You mean to spy on the people who come?"

"Yeah, all one of you. That's what we do."

"Well, you can go to hell, too," Kanetha said. "Just like that shit-for-brains priest."

"I believe you, you know."

"What?"

"What you said over there, about 'the murder plague,'" Marty said. "And what you and that doctor whatever-his-name-is said the other day about the virus. It makes sense."

"So you don't believe Mae-Lu was guilty?"

"That's kind of irrelevant now. They're putting her in the ground as we speak."

Kanetha was stunned. A chill ran down her spine. She tried to speak but could not think of a word to say and closed her mouth. She was suspicious of this man, and she despised him in the weeks since Mae-Lu's rampage.

"So you did get here in time for the funeral!" she said.

"I spy, remember?"

"Hardly anybody believes me—us. Why you?"

Marty adjusted himself on the bench, buying a few seconds.

"I've been a cop almost twenty-five years, the past eleven in homicide. I've seen it all, sweetie. Nothing about your friend's murders makes sense to me, though. There's no motive. There's no previous behavior, no stress points, no trigger, nothing. I know, I've looked. I've looked hard."

"There was nothing," Kanetha confirmed. "She was a good person."

"Sort of the same thing with the Veronica Van Zandt murders," he continued. "I've got her case too. Sure, maybe that first one. That lawyer obviously beat her that night, so there was at least a trigger in that homicide. The bastard. Never liked that guy. But for her to go door-to-door shooting her Johns? There's no explanation for that behavior.

"I hate it when I don't have an explanation."

Kanetha wiped her eyes. "That's it? That makes you jump on this fucked-up theory that we've got a murder plague going on?"

"That, plus we've got this shitload of murders going on everywhere. There's not a cop anywhere that doesn't suspect there's something, something different behind what's going on. We see it. It's not a hypothetical for us; it's our job. We know there's something going on. But it's not just that. We've also run so many domestics the past couple of weeks...it's out of control. Assaults. And none of them make much sense."

"It's gonna get worse," Kanetha said.

"I agree," Marty said. "It's gonna get bad, real bad. That's why I want to learn more about what you and that quack are up to."

• • •

It was getting worse even as the pair of them sat there, sharing a peaceful moment in the tomb. Orlando's third mass-murder already was underway, at a resort hotel in the tourist district, well outside Marty's jurisdiction.

A valet brought a Bushmaster Carbon-15 Special semi-automatic rifle and a Smith and Wesson .38 to work in a gym bag. At the valet desk, he shot his fellow drivers, then rushed into the lobby where pandemonium already had broken out. He chased and shot. His bullets cleared an elevator of very unfortunate tourists when the door opened. Then he headed for the convention center wing of the hotel, shooting willy-nilly. He entered a banquet hall packed with salesmen getting roused up by a loud, multi-media presentation. The valet ran through, endowed with a fresh magazine and shot at a rate of almost three bullets a second. Tables collapsed, chairs toppled, people fell, bleeding or not. He reached the employees' exit and disappeared from the scene of carnage.

Sheriff's deputies cornered him in a corridor, but he ducked through a "Cast Members Only" door, ran down an interior corridor and took a service elevator to the roof. He emerged next to a huge, bizarre twenty-foot-tall sculpture of a fish adorning the corner of the hotel wing.

The valet fired several shots upward at the fish, chipping chunks of concrete. Then he turned to the parking lot, where there were no longer any obvious targets. He moved to the edge of the roof and thought he might get a shot at people crossing a bridge to safety in another hotel. But as he took aim, so did a deputy sharpshooter a hundred yards away. One last shot echoed through the area and the valet tumbled down nine stories, crashing through palm tree fronds on the way. He ended the crisis by bouncing on the lawn beside the hotel.

In about twenty minutes, the valet had set several new records. When the conference center was finally cleared, the mighty power of a good assault weapon and a bagful of high-capacity magazines had brought death to fifty-seven people in that room, ninety-seven people throughout the entire hotel resort. Another forty victims survived, because of swift first responders and the heightened preparedness of Orlando's EMT departments. Orlando's emergency responders and emergency medical teams, sadly, had as much training and practice as anyone in the entire world to deal with mass casualties.

This bloodbath was the event that convinced the world, and it spoke with its feet. Conference cancelations fell like bowling pins. Families saving for years for an Orlando vacation cut their losses on deposits. Hotel bookings fell overnight and overtime, in a stampede away. The shutdown, caused by the consumers this time, hit with the same swiftness of the COVID shutdowns, without a single governor or mayor yet calling for them.

That night, the President of the United States, joined by the Surgeon General and the Attorney General of the United States held a joint press conference in prime time.

It was the highest-rated broadcast in television history.

President Olivia Leary was herself a medical doctor and a former dean of an Ohio university medical school. She had pursued the medical profession with international acclaim before she entered politics, becoming a United States senator, and then winning her party's presidential nomination as a long shot who stole early primaries with charm, wit, intelligence and bravado. She won the White House election by running when whipsawing political extremism had driven a major popular mood swing back to the center of American politics, where she had always lived.

None of that partisan backbiting mattered now. Everybody knew it.

She looked into the cameras with steely green eyes set in a wrinkled, almond-shaped face framed by short auburn hair.

"My fellow Americans, we have a national crisis of unprecedented proportions," she announced. "It is a public safety crisis. And it is a public health crisis."

Watching TV in his lab, Mike punched the air with a right hook of victory.

"It is time for hard acknowledgments and great resolve," Leary continued. "We are experiencing the spread of a new virus that is causing profound neurological changes in some affected people."

Mike's cell phone rang. It was Kanetha.

"She's doing it!" Kanetha said. "She's telling the world that we were right all along!"

The President and her Surgeon General discussed the spread of the virus and what they knew about its effects and consequences. They spent little time projecting its spread, and in the question-and-answer period, they largely dodged any commitment on that prospect. They spoke hopefully and glowingly about the research being done by the Centers for Disease Control and Prevention, noting that they were already further along than the world's scientific community had been during the early stages of COVID. They said nothing about Drs. Andrusek and Crosby, or the Nona Institute.

The announcement brought fear, doubt, denial and anger nationally. A chorus of nay-sayers and political opponents accused Leary of being another foolish over-reactor.

But those reactions quickly washed away in a torrent of terror that would open up and rain mercilessly over the globe.

President Leary herself would not survive long enough to see the worst. Three weeks after her announcement, and a commencement of daily press conferences on the epidemic, one of the Secret Service agents in her security detail helped her into her limousine outside the White House, pulled his sidearm, and shot her four times. He had turned to shoot others but was gunned down before he could aim at anyone else. Vice President Howard Tate was sworn in after she died the next day. He was never seen to leave the White House for anything, ever, after that morning.

The torrent flooded America.

It had started with those few squalls of death that had blown across, beginning with Mae Louise Vicar, and had picked up to a steady rain. Within weeks of the president's announcement, the full force set in, making every outing in every city in America a potential trip to massacre.

Within weeks, there was no denial, no point to debate.

Mass shootings, bombings, arson fires and crashes blazed everywhere every day, until only the most bizarre and heinous massacre would catch anyone's attention. Far beneath the level of horror required to gain attention, a broader, more insidious flood was washing into every community. Friends and family members were turning on one another with whatever weapons were available. Fists. Knives. Baseball bats. Gardening shears. Assaults, domestic attacks and lowly lone murder / suicides became the un-talked-about epidemic that everyone knew about.

No one was to be trusted anymore.

And yet, somehow an economy and a society carried on, swiftly transitioning to black-market and, wherever possible, electronic lifestyle.

COVID had been the dress rehearsal that showed that society and the economy could operate in lockdown. It came naturally to Americans to lock themselves in and find ways of acquiring the things they needed to survive, the things they wanted. People still went out occasionally, because they needed to; therefore, the supply of targets was never ending.

One industry that did very well during the transition, despite its role in the crisis, was the guns and ammunition business. Almost every state eliminated gun control laws and legalized open carry so that everyone could pack, all the time. And everyone who could, did.

Medical research focused on stopping the plague. The CDC, hospitals, universities, research labs, and amateur scientists everywhere dug in.

It took three months after President Leary's announcement before a breakthrough was announced. Researchers at the University of Michigan, backed by scientists at the Cleveland Clinic and the CDC, had determined why the disease affected some but not others. The virus triggered a gene that triggered massive cellular releases of an enzyme in the brain, which stimulated its rage and action centers to psychotic levels.

The gene was recessive, which meant only one in four people carried it in an effective pair. The virus seemed to have no effect on people who did not carry both ends of the pair.

They dubbed it the "warrior gene." Geneticists theorized it had evolved from many thousands of years of human warring, particularly as generations of family lines were pressed into service as their tribe's, their empire's, or their nation's warriors. Those people with the gene were capable of atrocious behavior when necessary. They had survived, they had procreated. Those warriors without the gene died cowardly deaths from inadequate action in battle. The gene carried on, especially since those individuals with the gene had returned as heroes and had mated like rabbits.

And now those biological warriors who got the virus responded as if they were Medal of Honor candidates surrounded everywhere, all the time, by the enemy. They did what came naturally. They killed until they were stopped.

Dr. Bernard Samuels made the announcement, cautioning that they had not determined how to turn off the gene, but that was the next step.

PART II

CHAPTER 13

DAY 174: WEDNESDAY, OCTOBER 2

Dr. Michael Andrusek was certain that Dr. Bernard Samuels was wrong, or at least not entirely correct. The "warrior gene" did not fully explain why the incidents of violent behavior affected so few people. The epidemiological models still did not work. If a quarter of the population was susceptible, then the outbreak should be even far more widespread than they had seen. It was bad. It was terrible. But one out of four? The world should be ended by now, he believed. Something was missing.

He also was concerned that Samuels' theory did not fully address the sudden onset of symptoms, how people went from crankiness to uncontrollable psychotic rage in a snap. But it was a good start.

This focus was in Mike's wheelhouse, studying neuron responses to proteins stimuli. The data Samuels and the others provided looked strong, but it was not entirely jibbing with Mike's results. To stop this thing, they had to figure out what triggered it, and this warrior gene just was not enough.

These past five months had been like a deep sleep during the long hours past midnight (ironically, that rest was something Mike rarely experienced since he had met Kanetha Wilson in May). So much of life was suspended. She had work, finding food, and eating. Rest, when and where it could be found.

Regardless, the identification of the virus strain had geared up the worldwide research for both a vaccine and a cure. Government research mobilized like army call ups, from Beijing to London, Tel Aviv to Atlanta. The Big Pharma companies lustily committed mega resources, just as they had with COVID.

Mike's little lab was all but forgotten in the worldwide effort.

Over the past few months, the violence peaked then fell away somewhat as people went out less and less, and virtually all public gathering places closed.

Mike and Dr. Crosby ran their research at record paces, skipping steps and moving on based on the slimmest of evidence.

Dr. Crosby was altering other virus strains trying to develop germs with many of the same connecting characteristics as the murder plague, but with different proteins.

Mike was looking at those viral connections to neural receptors, especially in the amygdala region of the brain. He was encouraged by all the autopsy results that had been flooding back, especially in the early weeks, indicating a consistent pattern of enlarged amygdalae. Stop the inflammation there, stop the disease, Mike thought.

Mike went through mice and monkeys as if they were insects, setting an uncaring eye to the mammalian slaughter he oversaw. He had always done so, tucking any shred of guilt behind the mantle of scientific progress, but if he had given it half a thought, he would have agreed with Kanetha that this rush was going beyond the pale.

Mike moved from observation to hunch to revision daily, recording little of it and leaving the sloppiness for grad students to document, if it ever was required. He knew. That certainty was all he needed to proceed.

This work was hardly peer-reviewable research. If anyone wanted high-quality science to back whatever he found, they would be sorely disappointed. Mike wondered whether he could ever sell whatever he found. He also began preparing for the prospect that he and Kanetha might have to take on the world again.

It was looking like it might not matter, anyway. Mike worried that neither he nor anyone else capable of figuring out this crisis would live long enough.

Anymore, any time he went out, he seemed to encounter someone trying to kill him. He had been shot at a couple of times, but fortunately by no one who could shoot straight. Twice he had survived other drivers trying to ram his truck off the road. His three tons of truck, thank you very much, was not at risk. The ragers never had a chance. Mike shoved each of them into ditches and kept going as if he was using his bumper to nudge a shopping cart out of a parking space.

Still, he had to get home daily to take care of Stranger. Outside of the lab, Stranger was all that mattered to him. Fortunately, Mike's commute was short, just a couple of miles, and he could drive it all on back roads.

Like everyone else, he had learned that the first rule about being on the road was to never stop—not for anything or anyone. Traffic signals, stop signs, someone running out into the street in front; those devices were all indicators to speed up, not slow down. Getting through intersections was tricky. Hardly any vehicles on the road nowadays—and there really were not that many—were free of war wounds.

`Mike narrowly missed the worst incident when a Nona Institute intern with some higher education in applied chemistry blew up half the cafeteria on the Fourth of July. Mike had just left the dining area. He was in the corridor and the blast knocked him down. He ran back in to find devastation. One of his research assistants was among the five killed. Mike tried hard to save lives, to stop bleeding and stabilize anyone who was still breathing. But with emergency medical service wait times running an hour or more, there was only so much he and a handful of others there could do.

Still, you carry on.

Spending downtime in his apartment with Stranger was the only therapy he got. He had not fished in months. Hiking was out of the question now. If you asked him, Stranger was the only therapy he needed. The hound always was positive, always optimistic, always there for him.

This day began as Mike tried to begin all his days. Weak black-market coffee, tortillas and an orange for breakfast, followed by walking Stranger. He gathered his hat, the leash, and his Smith & Wesson .357 Magnum snub-nose. Clint Eastwood was right, Mike believed, as he was about most things. You want a gun that puts someone down with the first shot. The damn thing weighed like solid brick.

Stranger started his "oh-boy-it's-walk-time" dance, lifting one or two paws at a time in a pathetic attempt to jump as soon as Mike put his hat on. Mike got the leash on, and the dog pulled it straight with strength that people who did not know bassets would never imagine.

Mike had a first-floor apartment. He had reinforced both doors but installed a doggie door on the back one, off the kitchen, so that Stranger could get in or out at his leisure. To get out regularly, though, required Mike to turn several locks. They emerged into a crisp, cool morning.

Directly outside was about thirty yards of lawn, then some woodsy growth and a small lake. The lawn had been abandoned and grew into knee-high weeds and grass, taller than Stranger. The dog loved it. Mike looked around and saw no one in the woods, no one on the lawn, and no one on the perimeters, near the parking lot edges. These apartment buildings were three stories, so the upper balconies were perfect for snipers. Stranger led them into the grass. Mike could see no one was out. He kept his right hand on the revolver's grip, swinging the gun by his side.

Stranger headed for the lake with a powerful pull. Mike did not like to take him into the brush, but relented. Stranger was following a scent, and this moment was the dog's time.

The woods were about ten yards deep to the lake's edge. They stepped from the grass and Mike saw where Stranger was headed. A woman's body, white and brunette, was behind some blooming azaleas. Mike felt a cold rush through his body, just under his skin. When they got there, he could see she was dead. Her chest had been blown open. Stranger alerted again, pulling to the left and found another body, a young white girl, perhaps eight or nine, with the same hair as the woman, shot several times. Both killings were fresh.

Mike clicked back the hammer, crouched, and looked around carefully. Stranger alerted again, pulling around behind him. Mike spun and saw an adolescent boy pop out of nowhere, wielding a small handgun.

The boy clicked a trigger against an empty gun. Mike's heart leaped. He almost pulled his own trigger, but hesitated.

He could not.

The boy sobbed.

Mike watched frozen as the kid pulled and pulled on his gun's trigger, but nothing was happening.

The boy sobbed.

"Die, asshole! Die!" he screamed.

Mike stepped toward him, holding his gun at arm's length for a careful aim, as if, just in case, he might get off a shot if the boy's gun actually fired. The boy stood his ground, clicking his trigger.

"Die, damn it!" he cried. "Then kill me!"

Mike took another step and the would-be shooter stood still. The boy screamed wordlessly, threw the gun at Mike, missing badly, and then charged him, head down and arms out as if he were going to tackle the big man who outweighed him by more than a hundred pounds. Mike let go of the leash and Stranger attacked the boy's leg as he came close enough. Mike swung his left fist and knocked the kid to the ground.

The teen sprang up, coming forward on his knees at Mike again. This time, Mike gave him a swift boot to the jaw, and the boy went down again. He lay on the ground thrashing his arms and legs, swinging wildly with closed fists at nobody, except Stranger, who barked and ducked in and out with cat-like reflexes, getting a bite in here and there.

"I'll kill them!" the boy shouted. "So help me, I'll kill them all!"

Mike secured and holstered his gun and climbed onto the boy's back. The kid's legs were kicking and his arms still flailing. Sitting on his legs, Mike caught the boy's right arm behind his back, then his left.

It was like riding a bronco. The kid, maybe one hundred and ten pounds, bucked, squirmed and struggled with surprising strength. He was putting every ounce of his energy into his fight. He pounded his own face into the dirt. He spit dirt and phlegm. He looked over his shoulder at Mike and his eyes rolled back into their sockets, as if he were seizing. He shuddered with another struggle, mighty this time, against Mike's hold.

"Die you! Why can't you just die? Or kill me," he spit out, partly in a sob, partly in a scream.

Mike got to his knees on the boy's back and reached for Stranger's leash. Got it. He pulled the dog close and unclipped him. He gathered the kid's wrists again and used the leash to bind them.

The boy screamed an unholy roar. He took a breath and screamed again. He took another breath and screamed again. This confrontation was getting annoying. Mike punched him, hard, in the back of the head and finally knocked the kid cold. Mike checked his vitals to make sure he was still alive. He scooped up the kid's gun. He picked up the boy. Mike maneuvered him over his shoulders and got his right arm around the legs, in case the kid came to and began kicking again. Mike worried for a moment. He could not reach his gun quickly if he needed to, but decided it was worth the risk.

A plan was emerging.

Back in the apartment, Mike dropped the kid into the guest bedroom. After looking around frantically, he cut strips of leather from his couch and fashioned them into bindings. He then cut Stranger's old leash. He rolled the unconscious teen onto his back and tied his wrists and ankles to the corners of the bed frame.

Then he called Kanetha, who now had a very expensive institute-provided phone, fed by a government-run network.

"We're taking a new direction in our research," he told her.

"What?"

"Never mind. I'll tell you everything when you get here. I need you to get out and find some medical supplies and drugs. Can you find them?"

"I think so. There's a guy I know who would know."

"Great, I'll text you a list."

Mike called in the bodies to the police, neglecting to tell them he had encountered and captured the likely killer. He settled into his computer and pushed out several frantic e-mails. He scrolled through the medical examiner's reports on Mae-Lu and pored through research reports he had assembled from throughout the country. Now and then, he texted Kanetha with requests.

He pushed his brain. What do we know?

He reviewed Samuels' report again. He called up the lab work they had done on their own blood: Kanetha's, Tim's and his own. Back to the research. Back to Kanetha's bloodwork.

Push. Push.

Where is it?

The teen looked as if he was seizing. Plenty of research had been done comparing the viral symptoms to seizures, all of it inconclusive. Mike himself found nothing by looking at the seizure angle together with the warrior gene.

His phone buzzed with a text. It was Kanetha.

"In parking lot. Got stuff. Brought someone."

Who? Mike wondered. Why? Mike ran his palm through his hair. Now was not the time to bring someone over, not with the kid tied to the bed in the spare bedroom.

Kanetha knocked. It was her signature knock. Mike checked the peephole. She was there with a man. They both were holding bags. Mike picked up his magnum from the table, pulled back the hammer and crept the door open.

"Who's he?"

"Can we come in? I feel like a sitting duck out here," Marty said.

"This is Police Lt. Francisco. Marty. You met him at the press conference," Kanetha said. "He helped us get this." She raised her bag. "He wants to help."

"A cop? Jeez, Kanetha."

"Just open the damn door. Hurry."

Mike stepped away, and the pair entered. Mike locked it behind them.

Stranger waddled over to greet them. He liked everyone.

"Did you get everything?"

"Yeah, but it wasn't easy. Marty was amazing. I..."

A howling scream came from the guest room. Marty pulled his gun.

"What was that?" Marty said.

"Nothing. The TV."

"Bullshit."

The kid cried out again.

"Mike?" Kanetha asked.

"Goddamn you! I'm gonna kill you!" the kid yelled. "Let me— Ouch! Shoot. I'm gonna kill you, so help me!"

"The TV?" Marty said. He smirked. "Don't you have it on a little loud?"

"It's my nephew," Mike said.

"Let me go!" the kid screamed.

"It's my other dog," Mike said.

Marty headed toward the screaming. The kid let out another howl.

"Don't go in there!" Mike ordered. "I'm warning you!"

"Bite me," Marty said. He pushed the door in.

"Ayeee!" the kid yelled. Then he spit, hitting his own shirt. I'm gonna kill you!"

And then he started hyperventilating with hard, grunting breaths. Marty watched him thrash and pull at his restraints.

"Jesus," Marty said. "You caught one."

Kanetha was at the door now. Mike stood behind them.

"Mike," she said. "What the hell are you going to do with him?"

"We're going to run clinical tests," he said.

"No. No, no, no, no, no!" Kanetha said, backing away and waving her arms. "This is way wrong. This is what the Nazis did. This is what they did at Tuskegee!"

"What? No, it's not," Mike said. "Anyway. He killed his mom and little sister. He tried to kill me. I should have killed him; he begged me to."

"That doesn't matter!" she yelled. "You can't run experiments on an unwitting human being. A child."

Mike shouted her down, with his I'm-right-and-that-certainty-ends-the-debate tone. "We're saving his life. And if we get lucky, we might just save all of our lives."

"Please," she shouted back. "Don't give me that 'ends' shit."

"Argh!" the kid chimed in, looking at them. But he could not possibly see them. His eyes were rolled back in their sockets again. He bucked against the ties. "I'm gonna kill all of you! Do you hear me? I'm gonna kill you all!"

"He's gonna break that right-hand restraint," Marty observed. "I've got some stuff in my car that'll work better."

CHAPTER 14

DAY 183: FRIDAY, OCTOBER 11

Doctors Michael Andrusek and Tim Crosby had to merge their labs for the most practical of reasons. Neither of them any longer had enough lab assistants to continue alone.

Mike was working on identifying genes known to be tied to epilepsy and other seizure disorders. Dr. Crosby was working on identifying other viruses' characteristics that mimicked those traits they had already seen regarding the warrior gene, as were scores of other researchers around the country.

Mike and Dr. Crosby had an advantage.

Their labs were almost empty of help. Two PhD candidate technicians, Pedro Alvarez and Dawn Riley, were dead. Three others had gone missing and were presumed dead. The others were afraid to leave their homes. Occasionally, two techs, Ken "Bubba" Walters and Sylvia Moreno, would show up, but Mike no longer counted on either of them, especially Sylvia.

Bubba showed up today, though. White, thirty-two years old with a grizzly red beard and greasy reddish-brown hair tucked into a Ron Jon's cap, Bubba was the only man in the lab who was bigger than Mike, about as tall, but at his peak well over three-hundred pounds. He had played lineman at the University of Central Florida. Back in the day, he was an impressive human specimen. But over the years, his bulk had slid from his shoulders and chest to his belly. His legs and arms, once described as tree limbs, now were more like overstuffed throw pillows. His personality was more like throw pillows as well. Soft and comforting, Bubba was someone who still wanted only to please the coach. During the past few months Bubba had dropped more than forty pounds through simple malnutrition, but still could stand to lose another fifty. Interestingly, Bubba walked like a cat. Agile. Silent.

Mike did not realize the big man was behind him and jumped when Bubba touched his shoulder.

"You need to see this, Mike," he said.

Bubba looked happy, almost gleeful. He moved his feet and reminded Mike of Stranger doing his walk-me dance.

He led Mike to the mice lab on the sixth floor. Bubba slid a five-gallon plastic bin, topped with wire mesh, from a wall of shelves holding dozens of such bins. He placed it on a lab bench. Inside, twenty mice scurried about. None were dead. None looked particularly menacing.

"They were exposed to K12Q a week ago Tuesday," Bubba said. "And K38M on Sunday."

They should be dead. They were happily being lab mice, as happy as lab mice ever get. Mike stared for a moment in silence. His first response was confusion. This should not be. What went wrong?

"Last Tuesday?"

"Eleven days ago."

"You're sure?"

"Sure as I'm standin' here," Bubba said.

Mike felt his heart skip a beat.

"These were from samples A and B?" Mike asked.

"A and B."

"No mix-ups?"

"No one's been in here since then but you or Dr. Crosby."

"Run a second batch."

"I did." Bubba withdrew another tray. More happy little pink-eyed white mice. "Last Thursday and Friday."

Mike stared long and hard at a tub of harmless, happy white rodents. The potential conclusion finally hit him like a slap in the back of the head, and he gasped.

Bubba giggled.

Mike laughed.

Bubba's giggle turned into a roaring laugh. Mike put his hand on the other man's shoulder and for a moment, the two were sharing an intimate, uproarious moment, as if their lottery numbers all checked.

And then Mike bolted from the lab and ran down the corridor. He threw open the stairs door, banging it, and disappeared into the well.

They had the kid doped up on both haloperidol and ziprasidone, under the mother-like care of Kanetha, who still was disapproving but was doing her damnedest to make the best of a bad situation.

They still weren't sure who this kid was. Every few hours he would come down from the injections and thrash about in complete, lost confusion. Though he often appeared to be awake, he never achieved full consciousness. Those periods looked more like he was going through a terrifying, half-sleep nightmare with his eyes open. Sometimes he would call out, "No!" or "I hate you!" or some other barely discernible words, but he never quite recognized the real world enough to respond to it.

Mike explained that his brain was wandering to the edges of a postictal condition when it was trying to reset, then bounced back into a rage. His brain was in a loop, never quite able to regain normal function.

As Mike had shown her, Kanetha would push another injection into his IV port and he would settle back into a docile state, still appearing to wake sometimes, but remaining completely unresponsive.

If there were any neighbors in the adjacent apartments—and Kanetha was pretty sure there weren't—they weren't complaining.

Otherwise, her job was to kill time. Mike had substantial collections of books and DVDs, and she was running through them. This day she was curled up with a Don Winslow novel that just did not seem all that violent anymore, despite its intense brutality.

She heard a key scratch in the door lock and reached for her revolver, even as she heard Mike's voice.

"Kanetha, it's me," he shouted through the door.

She kept her hand on the gun anyway, and he burst into the apartment.

"What's up?" she asked.

He did not answer. He went straight past her, directly into the kid's room, leaving her to get up to lock the door behind him. When she came back, he was pulling a dose from a vial into a syringe.

"What's up?" she asked again.

He still did not answer. He made his way to the side of the bed and pushed the dose into the IV port.

"We may have found a cure," he said.

"A what?"

"Or maybe an inoculation. I dunno. It would take weeks to see. Or I can just shoot him now and see what happens in a few days."

"What did you inject him with?"

"An anti-virus, I hope. It seems to block the receptors that trigger seizure genes to activate the rage fueled by the warrior gene."

"Oh my god," Kanetha said. "Will it work?"

"No idea. It worked on mice. This little guy's the first real test."

"What about side effects?"

"No idea. It might kill him, for all I know."

"Mike!"

He smiled at her and sat down on the corner of the bed. He had been at full speed for the past hour. He did not realize until this moment that he was truly, physically exhausted. Or maybe it was a psychological exhaustion. Either way, he needed to sit.

"You're joking," Kanetha said. "I get it."

"No," Mike said. "I'm serious. Look. None of the mice are dead. So there's that. But we know pretty much nothin' about this strain other than what Crosby's been able to determine it does in Petri dishes, and what Bubba and I have seen with mice. By injecting him now, I'm skipping about five years of necessary research. So, no. None of the questions have answers. Nothin'."

"What do we do?"

"We wait. And we watch."

•   •   •

With Mike at the apartment, a rare occurrence during daylight, Kanetha finally went home to check on her father. She had not heard from him in weeks. She had not heard from almost anyone in at least that long. That situation was not unusual anymore because almost no one had phone or internet service and almost no one drove around, as Kanetha was doing now, unless there was a damn good reason. She took Mike's truck because it had gas.

Her family home was in a small, older, working-class neighborhood a good twenty miles away, tucked in between a lake, two major streets and a big county psychiatric hospital. People only went into her neighborhood if it was their end destination. The broader community there had never been the safest of places, but people had gotten along. Normally, the streets were full of people during a day like this one. People here walked. They walked to the stores. They walked to the parks. They walked to the bus lines. They pushed strollers and clung to little hands. Some men were sure to be hanging out on front porches, spilling into the yard and streets, where someone was always working on a car.

Not on this day, though. Kanetha was grateful for the uneventful drive over. But the absence of any signs of life in her childhood

'hood unnerved her in a way almost worse than encountering random killers.

Her father's house, where she had grown up, was as still-looking as the street. It was a flat-roofed three-bedroom ranch, fronted with stucco, which he had painted pastel green. Pops had been meticulous about their lawn, but now it was wild like all the others, with tall grass gone to seed, and plagued by hip-high weeds that had flourished from lack of attention through the rainy summer and autumn. Pops had installed bars on all the windows a long time ago, and the glass behind them was not broken. That security was a good sign. His Nissan was in the carport. That sign could go either way. She parked behind it.

She knocked hard—the doorbell had not worked in decades. She called out.

"Daddy? Pops?"

There was no response. Kanetha felt her heart sink and her shoulders slumped. She knew the worst could happen, but she had refused to face the prospect until this very moment. She took a deep breath and bucked herself. She tried her key. The door only pushed open a couple of inches before a chain stopped it. She went around to the back and tried the rear door. It opened. She hesitated before she stepped inside. He had not answered. What would she find inside? Her heart ran a fast beat. She grasped her revolver and pushed the door all the way open.

Kanetha checked the pantry beside the kitchen.

"Daddy? Daddy? It's me, Kanetha!"

Silence.

The kitchen was clean. Her father always kept the kitchen clean. She opened the refrigerator. She spied a few bottles of condiments, but not much more. She held her gun in both hands and stepped toward the dining area.

"Pops?"

The wall at the far side of the dining area was, to Kanetha, her father's museum: a few scattered pictures of her mother from back when she was still around, and of her uncles and aunts and cousins from various family gatherings. Maybe fifty pictures, framed by Walmart. They captured Kanetha as a baby, as a toddler, as a six-year-old in braided ponytails headed for first grade, holding up one finger. Second grade, with two fingers and missing teeth. Third grade with three fingers. Her parents had made her perform this ritual all throughout school, and all the pictures were there on the wall in cheap frames. One showed her in her high school graduation gown, and there she was in her Florida A&M graduation gown.

Her mother appeared in some pictures through eighth grade. The progression of those photos of her mother was telling. First grade and second grade, her mother's almond skin shone, her eyes twinkled and her teeth flashed, looking much like Kanetha today. By the sixth-grade picture, her mother did not smile. In the eighth-grade picture, her mother's beautiful eyes were sunken and dull. Her skin had lost its sheen. Her hair was a mess. Kanetha hated that picture, but she dared not touch it.

Kanetha learned then how to lose someone. But not her father. She could not lose him. She felt her breathing pace her heart.

She stepped through to the living room. Nothing was out of place, but nothing looked in use either.

"Daddy?"

She ambled down the hall toward the bedrooms. The first was her father's storeroom. She opened it anyway. No one was there. The second was her room. She opened it and saw her own museum to herself, Kanetha's life, frozen in time at when she was a college student. Her bed was made, covered with the comforter her Aunt Jeannette had made for her as a high-school graduation present. She tried her father's door next.

"Daddy?"

She opened the door to find another vacant, well-kept room. Kanetha was both relieved and scared. Where was her father? His car was out front. What happened to him?

Perhaps he was out getting food or visiting someone. She sat on her father's bed, horrified that she had made this trip to check on Pops but had no information.

She heard the back door open. She lifted her revolver.

Someone entered the house. She could hear steps.

"Daddy?"

When there was no answer; she regretted yelling out. If it was not him, whomever it was knew she was there, and where she was.

The steps sounded like a big man in boots. They stopped in the hall.

"Whoever you are, come out!" a deep voice commanded.

Kanetha's hands holding her gun were shaking. She was not about to come out.

"Go away!" she responded. "I've got a gun."

"Get out here, bitch!" he replied.

Standoff.

He fired off a couple of rounds. It sounded like a semi-automatic. They were warning shots. Whoever it was had her outgunned.

"Now!"

"Don't shoot! Don't shoot! Don't shoot. Please," Kanetha said. "I'm coming."

She raised her hands, her gun held aloft, and stood from the bed. She took one step toward the hall door.

"Now, bitch!"

She inched toward the door, holding her breath. In the hallway was a large, heavy, bald black man about her age, holding an assault rifle. He was covered with tattoos, even on his face. He was poised, ready to shoot, and she winced, shutting her eyes to the blast.

"Kanetha?" he said.

She looked. It took a moment for her mind to sort through her fear to achieve recognition.

"Leonard? Leonard? What are you doing here?"

Leonard Fuller had been Kanetha's neighbor, a few doors down, and a schoolmate, gone bad years ago. She was not sure she had seen him in a decade. And as with a lot of guys like him, she would have assumed he was in prison or dead if she had given him much thought at all.

He inched the barrel of his rifle upward, toward the ceiling, just enough to signal a truce, but not enough to suggest he was ready to disarm.

"Pops asked me to watch his place."

"My dad? Where is he?"

"He went up north somewhere with Mr. Dugan. Said it was safe there. They took off."

Kanetha put her head down and her feet led her into a little circle dance of confusion, disappointment, and yet relief. She sat on the bed and placed the revolver beside her.

"My uncle has a farm near Gadsden. So, he's okay?"

"I guess."

"Do you know how to..."

"No. He and Mr. Dugan did not say. They just asked me to watch their places."

Her head flooded with so much relief and hope she almost swooned. And then another fear bubbled up. Pops left safe, but would he ever return? Would she ever hear from him again?

Kanetha was not sure she could talk. She felt a cry welling up in her. She fought to suppress it. She knew speaking was going to betray her, so she held herself silent, steady, unmoving. She tried to refocus her thoughts away from the uncertain hope and fear about her father. But a sob came like a hiccup anyway and gave her away.

Leonard shouldered his gun and stepped toward Kanetha. He put a hand on her shoulder.

"Pops is a good man. He'll be all right. Meantime, we gotta look after each other, right?"

"Leonard, how do we d-do it?" She said, her voice breaking. "I mean," she paused, trying to compose herself. She would not go teary. Not in front of Leonard. She spoke with anger. "All you have to do is go outside and anyone you see might try to kill you."

"You been gone from the neighborhood a long time, girl. That's been the shit around here a long time."

"Don't talk to me like I don't belong."

"Just sayin'. Some things you know how to deal with. You know?"

"People walking around with automatic weapons? People shooting you just because you're there?"

Leonard shrugged.

Kanetha laughed at him. She sucked back a gasp that would have shaken out tears, but then, against all her efforts, all her strength, a tear leaked. She felt her whole body shudder.

"Hey girl."

Leonard took her by the arm and lifted. He led her to the living room and made her sit down. He sat down in a chair across from her. She sniffled. She stared at the window, looking angry yet avoiding eye contact. She sniffled again. He got up, looked around, went into the bathroom, and came back with a wad of toilet paper. He handed it to her. He sat again, and she wiped her eyes.

CHAPTER 15

DAY 186: MONDAY, OCTOBER 14

Guy Phillips awoke slowly, and alone. When his head cleared enough, he realized he was in a hospital bed, in a hospital hallway. He looked around. An IV drip hung from a pole raised from a corner of his bed. The tube connected to his right arm. Electrodes coming from his chest connected to a monitor hanging from a second pole on his left.

He squeezed his eyes closed and then forced them open again. He had been shot. In the leg. At the open-air market. A shooter. Two. The second was a cop, who tried to finish everyone. Guy had shot him and then gotten away and had tried to walk down the street. How did he get here? He tried hard to remember. He remembered lying down to die. That memory was it.

His right leg was bandaged. He felt no pain, though.

There were several other people in beds in this hallway. He did not see any nurses or doctors or anyone else who appeared to be caring for anyone. He cranked his head around and could see the nurse's station behind him. Someone was there. One or two women—nurses?—working at desks. He closed his eyes again.

When he opened them again, a nurse was indeed there, checking his vitals. She appeared to be Filipino. He could not read her name tag.

"You're lucky you still have your leg," she said. "You're lucky you're alive. You're lucky you're here."

"Lucky me."

She removed the dressing and lifted his leg, examined both sides, swabbed it. Guy felt an acidic burn. He pulled his leg in reflex. She re-bandaged it.

She took his vitals and checked the chart.

"You'll be all right," she said. "You need a little more rest. We'll check on you again later."

She reached around him and pushed a syringe of something into his IV.

The next time he opened his eyes, there were three men standing over him, plus a different nurse. He immediately recognized one man as his neighbor and friend, an Orlando homicide detective, Lt. Marty Francisco.

"Hey, Marty," Guy said.

"Hey Guy. This is Detective Rosario and Detective Price. They want to ask you a few questions."

Both of them looked as taut and serious as FBI agents. Marty was not like them. He was paunchy under an old jacket, with a fluffy mustache and eyes that were never serious. Guy blinked and rubbed his eyes with his free hand.

"Am I in trouble?"

"You tell us," Rosario said.

"Look, Guy, I know this is insane," Marty said. "We had three shootouts yesterday alone. But we've still got jobs to do. We still need to investigate. Murder is still murder. And we've got two dead cops in this one. You were at that one? Nurse said you said you were."

"It wasn't me. I mean, I shot the guy, but it was him or me. He was shooting everyone."

"Who did you shoot?" Rosario asked. He opened a little notebook.

"The second cop. Look, first the first guy was shooting everyone. The guy with the Uzi. He shot me. Then we thought everything was okay. I'm? I'm the one who called 911. But these cops show up, they get out and then one cop shoots the other cop. Then he starts walking around, finishing us all off. I was hiding. He leaned over to see me, and I let him have it. But I did not kill him. Some other guy finished him off."

"And then?"

"Then I left."

"What did you do with your gun?"

"I don't know. I must have left it. I don't even know how I got here."

Rosario and Price pushed him with more questions, taking notes with those tiny little notepads. Guy had seen them use those notepads on TV, but he never believed detectives used them in real life. Their questions were about details, but they were not too pressing. They got his name, address, workplace and phone number and said they would be back in touch. And then they left.

Marty stayed.

"I'll take you home," he said. "The nurse said they've done all they can for you. You can go home soon as you're ready. I think they want you outta here because they need the bed for someone worse. And they don't want to waste any more time or this shit on you."

He swatted the IV bag.

"Thanks."

Marty went to talk to the nurse. She came around with discharge papers and a few words of advice and detached the IV and electrodes. She did it quickly. She was done with him.

When Guy tried to stand, he could not. He may have hobbled several hundred yards yesterday, but today he was convinced he could not make it from the bed to the wheelchair three feet away. His thigh had tightened up, and when he touched his right foot to the floor, sharp pain fired through his entire upper leg, hip to knee. It was as if the entire leg was squished right now.

Marty got him into the wheelchair.

Marty drove an unmarked, dark blue Dodge Charger police car, and he had left it parked in the valet circle just outside the door. The car said "Police!" in every way, except it had neither lettering on the door nor flashers on the roof. Marty drove toward home, and then took an odd turn, as if going somewhere else instead.

"Multi-car crash. Probably a suicide driver trying to take someone with him," Marty said.

The main roads on this route were lined entirely with businesses: trendy stores, restaurants, law offices. Some were boarded up. Some were busted open. All looked closed. Phillips had seen avenues like these desolate streets growing up in Detroit, so they did not look entirely strange, and he recalled seeing avenues like these in the newscasts out of New Orleans in the years following Hurricane Katrina. Yet here there were almost no pedestrians or moving vehicles anywhere. He spotted someone lurking behind an abandoned restaurant. They passed three cars driving the other direction.

Marty ignored the red lights. Why the traffic signals were still functioning was a bit of a mystery anyway, Guy thought.

"Do you think I'll be a suspect?" Guy asked.

"Nah. All the evidence says it went down exactly how you said. Thank God you're alive."

"You think God really gives a shit at this point?"

Marty looked at him, and then back to the street. Both men had suffered unthinkable losses already.

Guy had lost his wife Pam to a shooting early on, in the mall just down the street. The mall closed after that incident. So did the others in town. The coronavirus crisis a few years ago had led to government-mandated business closures, which had resulted in political backlash that had swept out the political leadership that had advocated closures for public health reasons. The pendulum swung the other way, but not for long. This time, there were no government mandates. Just, everybody closed up and left. This time, there was no backlash.

Back when she was killed, they still could have open funerals. Pam's was as beautiful as she had been. She had plenty of family and plenty of good friends. Pam was one of those people other people gravitated towards. She was the center of so many circles, the center of all Venn diagram overlaps. People Guy did not know packed the church. They packed the cemetery. And afterwards they packed their little three-bedroom house until her sister saw Guy could bear no more and shooed everyone away.

Pam and Guy had no children. That choice was Pam's. She was not ready yet. When they married, she was young, twenty. He was thirty. They celebrated her twenty-ninth birthday a few weeks before she died. He thought, however desperately, that maybe she was ready for children then, but the killings had begun, and they were both then worried about how long the craziness would last.

Forever, now.

Forever was taking a long time without her.

Pam had brought life to Guy, every day, in every way. He had never known anyone so outgoing and honest, so optimistic, so positive about everything, even their fights.

"This is our adventure," she would say when she was angry. "Learn to love it. This is what we'll be sharing, looking back."

And he did. An argument was something to be enjoyed. Terrible events, from financial problems to misunderstandings, were things to be shared. When she wrecked her Toyota, she insisted it was an adventure they would laugh about.

Guy was not like her. He had always suffered from shyness and low self-esteem, even as he succeeded in school, career and life. He was driven to prove himself against standards that only he saw. Falling short, he worked harder. That drive, he supposed, was why he gravitated toward mathematics and engineering, because they required little personal interaction. He would have starved as a salesman, foundered as an executive. He had always enjoyed solitude and always found himself uncomfortable trying to fit into any crowd.

Except with Pam. She understood him. She brought him along into the life of humans carefully, always watching over him in the presence of others. He also knew that she needed a strong, steady sidekick. She told him she loved him for that acceptance. She was Batman needing a Robin, The Lone Ranger needing a Tonto. She never, ever forgot how much she needed him for that role, or neglected him in any setting.

He always had been content to be in her background because somehow it felt like his place. It was a wonderful place to be. Most of their friends were her friends first. Most of their social outings were where she would rule, and he would be the strong, silent arm-candy. He was forever grateful that she would bring him along as her full partner in a life that was far more active and outgoing than a young Guy would have ever attempted. He knew shortly after marrying that she was leading him into more life than he would ever have had otherwise.

"This is our adventure," she would tell him anytime she saw doubt or discomfort lower his eyes.

What would she say about being gunned down in a shopping mall food court? Guy felt only pain, anger and grief for weeks when he gave that event any thought. One day, it occurred to him she would want him to absorb it and make her slaughter a part of them. Somehow, this boldness would be his way of carrying her on. The superhero has fallen. The sidekick must go forward for her.

"This is our adventure," she would say.

Marty grabbed Guy's attention by making a turn onto a side street far early of their neighborhood. This one featured big houses encircling a small lake. A fountain in the middle of the lake was off. This town used to be fountain city. Fountains even appear on street signs. All the best lakes had fountains. But Guy had helped the rec department take most of them offline a couple months ago.

Marty pulled over at a curb in front of a big brick colonial house with boarded-up windows on the first floor. Even the front door was covered with plywood. He turned off the car.

"Wait here," he said.

Marty got out, stopped, then climbed back under the steering wheel. He punched something under the dash. He punched it again, and a springboard swung down, holding a pistol. He removed it. He checked it and then handed it to Guy.

"I take it you already know how to shoot people. Anyone gives you trouble, shoot them. I'll be right back."

Marty went up onto the portico and pounded on the door. A slot in the plywood opened. Marty said something. The slot closed. Marty waited. The slot opened again. Marty withdrew bills from his wallet and handed them through. A moment later, a bottle emerged from inside. And then another. Marty carried them back down to the car. Inside, he handed them to Guy, trading them for the gun. Two liter-bottles of Jim Beam.

"Your medicine. Thank God you can still get whiskey in this town," Marty said.

Marty used the backstreets to get to Guy's tiny house. Guy's Toyota was still in the carport, undisturbed. Marty parked behind it.

Guy had bricked over all his windows a few weeks after Pam died. The landlord had started a patio project the very weekend she had died. He never came back to finish. Guy found a different, more practical use for all those bricks and bags of concrete. Each window still had an opening the size of a single brick. It made the house very dark, especially when there were blackouts, which could last for days. Darkness suited Guy anyway.

Marty got him inside, poured him onto the living room couch, and then wasted no time filling a couple of deep tumblers. He opened the refrigerator, then started banging cupboard doors.

"Where the hell's your food?"

"I dunno. I guess I left it in the market."

"I'll bring some over later. What's this? Oh, hello!"

He brought over the two glasses in one hand, and a bottle and a can of sardines in the other. Guy stretched his long body across his long couch but still overlaid the arm. His thigh felt as if it were twenty pounds of pain. He took his glass and drained an inch. He looked at it, winced, then downed the rest. Marty set the bottle on the coffee table, raised his own glass and drained it without stopping, but his wince at the end was far more pronounced.

"Ooh, wow!" Marty shouted.

He refilled both glasses. He opened the can of sardines and waved it toward Guy, who waved them off with his glass.

"Those were Pam's. I can't stand them."

"Good. More for me."

Marty put one between his lips and sucked it in. He chewed.

"So you never answered my question," Guy said.

"What?"

"Does God give a shit anymore?"

Marty chewed some more.

"After Eddie was killed, I had doubts," Marty said. "But do you remember? There was such an outpouring of love, commitment, and generosity. It changed me too. Remember? I lost Eddie and became a better man because of it. I did."

"I know you did."

"It took time," Marty continued. "But somehow that tragedy brought out the better man in me. This city became a better place. We all became better people. That was God. I'm sure of it."

Guy had watched Marty through that whole time. Eddie was Marty's twenty-three-year-old son from an unfortunate marriage that had lasted only a couple of years. In a paradox that haunted Marty, the boy and his father were both close and distant. Eddie's mother was a lifetime partier, an alcoholic who dabbled in drugs, and when Eddie moved out after high school, he wanted to be like his father. But Marty was busy then, like he always was. He found time to dote on his son but never quite grasped whom Eddie had become. Marty never picked up on the first clue, never imagined that his son was gay.

And so they never had that reconciliation, or showdown, between the gay son and the father he loved, who loved him, but who was of a generation, and of a society, and of a culture that was not ready to accept that Eddie's sexuality was the tiniest insignificant part of a terrific young man his father had loved.

Eddie was in Pulse, the popular Orlando gay nightclub, when the city's first mass murderer came in and fired more than 100 rounds. Eddie took two bullets to the head. Hours later, at first light, Orlando Police Detective Lt. Marty Francisco was out in the parking lot when someone else identified Eddie's body.

The pain, the horror, the sorrow, the disbelief, and the denial all were double-edged for Marty. Guy was among the first to see that struggle. How could Eddie be dead? What was he doing in a gay nightclub at two in the morning? How could he be gay? Marty could not process the double shock. He asked himself all the wrong questions.

The next few days, maybe a couple of weeks, Marty invented scenarios for Eddie to have been straight, in that club with friends that night. He felt an anger toward Eddie for being where he did not belong and paying for it. Guy quickly grew tired of them and dismissed them not outright, but just by not joining the conversation as Marty laid it out. Pam was different. She implored Marty to mourn for Eddie as he was.

Then, at Eddie's funeral, angel-winged volunteers created a wall between the gravesite and hate-filled protesters who had come from as far away as Kansas to denounce homosexuality. Eddie's gay friends rained tears on the sod. Those tears washed away what little hope Marty had for his invented excuses for his son. He had to choose a side.

Pam, ultimately, brought Marty around. She convinced him that what Eddie needed more than anything was to know in Heaven that, despite it all, his father stayed with him. She convinced Marty that he needed that to survive. It kicked in. One day Pam and Guy drove Marty back to the gravesite and watched the tough old cop fall to his knees, hug the gravestone, weep, and beg his son's forgiveness.

After that epiphany, Marty became one of the most visible, outspoken, and generous allies of Orlando's gay community. It was as if Marty had not only accepted that Eddie had been gay, but now needed him to be. This newly defined person was his son. This was the son he would mourn from here out.

Marty raised his glass to Guy.

"God gives a shit," he said. "I see it even now. I see, I hear about acts of heroism and kindness almost every day. Just like after Pulse. People are far more scared now. But, still, most of them are good."

"Probably not for long," Guy said. "I think we may be witnessing the end of the world."

"You're really getting cynical now that you've been shot at. You know that? Geez. It was just a flesh wound. Get over it."

"Kiss my ass."

"I would, but it probably stinks, and I don't want to vomit sardines all over your couch."

Guy laughed. "I appreciate that." They clinked glasses.

"Things have slowed down, you know," Marty said. "A month ago. Two months ago. Shit. We were having so many shootings, bombings, crashes, stabbings, beatings, brickings, bitings." Marty laughed at the absurdity of some of the killings. "We weren't even taking reports on all of them. Not even taking reports! And you know where most of the bodies have been going? Do you? Do you? Not all. Some. If families aren't claiming them right away?"

Guy did not respond.

"The landfill. The goddam landfill."

"Ha!" Guy swatted with an open hand. "I've heard that rumor. It's bullshit."

"Swear to God. They cremate. Then they ashcan the ashes."

"Bullshit."

"Asses to ashes. Your ass to trash."

Marty sucked in another sardine. "Things are better now, though. It has definitely slowed down."

"That's because no one goes out anymore. It's harder to find anyone to kill," Guy said. "Everyone who's still alive is boarded up inside."

"Or bricked," Marty said with his mouth full. He nodded to the window. "Nice job, by the way."

Marty was acting sarcastic, as usual. Guy had bricked the windows from the inside, sloppily, though effectively. Big chunks of dried, spilled concrete stuck to the sills, the floor, even on the coffee table next to the bottle.

It occurred to Guy he had not had Marty over in a couple of months, so Marty had not seen the brickwork before. Like everyone else, they'd both hunkered down. They'd missed a lot.

Marty turned his attention to Guy's wedding picture on the table.

"Pam's was beautiful," Marty said.

"There's that. Damn, this leg hurts," Guy said. He chugged more from his glass, and Marty topped it off for him. "You ever been shot?"

"Never had the pleasure. You need some pain meds? I can get you some."

"Thanks, no. I'd probably get hooked. How much was this? What do I owe you?"

He picked up the Jim Beam bottle by the neck.

"Fifty bucks a bottle. It's on me. I still owe you."

"Fifty? Wow! Now there's a crime for you."

Guy shifted his weight and his leg reminded him of the hole blasted through it.

"Ow, shit," he announced.

He raised his leg as best he could and peeled back the backside bandage and dressing a little to examine the wound.

Marty sucked in another sardine and topped off his glass.

"You know how to change that dressing, right?" Marty asked.

"The nurse showed me."

Marty was there when she showed him. Guy's entry wound was no big deal, stitched closed and scabbed now about half the size of a dime. The exit wound took a chunk of flesh a couple inches across and a half-inch deep.

"Four times a day. It's important, Guy. I'm surprised they did not pack it."

"Pack it?"

"Yeah, they. They fill it with gauze all the way in. Let it heal from the inside out. Otherwise, it. Never mind. You know you were lucky."

"I'm telling you what," Guy replied. "If the shot was a few inches higher and a coupla inches over, he'da taken out my junk."

They both laughed at that concern. They sat in silence for a while. The room was pretty dark. A single floor lamp, with a high-efficiency bulb, plus the TV, lit the entire room. Guy studied his iceless drink, then sucked on it.

"Is the world ending, Marty?"

"Nah. Maybe America. I hear most of Europe's pretty plague-free compared with us. They shut down right away, and it made a difference. Canada, Mexico, they're not so bad."

"That's malarkey. Canada's got it bad."

"That's not Europe."

"England's got it. What? Africa? Brazil? It'll spread."

"I dunno. Most borders are closed."

It was true. Canada and Mexico both had closed borders with the United States and were guarding it with their armies. Remarkably, a southern United States border that had seemed so porous to illegal crossings heading north before the murder plague broke out now was remarkably tight. Mexico's army patrolled with gunship helicopters and rarely left any runners standing. Word got around. No airport in the world would accept a flight from the United States. Other international flights were subject to in-airport quarantines. No seaport would allow a ship or boat from America to dock.

Floridians were trying to get to the Bahamas, Puerto Rico, even Cuba by boat, by raft, by anything. If they made it and were caught, they were escorted back and dropped on rocky shoals along the Florida Keys. Cuba was shooting without warning shots.

"It'll spread," Guy said.

"Hey, we had a woman last week try to kill some people at a gas station on Michigan Avenue by running around throwing rat poison at them."

They laughed. They clinked glasses and drank.

They had reached the point that the shit was getting amusing.

"She had this box. She was doing this." Marty got up and acted like he had a box in his hand and swung it the way a priest sprinkled holy water from a scepter. They laughed some more.

"No. It was like this."

He made his motion more like a lunge, to fling the contents farther.

"What'd you do with her?"

"Someone shot her. People are getting impatient, I tell you."

"I'm telling you what. It's getting harder now. We're all holed up in our bunkers."

"There was a guy I heard about in Winter Park last week. He was walking up and down the street knocking on all the doors saying things like, 'Package.' 'Police.' 'Candygram.' Only he had his gun in his hand the whole time."

"Land shark!" Guy offered.

This time, they laughed harder. "Land shark!" Marty repeated.

When Guy caught his breath, he asked, "Anyone open the door for him?"

"Sure."

"What happened?"

"Some old lady shot him."

They laughed hard again, and Guy twisted on the couch. Then he screamed with pain because that move shifted his leg. He imagined his thigh like a loaf of bread connecting his knee to his hip. Every movement squished it and every squish radiated pain.

Yet Marty pointed at Guy's leg and laughed even harder. That mockery made Guy laugh harder, which made his leg hurt.

Marty refilled both glasses.

"Jeez, there are so many guns," Guy said. "I lost two of them yesterday. I still have two left. Six months ago, you could not have paid me to have a gun in my house. I guess that's finally a good thing to have, huh?"

"No, it's not," Marty said. "If we didn't have so many damn guns out there to begin with, most of these attacks would be with knives or cars or boxes of rat poison. I can't tell you how much harder my job is because the sick people have guns, the bad guys have guns, the good guys have guns. Damn kids are walking around with guns."

"We have to."

"Yeah, maybe. Maybe now. But if we would just run out of bullets, we could survive this thing. I can deal with people throwing rat poison around."

They clinked glasses and drank again.

"I expected to die, Marty. I really..."

"Stop."

"No. I've never been so scared. I..."

"Don't."

"Three times, Marty. When that first guy started blasting away and hit me. All I could think was, this is it."

"Guy, don't."

"Then that cop was walking around, so calmly, so confidently. So coldly. He was..."

"I said stop it!" Marty screamed. He stood up. Marty had a temper, usually triggered by impatience. It sparked a little here, and for a moment Guy shut up. Marty paced the length of the coffee table, four feet. Back. Forth. Back again. Then he turned to a still shocked Guy on the couch.

"I..." Guy tried again.

"But you did not die! You did not die! Jes-us, Guy! Don't you dare feel sorry for yourself for almost dying! Lots of people really have died. Lots. They're really dead. Don't you compare yourself to them for one moment! You're alive!"

"I..." Guy tried yet again.

"Eddie really died! Pam really died."

"I know Pam died!" Guy shouted back, with more than an edge of anger, shutting down Marty's rant. Guy swiveled on the couch a little and grimaced when his squishy leg squished. "I think about Pam dying every goddamn second."

"Well, you. Did not. Really. Die," Guy said as coldly as he could manage. "You're still one of us. One of the living. So don't you dare think you were almost dead. Not for another minute! Do you understand me?"

"Have you ever faced your own death?"

"Of course. I'm a cop. I—Well. I—No. Not really. I've been shot at. Aimed at lots of times. But not close-up like you. But that doesn't give you the right to think of yourself in the same context as them. As Pam! As, as, as God knows how many people. You don't have the right to feel sorry for yourself. Not one second. You're still with me."

Guy nodded his head in defeat. A sly smile squeezed into tightened lips.

"This is our adventure," Guy said, softly.

"Huh?"

"Nothing. That's what Pam used to say all the time. She'd say that to remind me that it's never about situations. It's always about the people in them."

"Whatever."

Marty rolled his eyes as if he would not let that little nugget of philosophy get any credibility. He sat down again. They drank. Marty filled their glasses, and they sat in silence for a few minutes, worn out by their spat, absorbing it, and finally assimilating it.

Guy swirled the whiskey in his glass. He looked up, and Marty responded by looking up.

"We're fucked, Marty." He said. "America's fucked."

"It's worse here in Orlando. Way worse. We're ground zero, man. It's not so bad elsewhere. Just seems like it. Maine? North Dakota? They're probably fine."

They tapped glasses in a solemn toast. They drank. Marty shook the bottle, then refilled.

"Look at the bright sides," Marty said.

"Bright sides?"

"No traffic. Parking anywhere you want. Rents are down."

"I haven't paid rent in three months," Guy said.

"There. See?"

"I think my landlord's dead. Gotta be. Otherwise, she'd have come over here in a tank."

They clinked glasses again.

"My bank closed. I haven't paid my mortgage," Marty offered. "But they took my savings with them. Fuck 'em."

"You can get that back, you know. Through the FDIC."

"Yeah, right," Marty said, sounding a little sour. "You tried to call a federal office lately?"

They drank. Guy choked on his and put his glass down with urgency.

"Hey. I just thought of something," Guy announced. "This shit might spread worldwide. But the world won't end."

"No?"

"No. There'll be some shit hole little island in the middle of the ocean somewhere that'll never get it. Some tribe way back in the Amazon. Waaaay back. They won't get sick. Way back."

"Fiji."

"Nah. Not Fiji," Guy said, waving his hand. "Too many tourists go there. You go to Orlando. You go to Fiji. They're screwed."

"Tahiti."

"No, no, no. no, no. I mean, some little shit place between Tahiti and Fiji. Maybe."

"Fahiti."

"Fajita."

"Tahiji."

"Tafijihiti."

They both laughed until they both were coughing. The sight of each other coughing made them both laugh at each other more.

• • •

Marty took a bathroom break and when he returned, Guy had curled onto the couch, carefully, to keep his leg straight, and made do by bending awkwardly at his waist.

When Marty finally looked over, he realized his friend's eyes were closed. Guy was asleep.

Marty picked up the bottle. Only a little was left. He found the lid with a little trouble and screwed it on. He put it on the kitchen counter with the other bottle and headed for the door. Marty reached to unlock the door but stood frozen a moment in drunken contemplation. He turned and went into Guy's bedroom and returned with Guy's bedspread. He spread it over the tall man curled up asleep on the couch. Marty switched off the light and went back to Guy's bed and collapsed.

CHAPTER 16

DAY 187: TUESDAY, OCTOBER 15

It poured rain the next morning. October was normally the first month of the dry season, but Tropical Storm Something was drifting outside Florida's Atlantic coast and doing what storms like that do, throwing its rain bands at the Sunshine State. When a band passed overhead, torrential rain would pour for about a half hour. Then there would be a lull until the next band.

Marty went looking for food. He needed some himself, and he promised Guy he would bring some over, rain or not.

Most stores were long closed, so there were two easy ways to get food. Open-air markets sprouted overnight, here, there. They had combinations of stolen or resold goods, fish, and garden-grown foods. But they were notoriously dangerous—as Guy would attest— and painfully overpriced. The other source was the U.S. Department of Agriculture's food trucks. They roamed neighborhoods all week long, accompanied by trucks full of National Guard troops, stopping here or there for an hour at a time and tossing bags of free food out the back. You never quite knew where to find one, but when you saw one, you grabbed your ration.

Marty found one about a half mile from home. A few dozen hungry, drenched citizens stood in line behind it and another couple dozen nervous National Guardsmen stood watch with their guns loaded and ready. Marty parked and got in line in what was now a steady drizzle. Today's ration was a half-gallon sized bag of rice, a bag of beans, a stack of tortillas, a half-dozen oranges, carrots, celery, tomatoes and a pint-sized bag of powdered milk. All the little bags and oranges and veggies were put together inside the trailer by guys with barrels and scoops, then dropped into bigger plastic bags, which another guy heaved out the back to waiting consumers.

Marty wore his wide-brimmed, brown bush hat as his only protection from the rain.

"I need two," Marty said.

"One bag per person," the dry man called from inside the truck.

"I got a friend, shot up. I'm getting food for him."

"My heart bleeds. One bag per person. Next!"

Marty stood his ground until he saw a National Guardsman raise his rifle toward him and motion the barrel. Move along. The young man had rain gear over his armor. Drops rolled off his helmet.

Marty flashed his badge. "For a brother. Come on."

Marty stared him down, and the kid got it. He nodded his head back toward the line.

"Just get back in line again," he said.

So that is what Marty did. He tossed his first bag in his trunk, got back in line, got a second bag of food for Guy, and tossed that bag in the trunk, too.

Moments after Marty pulled the Charger away from the curb, communications reported a multiple shooting downtown, not far away. He popped his light onto the car roof, squealed a U-turn and headed that way. No traffic. No traffic lights to worry about. Marty was cruising.

As he turned into downtown, Marty's passenger side window exploded. He screeched the Charger to a stop and heard two more shots. He rolled out the driver's door and assessed the area. Another shot fired. He saw the guy, standing under an overhang to get partial relief from the rain, taking aim at him.

"Really?" Marty said to himself. "You don't want to get wet?"

He ducked and the man's fourth shot plunked the car's front right quarter panel.

When he looked up, he saw another man, maybe a teenager, running with pistols in both hands at the man. The kid shot with both hands and the man went down. The kid came up next to him and fired kill shots with both guns.

Marty popped up from behind the car.

"Freeze! Police!"

The kid shot wildly in his direction. Marty aimed and fired back. Pop. Pop. Pop. The kid went down. Marty ran low toward him, keeping him in his gunsight. The kid was squirming, but he also looked as if he were still holding one gun in his left hand.

"Drop it! Drop it! Police!"

The kid rolled and pointed the gun in Marty's direction. Marty was now only a few feet away, and he ducked, and then kicked the kid's arm. The boy's gun flicked away. Marty could see now he was no more than fifteen. Marty's heart skipped a beat, and he felt a swoon of grief for the kid. He pulled the boy's arms back, and the kid screamed as the wounded and clearly broken right arm protested. Marty cuffed him, then checked the first shooter, who was absolutely dead, face down in a deepening puddle. Marty gathered the guns, then came back to the kid and rolled him over. Marty's bullet had hit the kid in the right wrist, breaking it. He lifted him to his feet.

The kid, white, athletic, and tall, spit in Marty's face. Marty punched him in the mouth with his empty left hand and the kid flopped to the ground.

"Little shit," Marty said. "Do that again and I'll kill you."

Marty wiped his face, then lifted him again. Again, the kid spit at Marty, this time missing. Marty just shoved him forward this time.

"Better yet, I won't kill you. How about that? Huh? How about that?"

Marty dragged the stumbling kid back to the Dodge and threw him in the backseat. He found a towel he kept stashed underneath, wiped his face, and then wiped the shattered glass from the driver's seat.

"You're gonna die, pig," the kid said. "All of you bastards caused this. I hate you."

Marty put the car in gear and floored it.

"What's your name, kid?" Marty asked.

"Malfoy. And you're a dead man. Do you hear me? DEAD!"

"You're a Harry Potter fan? Me too. Who are your parents?"

"They're dead. I shot the bitch right in the eye."

"Don't call your mother a bitch."

"I made Dad beg for his life. I killed him a little at a time. A bullet here. A bullet there. Then he was begging me to finish him. I let him bleed to death, like the stinking rat he is. He was crying. It was so cool."

"Yeah, I bet he deserved that. What did he do, ground you for smoking?"

"I don't smoke. I'm not stupid."

Marty called in his arrest and checked on hospital availability. The only one that had secure beds available was down south in the tourist corridor, a pretty good ride away. He pulled out and headed for the expressway.

"You're going to the hospital," he announced.

"I want to die."

"Cheer up, baby. You probably will. The docs will patch you up, but most of you guys wind up getting killed in jail. Pretty little thing like you, you'll probably last a week under someone's protection as a girlfriend. But then he'll get killed and then you'll be next."

"You don't give a shit, do you?"

That challenge was a tough one.

Marty did give a shit. He saw this kid as Eddie at that age and wondered just for the tiniest fleeting thought what he would do if it was Eddie in the back of his car, having gotten the disease and killed people. Marty went through the motions, knowing they were futile. But not pointless.

He wondered if Andrusek had room for another guinea pig in his apartment. Marty realized it was the only acceptable answer. He would take him to the hospital, get his hand fixed up, and then call. Hell, this one even talked. He seemed to go in and out of reality.

Marty heard the sound known to all teenage boys and anyone who ever knew one, the sound of someone sucking together their spit to make a loogie. Marty looked in his mirror just in time to see the kid spit it at him, though he missed. It hit the side of Marty's seat.

"So if you're not stupid, how come you made it so easy for me to get you? You look pretty dumb to me."

"I'm an honors student at Boone," he said.

"Oh, at Boone, huh? That school sucks. I bet my golden retriever could be an honors student at Boone."

None of it was true. Boone was a pretty good high school. And Marty did not have a dog.

"You don't know," Malfoy replied. "My dad had connections to Duke. He said he was going to get me in there."

"This is the same dad you left crying on the floor?"

"He lied. You guys screwed up everything. There's no future for my generation now."

"Play any ball?"

"Baseball," Malfoy said. "And I was good, too. I started in center field last year, and I was only a sophomore."

"So, what set you off?"

"You're a flaming idiot. Don't you get it? There's no school anymore! Do you know, I was going to run for class president? I woulda won, too. I was pretty popular. Now there's no school. There's no girls. There's no baseball. There's no Duke. There's nothing for me. Nothing for any of us. NOTHING!"

"But what set you off? It had to be something."

"You're so stupid. You'd never understand."

Malfoy struggled mightily against the handcuffs and the seatbelt that Marty had fastened to restrain him. He kicked at the seats and pounded his head against the headrest, grunting and breathing violently. He rocked hard. He screamed.

Marty glanced in his mirror and saw Malfoy was drooling. Marty got a glance at the boy's eyes for just a moment before they looked rolled back in his head.

"Argh!" Malfoy screamed. "Crash this car! Crash this car, damn you! Argh!"

The highways were empty, not including an occasional steel carcass of some abandoned suicide-murder wrecks pushed onto the shoulder or median here and there. Rain began again, first as a driven mist, then coming down in almost horizontal sheets. Rain splashed in through the missing passenger-side front window. Most of that spray was hitting Malfoy. Marty shot along the freeway at ninety-five miles per hour, passing only a National Guard convoy. He saw two, three cars heading the other way. He was going to make this trip in record time.

But as he approached his exit, communications beckoned again. Duty called. Again.

There was an active mass shooting going on at a water park.

Of course, all the water parks, all the theme parks, all the tourist attractions were closed. For good, probably. But this one's owners never drained the pools or lazy rivers. They just padlocked the place and ran. Orlandoans who missed the fun, needed a place to cool off and did not mind the risk, broke open the gates pretty early on. They just made themselves at home. The percentage of people so daring was tiny, but there still were dozens who showed up on a nice day, especially on a rainy day when God made the slides work again. The owners were long gone, and the police figured that on their list of priorities, chasing away trespassers ranked about one hundredth.

Now there was trouble.

Marty took the exit, but instead of turning right, he turned left and headed for the water park.

"I gotta take a leak," Malfoy announced.

"Shoulda thought of that before you went on your homicidal rampage."

"So I'm just going to wiz in your car, then, okay, asshole?"

"Good luck getting that zipper down with your hands cuffed behind your back."

Marty screeched the car to a stop.

"Come on, man, I gotta go. So help me! I'll kill you for this! Bastard!"

"Hold that thought. I'll be back."

Marty was the first on the scene. That distinction was not surprising or unusual anymore. Most patrol cops reacted to "active shooting scene" with about as much eagerness as they might have had months ago to a report of "homeless man urinating in an alley."

The rain slacked off to a steady, light drizzle the moment Marty got out of the car.

Someone pushed open the gates. Marty two-fisted his gun and stepped over the turnstile. He heard a shot from his right and started in that direction, but then he noticed the big wave pool right in front of him. People were in it. He approached the pool, which was still filled with water, though it had turned green with algae from months of lack of maintenance.

There were four or five people floating in the water. Around them, pools of blood spread red smears in the green water. Marty felt sick. Two of them were children.

Who brought their kids to trespass in this day and age?

Families who needed the entertainment, the moment of old-style family fun normalcy, that's who.

Well, this is normalcy today.

He heard another shot, still to his right, and he left the pool. He passed a couple of unused attractions and then came across the body of a woman who had been running in his direction. She was young, attractive, wearing a bikini, and she had taken a bullet in the back. Marty checked on her. She was still alive, but unconscious. She was pooling blood. She would not last long.

Still, that kill meant the shooter could shoot here, recently. He looked around and up.

There he was, standing brazenly on the high platform of a tube slide, with a high caliber rifle. The top platform had a mushroom-top roof and the supports partly hid him. At the moment, he pointed his the rifle in a different direction. It fired. A painful roar drifted over through the rain.

The guy was an excellent shot. Marty was not that good. Not with a handgun. If he tried to shoot from here, all he would do was annoy the guy.

Landscaping surrounded the walkway heading that way, and Marty used it for cover. He reached the stairs behind without being noticed. The gunman was still shooting. Marty's ears tuned now to moaning, crying and screaming, cutting through the drizzle's patter from all over the park. He ascended the stairs quietly.

There were more shots.

Marty reached the top, crawling, raising his eyes and gun above the last step. He saw the shooter: a short, long-haired man in his thirties, wearing a baggy bathing suit and an oversized black T-shirt. The shooter looked Marty's way and quickly raised the rifle toward him. The detective ducked, and a shot skipped off the metal landing. Marty looked up to see the man pulling himself into the tube slide and disappearing.

"Ah, hell," Marty said.

That development meant running down the stairs and chasing him across the park. He turned and ran down the stairs. At the bottom, as he rounded the landing area, he saw the shooter was already running through landscaping. He jumped into a lazy river canal. The lazy riverbed was actually pretty deep, and the walls were steep. Marty figured he had the shooter trapped in there and ran along the bank to catch him. But Marty underestimated the guy's athleticism. He tossed his rifle onto the opposing bank, jumped, grabbed the top of the river wall, and popped himself out onto the other side. He was now inside an island. Marty preferred to take the bridge, which required doubling back from where he was.

The shooter had his rifle in his left hand and a handgun in his right. He saw a woman crouching inside a cabana and he aimed at her with the handgun. Marty used the moment to shoot at the shooter. He missed, but he got the shooter's attention. He spared the woman. He ducked into another cabana, and Marty found himself exposed to someone in hiding. The man had him, but he did not shoot. Instead, he broke out running again, heading for the barbecue tent.

The rain picked up.

Marty followed. The short guy turned and fired once over his shoulder, but it was a wild shot. Marty returned fire and came close. They ran again. They came out the other side, back into the hard rain, crossed another bridge off the island. The man headed for a spiral ramp climbing up to another slide.

Marty followed and fired. Shorty ducked and ran. Marty turned the corner, and the man fired at him. Marty ducked. Shorty ran. Marty came over the top of the ramp the same way he had on the last, laying down, gun first. But Shorty was already leaping down the slide.

The slide was designed for tubes. It was not rushing with pressurized water, but it was running plenty of rain. The man disappeared quickly. He was rolling, moving fast. Marty took aim, but he lost any angle when Shorty disappeared over the first big drop. No place to go but down. Marty grasped his gun and hat and went down feet first. Gravity took hold right away. When he came down the first big ramp, he banged hard and lost complete control of his descent. It became a free fall. The second bump dislodged the gun from his hand and whacked his head. Marty tumbled, rolled, fell, smashed against the next level and rolled again. His left shoulder, his right knee, his jaw all took a beating. The last drop rolled him through the finish gate. When he regained his senses, he saw Shorty, also disarmed, also staggered, getting up, looking for his guns. He found one. But as he leaned to reach for it, Marty got up and ran at him.

Marty tackled him hard. Shorty went flying back-first. His head whipped back against the concrete landing pool.

Marty heard the man's skull go plock. He rolled off and Shorty lay there with useless eyes staring skyward.

Marty staggered around in the rain for a moment. He found his hat and put it on. Shorty did not move. Marty found his gun and gathered Shorty's, too. He withdrew his cell from its holster. The phone was tough. It had survived. He called the incident in, declaring that it was over and the park was secure. Then Marty made his way back to the gate.

There was a fire out in the street.

Marty broke into a run. His car was blazing. He got up close to see Malfoy on fire in the back seat, making his last flails. Fire filled the interior. Flames blew out the broken window. Marty peered in to see pieces of a bottle there. Someone had tossed a Molotov cocktail at Malfoy through the shattered window.

Marty tried to open the back door to help Malfoy, but the handle was too hot. He looked in again. Malfoy was gone anyway.

So Marty opened the trunk.

He rescued the two bags of food, closed the trunk and then walked back to the gate, far enough to get under the entrance canopy. He sat on the concrete to wait for his backup to arrive. In that moment, rage, fear, frustration and grief all swept over him.

Malfoy was not Eddie, he told himself. He could have been. He could have been. They both died violently. But Malfoy suffered a fate far worse than death. Eddie only died.

Marty clapped his hands, as if that signal would make it all go away. Then, as his car burned, and as the sirens drew close, he peeled an orange and took a bite.

CHAPTER 17

DAY 188: WEDNESDAY, OCTOBER 16

When did it all become such a farce? Tim Crosby had accomplished just about everything he had set out to do so far in life and yet none of it seemed to matter much to him anymore.

He had pursued the science he loved in a well-respected position in a quality lab. He had a beautiful wife, two beautiful daughters, a beautiful home. A fine car. He and Nadine went to Hawaii, again, last winter and had a great time. After taking some losses in the post-COVID economics, this time, at the first hint of a worldwide pandemic, he had pulled his money out of all the markets. Financially, he was set, provided the world ever rebounded from this collapse.

Yet everything Crosby had ever wanted never quite seemed to be as satisfying as it should have been. In the new reality of the K12Q virus outbreak, none of it really mattered. The shadow of a doubt that darkened Tim's life extended far beyond that professional responsibility. And he knew it.

He had married for beauty and because Nadine adored him and dedicated herself completely to him, characteristics no man could resist. But she bored him. She wrapped her whole life around him, the girls and the social life of this suburb, and, frankly, her average intelligence wore on him. It was not long before he started cheating on her, first non-sexually, just seeking the challenge and excitement of intelligent conversation with gifted women. It was so easy and it felt so good; it was not long before he sought it all. By now he had pursued several full-blown affairs, most recently with Dr. Caroline Pasquale, a microbiologist he had met the previous year at a conference.

And that frolic did not bring any satisfaction to his life, either.

Sometimes he felt driven into a corner, all alone, despite his family.

And now this. That damned Andrusek and his enforcer, the Wilson girl, were driving him when he did not want to be driven, forcing him to cut research corners and take protocol risks he knew they all would one day regret. It was a sloppy hellbent rush toward an answer he did not expect to find, a fools' gambit when there were real scientists out there doing science the right way, and they would surely win this race, simply by using confirmed evidence to stay on the right course.

So Crosby felt cornered again.

How did he always wind up here?

The moon was full and Orlando was mercifully quiet as Dr. Crosby cruised home from the lab, wallowing. Only three or four places on his route left him vulnerable to attack, and he slipped through them all without incident. All he wanted now was to eat and go to bed. It was after ten p.m., and he knew his depression was partly because of hunger and exhaustion.

The garage door slipped upward, and he rolled the Lexus to a stop beside Nadine's Mercedes E350 wagon.

Nadine, trim and fit from an obsessive concern over her own appearance, awaited him in the kitchen. They had relatively little food in the house, but she was ready to prepare him a plate of scrambled eggs from her backyard coop and a side of tomatoes from her garden. She kissed him on the cheek as he passed.

"How was your day, dear?"

"Fine," he replied.

"Kelli did really well on her history exam and Cindi is upstairs studying," she replied.

Nadine had taken on home-schooling the girls since the schools were closed now. The schools were trying again with distance learning, but it was a fiasco during COVID and Nadine did not want any part of it this time. It was not a big leap for her; she had an education degree and had volunteered at her daughters' schools for years.

"Good, good," he said. "I think I'll check on them while you cook."

"OK, dear."

Their oldest daughter, Kelli, fifteen years old, was in the living room watching a video of a Matthew McConaughey movie. She had filled out already; she had her mother's blue eyes and full red lips. She and Cindi had been cutting each other's hair, and it was short and curled.

"Hey, Daddy! Care to join me?" she asked.

There would only be electricity for another hour before the nightly brownouts took effect, but even that sacrifice was too long for him.

"Not tonight, sweetie," he said. He headed toward the stairs.

"Cindi's sleeping," Kelli said.

He turned to her.

"She said she was tired, and she went to bed early."

He headed up the stairs, anyway.

"Daddy, don't disturb her. Please. She had a busy day."

Crosby quickened his pace. He knew a cover when he heard it. His daughter Cindi, thirteen, had the room right at the top of the stairs. He knocked. No answer. He pushed the door open. She was not in there.

"Cindi?" he called out.

No answer.

"Cindi?"

He stomped back down the stairs.

"Where is your sister?"

"Daddy!"

"Where is she, Kelli? So help me."

Nadine emerged from the kitchen to check on what was going on.

"Cindi's not here," Crosby advised her.

Nadine's eyes broadened in terror.

"Kelli?" she asked.

"She's over at her boyfriend's house," Kelli finally said, looking at her feet.

"Her? What?" Crosby asked.

"Salim," Kelli said. "You've met him. He lives over on Myrtle Avenue."

"Did you know about this?"

"No dear, I..." Nadine said.

"What the hell is she doing going out?" Crosby said crisply, angrily.

"Daddy, you can't keep us in here all day, every day. We have lives too!"

Crosby paced toward the stairs, and then back toward Nadine. He shot her his angriest, "I'll deal with you later" look, froze, then turned back to his daughter.

"Am I the only one in this family who knows how dangerous it is out there? God damn!"

"Don't swear, dear," Nadine cautioned.

"Damn it, Nadine! Our daughter is out there who knows where, with who knows whom, doing who knows what. And there are killers everywhere!"

"Did she walk?"

"I don't know," Kelli said. "Yes, probably."

"You're coming with me," he said to Kelli. "You're going to take me to go get her."

He felt his hip for his gun and his pocket for his keys and stormed back toward the garage. Kelli followed.

The house was only three blocks away, a white stucco two-story like all the other white stucco two-stories, except this one had green trim that looked decidedly awkward. Tim's first thought was wondering how the homeowners' association had approved the color.

He parked in the driveway, locked Kelli in the car, looked around and stormed the door.

"Who is it?" a man demanded from the other side after he rang the bell.

"Tim Crosby. I'm here for my daughter Cindi."

There was a pause of ten or fifteen seconds, and he heard Cindi's voice declare, "That's him."

The door opened and Crosby found himself face-to-face with a heavy, olive-skinned man about forty-five years old, with a face so full of deep, fleshy wrinkles that he looked like a manatee with glasses. Crosby figured he might be Arab or Indian or Pakistani. He did not look Hispanic, and he sure as hell was not white.

"Come in," he said.

Crosby pushed through the door. His daughter, tall for her age with Nadine's oak hair (which Kelli had just cut into a girl's pompadour) and dressed in a pink-and-white striped shirt and pink shorts. She stood a few feet behind, with a boy about the same age, but a little shorter than she, with a heart-shaped face and dark hair. They were holding hands.

"I'm Kamran," the man said, offering a handshake.

Crosby ignored him, looking past him.

"Cindi, get in the car."

"Daddy, it's okay," she said.

"Cindi, now!"

"She's fine," Kamran offered. "She's safe here. We were just playing Hearts together."

"You stay out of this," Crosby said. "Cindi, so help me, how stupid could you be? Just walking here, you could have been killed. Or infected."

"Now just a minute, Mr. Crosby," Kamran protested.

"Dr. Crosby."

"Dr. Crosby, I picked her up, and I was going to drop her off just as soon as we finished this game."

Crosby looked at him incredulously.

"How dare you!" he said.

"Dr. Crosby, the children need social interaction. We cannot expect them to stay locked up all the time. And Cindi is a fine girl. You've raised her well. You should be proud."

"I'll thank you to stay out of my family. Cindi? Let's go!"

He watched in utter anguish as she kissed the boy lightly and pulled away until their arms could not reach one another anymore and their hands pulled apart one finger at a time Crosby opened the door and followed her out.

"I will never speak to you again!" Cindi shrieked as she led him down the walk toward the car.

"Get in the damn car!"

She turned and looked at him. She bolted.

"Cindi!"

She ran toward home. He ran after her, but she was quick. Crosby was a good athlete, and so was Nadine, and both of their genes had produced daughters who ran track. Crosby knew he could not catch her.

He darted back to the car and fired it up.

"Daddy, you want me to...?" Kelli offered.

"Shut up!"

He caught Cindi at the corner, but she cut through a yard and headed for home.

When Crosby turned the corner, he saw another car approaching from down the street.

Crosby's heart sank. That car was creeping along. A terrible sign. Anyone on the streets at this time of night who was an innocent driver raced home to avoid cars that creeped.

Cindi was running on the sidewalk, a sitting duck. About one hundred yards separated her from the oncoming car, but that space would be made up in a few quick seconds. The time it took Crosby to turn the corner had allowed her to build another lead.

Crosby floored the Lexus to cut Cindi off. He also reached down and un-holstered his gun.

The driver down the street also floored it. The little, tricked-out Civic raced under neighborhood streetlights toward helpless prey.

"Oh, my God!" Kelli said as she realized what was happening.

The Civic was set to reach Cindi first. It bumped over the curb, took out a mailbox and turned onto the sidewalk. Cindi, aware now, had nowhere to go. Nowhere but up.

But she had up.

She was just coming under the branches of a young live oak tree. She leaped and grabbed the lowest bough and swung her legs forward. Her feet just cleared the windshield, and the Civic slammed the tree, bringing it and Cindi down.

The collision stopped the car and blew out the driver's airbag, stunning him and temporarily trapping him in his seat. Cindi still was in the tree, which lay on its side in the lawn. She appeared to be stuck in what now was a high branch, trying to make her way down.

Crosby's car arrived just as the man started opening his door.

"Brace yourself!" he yelled. The Lexus broadsided the little car hard, smashing the driver's door and rocking the Honda.

That crash exploded Crosby's airbags.

As Crosby and his older daughter struggled to escape the bags, the man escaped the Honda through the passenger door. Cindi dropped from the tree, but when she tried to run, she stumbled over another branch and, like a cheetah, the man pounced on her.

Crosby finally wrestled his way out of his car, his revolver in the air. The man, young and bearded, was up with Cindi. He had a knife to her throat.

"Drop it or I kill her now!" the man shouted. He licked Cindi's left ear. She squirmed, and he tightened his grip.

"Drop her or I kill you now!"

Pulling Cindi, the man circled a little and put much of the tree between them and Tim.

"Put the gun down or I will slice her pretty little throat."

He raised the knife from her neck to show it to Crosby. It was big and long.

Cindi took that moment to act, stomping the man's foot, and then rotating to bring her knee, hard, into his groin.

"Uhhhgh!" he shouted, losing control of her entirely.

She kneed him a second time and stepped free as he collapsed.

"Get in the car, Cindi!" Crosby shouted.

She did, scrambling around the tree and Honda and coming into the far back door of the Lexus. The man had fallen to his knees, and then rolled. Crosby strode over and took aim at the back of his head. The man spit at the grass. Crosby reached down and picked up the man's knife. He pulled the gun's hammer back.

He could not do it. He could not shoot.

As dangerous as this man was, and as horrible were his plans for Cindi, Crosby could not pull the trigger. He felt sweat drip on his temples as seconds clicked. The man was not getting up, but eventually he would. Crosby refocused and aimed the gun again.

And nothing happened.

Crosby aimed the gun skyward and gave the man the hardest kick he could manage into the lower kidney. Crosby kicked him again, this time catching the side of the guy's face. Then he backed away, all the way to the car.

He got in. He used the knife to cut away the airbag. The knife was, in fact, sharp.

The car would not restart, though. It cranked and cranked.

"Daddy?" Kelli asked.

"Get out. We're going to have to run for it," he told his daughters. It was not that big a deal. They were just a little more than a block from home. The Honda driver was not getting up soon, and no one else was in sight. But it would still have to be quick.

"On the count of three, I want us all to get out together. Kelli, you take the lead. Cindi, stay at her pace. I'll follow with the gun."

And, on three, the Crosby family went home together.

CHAPTER 18

DAY 189: THURSDAY, OCTOBER 17

When Guy awoke the next morning, his pain was shallower, but his funk was deeper.

What was to be sad about? The world was ending. Pam was dead. He had lost contact with almost everyone else. He bunkered in this dark, hot house with nothing to do. All of that isolation was depressing as hell. He had nothing to eat but rice, beans, oranges, and tortillas.

And his leg looked as if it might get infected.

He had called in sick for a few days.

"I was shot Sunday, in the leg. I'll be okay, but I need a few days off. ... Thanks. ... No, Darcy's taking care of that; check with her. ... Good to hear; I was worried about that. ... I'll get online today and check, but I need some downtime. ... Okay. Bye."

The "I got shot" line worked. Always does anymore. It was the new "I've got COVID," Guy thought as he hung up.

He meandered into the kitchen to get something to eat. Marty had dropped by with a bag of food and some bandages he had scrounged from somewhere. They shared another drink, but only just the one. Marty had wanted to go home. He had gone through a tough day. Still, he tried like hell to break through Guy's emerging funk.

At least Guy could get around now.

Guy and Pam had a canoe, chained to the back porch roof posts. Two oars were tucked inside.

Guy stared at the oars, thinking of crutches. The hospital, of course, had run out of crutches months ago.

He sawed off the paddle ends to make them the right length. He had enough hardware to attach handles made from sliced pieces of broomstick, wrapped in foam rubber packaging. He wrapped the business ends of the paddles in rubber too, anchoring it with bolts and wing nuts.

The bolts were way too long and stuck out two inches, but they worked. He got around the house just fine, thanks.

He also affixed a holster to one crutch so that it was convenient to his handgrip.

Have gun, will hobble.

Of course, if he ever wanted to go canoeing again, he would need new oars.

Pam loved canoeing. Guy had never been much of an outdoorsman before he met her. He had never been in a canoe. She introduced him to the glory of the inland waterways that surrounded Orlando.

Their first stop when they were dating was the St. John's River, just north of town. They put Pam's canoe in at Blue Springs and headed north with the current. The lush, full forests quickly gave Guy the feeling that they had traveled a thousand leagues from civilization, even though they had gone just a couple of miles. They drifted past rolling manatees. They spotted an eagle overhead and a fox on the shore. They saw gar splash. The sun shone on them that day in glorious splendor. It was all new to Guy. Pam made it all seem so, so natural.

Over the years, they did not get the canoe out often enough, but there were plenty of times. The Wekiva River. The Econlockhatchee River. The Kissimmee River. They also put in on some lakes. Each of them gave a novel experience. Pam had always understood the healing power of bird calls, the rustle of wind high in the trees and the steady slop, slop, slop sound, not to mention the honest, worthy muscle burn of pulling oars.

Raised in a small town outside Gainesville, she was Earth Mother to his urban essence.

God, how he missed her right about now.

Guy had this picture of Pam standing by the river, holding one of these very crutches back when it still was an oar. He pressed the button but the camera's aperture delayed snapping for just long enough for Pam to raise her right hand to brush hair out of her eyes. Click. Her gentle fingers were caressing locks beside her right eye. Those deep brown eyes glittered in a strong, horizontal morning sun. Her glowing, chocolate-milky skin pulled tightly across high cheekbones, and her dark, thin lips pulled tightly around her luminous teeth. She was not smiling for the camera. She was smiling because she was happy. She looked perfect.

Nowadays he often spoke to this picture.

It always spoke to him, too.

"Sugar," he said. "Marty says I should be thankful I'm still alive. I'm not sure I know why. I. I don't know how much longer I can hold out. I don't know if I want to anymore. It's getting worse. Every day without you is worse. God, I need you."

Baby, I need you to stick it out. I need you to make sense of this anguish. I need you to make sense of my death.

"I know you do, Sugar, but I can't."

I'm with you. This is still our adventure. Find your way. Find your role.

Guy put the picture down and was left with this question: What now?

Being a shut-in was making things worse. She would tell him that warning. Under the best of circumstances, he was not naturally communicative; he could not just pick up a phone and call someone to chat. It just was not in his nature.

And going out could be suicidal, especially since he could barely walk, let alone run.

The hell with it.

Guy lurched into the bedroom and took in his reflection from the mirror over Pam's dresser. Guy had aged about ten years in the past few months, maybe five this week. He had let his nappy hair go to seed, without so much as a trim in months. He shaved twice a week with a battery-powered shaver, and that grooming had not happened since Friday, so a mix of salt and pepper bristle infected his face. He rubbed it, considered it, and decided against doing anything about it.

Guy gathered his wallet, keys, sunglasses and cell phone. He checked the cylinder of the Smith & Wesson he had bought at a gun store. He holstered it. He shook a few more rounds out of a box and dropped them into the pocket of his shorts. He kicked his feet into a pair of sandals. He went to the kitchen and filled an empty plastic water bottle with water, then shoved it in his other pocket. Finally, with no hesitation, Guy ventured out.

The sun met him with a jolt. The storms were over South Carolina or some place today. Behind them was a clean sky. He put on his sunglasses.

Immediately, he felt vulnerable. If someone wanted to kill him now, he was not sure he could do much about it. But he also felt a fierce determination to go somewhere, to just get out. To do.... To do something. He reached the sidewalk, stopped, then turned left and headed down the street.

These houses were modest-sized homes, in a fashionable neighborhood, old by Florida standards, about a mile from downtown. He was two blocks in from the main drag, where he had been shot just three days ago. He had not consciously decided this point, but that spot was where he headed. Two doors down, he stopped in front of Marty's bungalow, a nineteen-forties-era house with a high-pitched roof and a screened-in porch. Marty had a new car—the department had extras now—but no car was there. Guy kept going.

In front of the next house, where a retired Disney bookkeeper named Hal lived, he stopped and looked about carefully. No one else was out. Nothing was moving.

A squirrel shrieked.

Birds were about. Guy saw one flutter from one tree to another. Pam would have seen them immediately. She always saw. Nature often took Guy by surprise.

He was stuck in neutral, trying to decide to go on, against all wisdom, or go back, against what he felt was Pam's inspiration.

He positioned his hand near his holster just in case someone shot at him for being out and about in the neighborhood.

Nothing.

He slowly progressed forward. Oars, good leg, touchdown with the foot of his bad leg to rest as much weight on that foot as he could, while still favoring his left foot. Then, oars again. He pulled himself upstream, crossed at the corner, and headed toward the scene. The scene of the shooting.

Now he knew where he was headed. Was it too soon? Guy thought it was too late, or would be with another passing day, or another. He had to see evidence of what he had experienced. He had to see it was as real as it felt.

Vietnamese businesses, particularly restaurants and Asian supermarkets, lined this stretch. Nail salons, law offices, jewelry stores, and travel agencies featured signs announcing Vietnamese names displayed both in English and Vietnamese script.

A car passed from his right, and Guy positioned his hand for defense. It drove away in a hurry.

He reached the corner across the street from the grocery store where he and Pam had shopped together for years, and where he had shopped alone, in the parking lot, for months. And where he had suffered unspeakable fear and pain that Marty made him promise to forget.

Another car, two, came from his left. The second car, a red Accord, seemed to slow down, and Guy took a deep breath. Guy saw a terrified male driver. The Accord changed to the inside lane and blasted away. Guy crossed.

As soon as he rounded the retention wall and the shrubs, he could see what he surmised were bloodstains on the parking lot's bleached concrete surface. He made his way to them. Oars, good foot, bad foot. Oars, good foot, bad foot. He kept going until he figured he was standing about where he had been shot. He saw no particular blood stain that he could conclude was his own. There were planters and stripes that should have given him some sense of perspective, yet none of them seemed quite right. The tables, the boxes and everything else, except the rain-washed but still apparent blood stains, had been cleared away.

Just then, another man approached from the back alley, into the other side of the parking lot. They stared each other down. The man was in his seventies, at least, wearing jeans and a long-sleeved, white, collared shirt. He had not shaved in weeks. It was not a beard exactly. It was more like a coarse, white rag. He shouldered a rifle.

"Where's the market?" he called out from the other side.

"It closed. A shooting. Sunday," Guy shouted back.

The man nodded and approached.

Guy stood still, ready. Small talk was no indication of safety. The man had a round face, a mottled nose and round eyes behind regular glasses. He was more tanned than most white people were nowadays.

"I'm so disappointed," the man said. "I hate rice and beans all the time. Was it bad?"

"Yeah, it was bad."

The man looked at Guy's leg. "You shot here?" he asked.

"Yeah."

"Why are you here?"

"I don't know. I just came."

The man nodded again. He looked around. "Damn this disease. You know, it's always nice to find someone to have a face-to-face conversation. I'm glad you came. My name's Rob. Rob Petry."

"Like Dick Van Dyke?"

"Only spelled differently. Let's sit down." He nodded toward the wall.

"I'd rather stand."

"You think it's safer? We're out in the open. Over there, at least we have some shield."

Rob walked over and sat on the edge of the wall, which was only about three feet high on this side. Guy watched him, but he really did not want to leave his spot amid the blood stains. He was expecting to draw something from them, and it had not come yet. But he relented. His leg had been killing him. He forcefully ignored it. Sitting down was good. Better. He looked around. They looked like the only people outside for blocks.

"I'm Guy Phillips."

"Did you feel it?" Rob asked.

"The bullet? Hell yes. Still."

"No, the power of life."

"Come again?"

"We're out here, we're both out here searching for some something. Yes, I need food. But the real reason I come out is to tell myself I can. When you came to visit that spot, you were just trying to prove to yourself you could do it. It's like getting on a horse again. Right? I bet I'm right. If you don't, you can't. If we can't go outside, we'll never go outside. I've been walking to some place every day. Just because I can."

Another car passed. Both of them turned to face the vehicle as it came and went.

"It's dangerous."

"Sure it is," Rob said. "But we're here anyway, right?"

"Facing our fears?"

"Kind of that. But it's more than that. I could get murdered walking home. But I'll be walking home. I will have lived until then.

"Have you lost anybody, Guy?"

"My wife Pam. Back in July."

"That makes a difference. My wife Lara…"

"No. Her name is not Laura. No."

"Again. Spelled differently. L.A.R.A. I lost her to COVID. She was fine. She got sick. She went to the hospital. She got better and then she got worse. They had to put her on a ventilator. She died the next day."

"I'm sorry."

"I was so angry. I was angry at the doctors. I was angry at the virus. I was angry at the whole world, at God, you know? And we were stuck indoors. I got to the point where I was so depressed and fearful. I never went out. You remember what it was like."

"Yeah."

"It must have been a year. I was pretty much locked in the house or my car. Home deliveries. Jeez. First, I hated them. Then I came to rely so much on them. I think I went a year without having any human contact, except by phone."

"You get the vaccine?"

"Sure, but even then, I didn't change yet. I finally, just one day, just took off my mask and went out. You know? I think it was Lara, somehow, pushing me out the door."

"Really?"

"I truly believe that."

"Because I think Pam pushed me out the door today."

"I'm still missing her every day. That never stops. The missing her will never stop, Guy."

"Why is all this happening to us, Rob?"

"Don't think of it that way, Guy. We're two guys, well, one Guy and a Rob, I guess, right? Heh, heh. We're sitting in paradise on a beautiful October day. The world has gone to hell. But for us, living is now moment-by-moment, right?"

Guy did not respond right away. Finally, he asked, "Is that what God wants of us?"

Rob stared deeply into his eyes, trying to find Guy's answer there. He reached out and put his hand on Guy's.

"Do I look like a man of the cloth? How should I know what God wants? It just seems to me we can't live our lives in fear."

The old man took off his rifle and placed it across his lap, pointing away from Guy. He rubbed his beard and looked skyward.

"I have a son, Caleb, and a daughter, Linda, and four grandchildren. Caleb and Rebecca live in Colorado, Linda and her second husband live in New Jersey. Caleb and Rebecca have three kids. Noah's the oldest, he's sixteen now. Linda's got a daughter, Debbie, from her first marriage. She's fourteen and so pretty. I haven't heard from any of them in months."

"That's tough. I can relate."

"Argh! I didn't see them for more than a year, during COVID, but at least we'd call. We'd Zoom. Zoom. Ha. But now it's nothing. There's nothing. My phone doesn't work. I don't have internet anymore. No one knows how to write a letter and put a stamp on it. It seems to me this is not unlike what life was like one hundred fifty years ago, before phones and the Internet and all of that. Only you might get a letter. Now, not so much. Back then, though, I can't imagine people just assumed the worst while they waited for a letter. We can't assume the worst. We just have to hope. We have to have faith in our people, and God. We have to assume the best."

"It's not like it was a hundred fifty years ago."

"Sure it is. They had diseases, accidents. You never knew. A month without a letter could mean anything."

"So we're just supposed to forget about them?"

"Of course not!" Rob snapped. "You deal with what you can deal with. You try to live your own life. You have faith in the rest. You asked what God wants. Surely, doing what we can with what we have, he'd want that."

When Guy did not reply, Rob asked, "Do you know of any other markets?"

"I hear there's a big one down at Lake Eola, but I've never been to it. They've got armed guards and everything. Long lines, though. That's what I hear. And there's a 7-11 that's still open and sells food downtown. It's tough to get into though. I hear some places in Winter Park are open too."

Rob nodded. They sat in silence for a while.

"Well, I'm off, then. This is why we venture out. For a little human contact. To remind us that we're not alone. There are killers. There are assholes. But there are the rest of us, too. Don't forget that. Very nice to have met you, Guy."

"You too, Rob."

"Good luck."

"You too, Rob."

The old man got up and then turned back to Guy.

"Remember, when you get the choice to sit it out or dance," he said, "dance. Lee Ann Womack. I'm not much for country music, but I like that."

The old man stepped off a little jig, shaking his butt and turning away again. Without looking back, he raised his right hand in a farewell salute and walked away along the wall, still dancing. When he reached the parking lot's drive entrance to the side street, he slipped onto the sidewalk and headed back toward the neighborhood. Or toward Lake Eola. Someplace else, anyway.

Rob was halfway down the block, almost out of Guy's sight because of the hedge, when another vehicle, a big pickup truck, approached, slowed at the intersection and then turned onto that street.

"Rob!" Guy screamed. But the old man did not respond. "Rob!"

The driver goosed the heavy eight-cylinder engine with a mighty roar and swerved across the opposing lane and up over the curb. He ran right over Rob, who had turned toward it only at the last moment. Guy saw the fuzzy face for an instant, but saw no fear before Rob disappeared. The truck's rear left wheel bounced over him.

"Asshole!" the driver yelled.

Then the driver gunned the engine again, and the truck quickly disappeared down the street.

CHAPTER 19

DAY 191: SATURDAY, OCTOBER 19

Survival was now life, and life was survival. That cliche was the lesson that Guy Phillips took from Rob Petry, minutes before he died. Rob looked as if he was okay with dying, because he was living.

Guy's leg was getting better only in degrees. He had wasted much of the booze that Marty bought for him by using it to clean the wound, an action that caused howling pain. The leg still offered little support. It was purple-blue from his crotch to midway to his knee. But it looked better. It no longer looked to have any sign of infection, and the wounds were closed. It was not just that Guy was getting used to it. He was sure it felt a little better, too.

So he picked up Rob's mission, to wander forth into the world daily, to dare the world to kill him if it could.

Guy decided he could work from home no longer. This morning, Marty was on his way over to give Guy a ride down to the water treatment plant, where Guy intended to spend the day recalibrating flows. But with Marty, "on my way over" sometimes meant hours of delay, and Guy knew to dig in.

Marty arrived on time, though. Guy wordlessly loaded up and joined him in the new black Charger.

"Like it?" Marty said. "I sorta burned up the old one."

They headed for the expressway, but when he turned onto the steep, narrow on-ramp, they encountered trouble. Four cars collided on the ramp and a fifth one was turned sideways, blocking the entrance. Marty saw a killer standing beside a white sedan sandwiched in the pileup, firing into the window for what he presumed was a kill-shot.

"Get down!" Marty yelled.

He slammed on the brakes and skidded the car sideways with Guy's side turning away. The man, white, elderly, almost completely bald and grizzly, stood as Marty rolled out and ran behind a small, red car that was last in the pileup's line. The man fired at Marty and missed everything. Marty fired back and the man dove behind the car he was standing beside.

Marty's cell phone jingled. He glanced down just for a moment and saw that it was Kanetha. He turned his eyes on the car hiding the man and put the phone on speaker.

"Not now Kanetha. I'm busy," Marty said.

"It worked!" the phone shrieked. That declaration got his attention, and he glanced down at his phone. The man popped up and fired a shot that dinged off the Caprice.

Marty fired back.

"What worked?"

"The antidote Mike gave the kid!" the phone shrieked again. "He's coming out of it! He's talking to me like a kid, not like a crazy. He's..."

"I'm real busy right now, Kanetha. Can you call me back?"

He saw the man run from the bumper of the sedan to the back fender of a big pickup, ten feet closer, now just twenty feet away.

"Don't you get it?" Kanetha implored. "This might be the cure! This might be the end! The kid's coming out of it! He's even told us his name! It's B.J.!"

"Kanetha, it's not that I don't care. I'm just tied up right now," Marty replied.

"We got it! We got it! We got it!" she shouted gleefully.

Marty checked his clip. He had plenty of rounds left, unless this skirmish went too long, in which case he would have to make it back to his Charger. He looked up again. The man hunkered behind the pickup. He could see the man's feet and wondered if he could get a low shot off that might bring him down.

"Marty!" Kanetha cried out. "We need your help, now! We need you to help us get more study subjects!"

"What?"

"Murderers! We need you to help us get some more to test!"

"Are you out of your damn mind?"

He saw the feet shift. The man was making his move. He came around the truck bed firing a small handgun and damned if his first shot did not hit Marty right in his gun. The blast popped the pistol from his hand and sent it skidding across the pavement. Marty grabbed, not for the gun, but instinctively for his hand, which was unshot, but bruised and possibly broken. The man came around the pickup and then the small, red car with monster steps, handgun held tight and stretched out, ready to first terrify, then kill.

"We need you to bring us four or five more people," Kanetha said.

"Five," Andrusek called out from somewhere near the phone.

"Five," Kanetha repeated. "We need variety. Old, middle-aged, young. White, black, Asian. Male, female. Can you do it?"

The man got to within about eight feet, standing by the back fender of the red car, and took a steely aim.

The old man grinned as if this shot would be the greatest thing he ever did. He enjoyed the moment for just a few seconds.

And then the man took a canoe oar crutch, on edge, to the back of the head. He surged forward and toppled, slammed his face on the pavement, bounced, and came to rest on his back as his gun skittered away. Guy stood behind him on one leg, leaning against the back of the red car.

"Marty?" Kanetha asked. "Can you help us out? Marty? Are you there?"

Marty grabbed the man's gun and held it toward him. He was out cold, if he was not dead. Marty checked his pulse. He still had one. Then Marty picked up the cell phone.

"Okay," he said. "I think I can get you at least one for now. White, male, age seventy-five to eighty. The others we'll have to see about."

He hung up.

• • •

When Marty and Guy arrived at Andrusek's apartment, the man was still unconscious. Mike and Marty got the man into Mike's bed and tied him down. And then Kanetha led them all into the guest room.

B.J. was awake, still restrained. They stood at the door and stared at him, and he stared back.

"He knows why he's here, but he doesn't know… what he did," Kanetha said. "No memory of it whatsoever."

"B.J.," Marty said. "Is it B.J? My name is police Lt. Francisco. "Can you hear me?"

The boy nodded.

"Dr. Andrusek tells me you're feeling better. How are you feeling?"

"Why am I tied up?" he asked. "Where is my mom?"

Marty and Mike exchanged glances.

"It's all right, baby," Kanetha said. "Your mom can't be here."

The boy looked around. "My head hurts," he said.

"I want you all to leave the room," Marty said.

They hesitated, but left. Marty closed the door behind them. He withdrew his knife and the boy's eyes widened.

"It's okay. I'm going to cut you loose," Marty said.

He started with the feet. The boy brought them together. Marty cut the restraint on the boy's right hand and the boy only withdrew the hand to his belly. Marty walked to the other side of the bed and freed the left hand. The boy rubbed his wrists.

"Better?"

"Where's my mom? Where is my sister, Madison?"

"You don't remember?"

B.J. shook his head.

Marty turned his back, tensing for the kid to pounce. Nothing but silence. He slipped his service revolver out of the holster and quietly unloaded it.. He slipped it back into his side holster and turned back to B.J.

"B.J. Listen to me very carefully," Marty said. He pulled the gun again, this time holding it gingerly by the handle. He tossed it on the bed beside the boy. "I want you to shoot me. I want you to kill me, and then I want you to kill all those bastards in the other room. Can you do that for me?"

The boy cried. He shook with sobs.

"Why?" he asked.

Marty just watched and waited. B.J. broke down into a full cry.

"I'm sorry to tell you this," Marty said. "But your mother and sister are gone."

The boy wailed.

Kanetha burst back into the room.

"A killer got them. But you survived," Marty said.

Kanetha shot Marty a fierce look and ran to the bed. She pulled B.J. close and cradled his face to her chest, and the boy sobbed there.

"You asshole!" she whispered.

Marty retrieved his gun and holstered it.

"He looks cured to me," he said.

• • •

Mike was in touch with the CDC and other researchers, but he was careful about details, knowing that no one would approve of his methods. The initial responses were cool. Hopeful, cautious, skeptical. Suggestions and protocols poured in, but most of them were traditional and would take weeks or months. Researchers on both the West Coast and in Atlanta had access to some patients and will try out K38M there as soon as Mike could get samples sent over, but even the protocols they intended would take weeks to produce more results. Mike argued for shortcuts and got shot down every time, though there were some not-very-helpful compromise methods suggested. He thought they all were out of their minds.

Mike, too, was cautious and skeptical, slapping down the greatest hopes Kanetha voiced. Yet he was resolved. He believed they had two choices: break all the rules to see if this breakthrough would work or die trying. He settled into his desk and spent the rest of the morning writing notes, organizing, carving out a plan that would touch enough bases, but fast.

B.J. was confined to his room, and Kanetha spent plenty of time with him. He had chronic headaches, but Mike was concerned about giving him anything for it. He wanted to observe him as he came completely out, with nothing in his system.

The old man that Marty had dragged off the freeway offramp, put to bed in Mike's own bed, woke up yelling and wrestling against his restraints, so Mike gave him a shot and he went right down. Mike also gave him K38M.

Marty left, but the other guy Marty had brought with him, Guy Phillips, stayed in the apartment. He said little, but he was the most positive man Mike had encountered in a long time. Guy spoke of remembering those loved ones lost with the greatest reverence. He spoke of hope for those people who were surviving, and the need to savor everything, even the rice and beans they had for lunch. Spiritual without sounding religious, Guy struck Mike as a rock of life in this thrashing sea of death.

They all got together that evening for dinner, including Marty and Dr. Crosby, who usually went home to his family, but this time did not play that card. They crammed five chairs around Mike's little table. Marty brought a bottle of rum, and they all hit on it.

Marty had some good news and some ideas, but there was nothing easy about any of them. He intended to get a court order signed by a judge to transfer some prisoners from the jail to a fictitious facility. Then they'd go get some hand-picked subjects for Mike's tests. Even in this age, getting a judge to go along with their plan was too long a shot to pursue, and to get one to sign a phony order just would not happen. What could they tell him? How could they make their story believable and the science credible at the same time? And they could not convince a judge to agree to submit prisoners to unauthorized human drug tests.

Getting the prisoners was one thing. They also needed a place to house them because Mike's apartment already was overbooked. Fortunately, Orlando had no shortage of hotels, motels, vacation rental homes and assorted lodgings, and most of them had been abandoned. No one wanted to come to the city. More than a few had become flop houses for anyone.

Marty had scouted a place near downtown he already knew about, a two-story vacation rental that was padlocked and boarded until Marty broke in. A former Victorian mansion, it had eight bedrooms, a full kitchen, a servants' area that could easily be converted into a lab, several other rooms, electricity and running water. And it had been well-secured and was therefore vacant.

"I'm gonna need some help," Marty said. "Guy, you in?"

"You know I am."

"I need one more. Someone big and intimidating. Mike?"

"I've got too much to do."

"How about Bubba?" Kanetha offered.

"That's great, but let's look ahead," Dr. Crosby said. "How are we going to inoculate three-hundred million people? No one is going to approve this, not for many months at least. I promise you that. And even if you got permission, how are you going to distribute it?"

"That's true," Guy offered. "Everyone's in hiding."

"And since COVID, about half of the population has lost faith in anyone saying, "Here. Take this. It'll protect you," Dr. Crosby said. "That's probably up around ninety percent now."

"And if you go to the door and say, 'I'm from the government, I just want to give you a little shot,' you'll get your own shot," Dr. Crosby added.

"Isn't this stuff a live virus? Isn't it contagious? Won't it just spread naturally?" Marty asked.

"Sure," Dr. Crosby said. "But it took, what? Three months for the first virus to spread, and that was when everyone mixed freely. That doesn't happen anymore."

The table fell into silence. Guy took a sip of rum and studied his glass.

"What about water?"

"It is waterborne. So what?" Dr. Crosby said, though he guessed.

"What if we contaminate the Orlando water supply? Everyone drinks it. It's the only hydration you can get right now, unless you risk buying black-market bottled water. If you're holed up, you drink my water. If you're out and about, you drink my water. I've got a monopoly."

"Can you get it to everyone?"

"If we can pump enough of the anti-virus into the system, it'll go everywhere in Orlando. At least in the city limits."

Kanetha waved her arms and shook her head.

"Stop. Stop. Stop. Stop. Stop. Stop. Stop. Stop! You've all gone bat-shit crazy now," she said.

"Listen," Guy said.

"No! You listen!" Kanetha said. "You want to poison the entire municipal water supply with an unproven virus so everyone gets sick with it?"

"I think that's what we're talkin' about, yeah," Mike said.

"Fucking nuts."

Dr. Crosby said, "And how do you go about that?"

"We make a big-ass batch," Mike said.

"Um-hum," Kanetha said. "And what if it makes everybody sick? And kills people? You'd be the biggest mass murderers yet."

"That's why we've got to test it on more people," Mike said. "And watch them for a few days."

"A few days. Five more people. That'll tell you what? That five people, six, seven, did okay. And what if they get sick? That boy in there has a migraine right now. What if he gets sicker? What if he dies?"

"It won't tell us much," Dr. Crosby agreed. "It won't tell us what we need to know."

"But you're okay with this?" Kanetha asked him.

Dr. Crosby shrugged his shoulders.

Guy got up and stretched his leg. He hobbled around the table.

"I..." he said.

"Why?" Kanetha interrupted. "Why are you okay with this?"

"It doesn't matter," Dr. Crosby said.

"No, it does matter. Let's get this out now. You've been sitting on this for months. There's something about you."

She was standing now, shaking a finger at Tim.

"You've never acted like you were on board with any of this, but you've always gone straight forward."

"It doesn't matter."

"I want to know."

"Fine. I did it," Crosby said. "There. I said it. Is that what you want? I contaminated the lab that day. I infected myself. I infected Dr. Vicar. This is all my fault. Satisfied?"

Silence lasted about a minute.

"You said you infected yourself. How did you know?" Kanetha asked.

"I tested my own blood."

"You knew before then! How did you know? So help me Tim, tell me the truth."

He rimmed his glass with his right forefinger's tip. He stared at the rum at the bottom. He smiled and shook his head.

"Let's just say I had more evidence."

"He went to Des Moines," Mike said.

"What?" Kanetha shrieked.

"You were in Chicago that weekend, for the American Society of Microbiology conference," Mike accused Tim. "I checked. Des Moines is only an hour flight side trip from there."

Dr. Crosby said nothing. No denial. No confirmation. They all took that silence as guilt.

"Why?" Kanetha asked.

"Never mind why."

"No. I want to know why, you son of a bitch. You kept that from us all this time. I want to know why or so help me. I'm going to go murder plague all over your ass."

"It was a woman, right?" Marty asked. He looked around at the others. "It's always about sex."

"Look, never mind why I did not tell you."

"You took a side trip. You could not tell anyone because you're a happily married man with a lover in Des Moines," Marty explained. "I've seen it too many times."

Dr. Crosby swirled his drink.

"Yes, I went to Des Moines that weekend. That guy who shot up that Walmart store? He cut my hair at the airport."

"Why didn't you say anything?" Mike asked.

"I, Nadine can't know," Dr. Crosby replied.

"Fuck!" Mike shouted. "You covered this up because you were hiding a goddamn affair! How much time did you cost us?"

"None!" Dr. Crosby shouted back. "After you came and got me that morning, I never dissented on your theory. I never once slowed down your efforts or changed your direction. I bought in. We went forward!"

"Blindly!" Mike shouted again.

"For you? So what? I knew what we were doing! And you sure didn't deviate. I made you go through steps you needed to go through. We got there."

"You think the CDC woulda bought in a little earlier if they'da known about Des Moines? You think we mighta had, I don't know, some help? If the world knew every known case was connected to you?"

Dr. Crosby was up now. "What are you trying to say, Mike?"

"You little shit!"

Mike moved toward Dr. Crosby. He moved toward Mike.

Marty spoke up. "Wait. Let me get this straight. This is all your doing?"

"Sounds that way to me," Kanetha said.

"It was an accident. I went to get the kit to decontaminate, but Dr. Vicar beat me into the lab. At that point, I did not think there was a problem."

"Damn you!" Marty said.

"I didn't know!"

Marty pushed him hard, nearly knocking him down, then stepped toward him as if he was going to grab him again.

Guy slammed an oar-crutch onto the table between them. Glasses fell over and spilled.

"Gentlemen! We digress!" Guy said softly, but in the silence it sounded like the wrathful voice of God. "Back to the subject, please? Are we or are we not going to contaminate the city water supply? Because if we are, I have some planning to do."

Marty froze. Kanetha leaned against the wall and folded her arms.

Guy looked at his friend and saw him troubled. "You okay, Marty?"

Marty shook his head as if he had just gotten his bell rung, then looked around.

"Aw, Jesus, Guy!" Marty said. "I just topped off my glass, and you went and spilled it. Lost rum's a shame you know! A damned shame."

CHAPTER 20

DAY 192: SUNDAY, OCTOBER 20

Marty had a plan to get a judge's order without all the wrong questions leading to the wrong answers.

Blackmail, of course.

For that mischief, he needed dirt.

For that currency, he needed help from someone who had dirt to sell.

And for that commerce, he figured he might need Mike. So he convinced Mike to take the morning off for a brief drive and to help with a little arm-twisting.

They left early.

South Semoran Boulevard was the aorta of the heart of Orlando's Hispanic sector. It still was not quite as overtly Latino as communities in Miami or Tampa, but a close look at the rag-tag businesses lining the wide boulevard revealed many were Spanish- or Caribbean-flavored. And the rest, the English-named fast-food restaurants, auto-body shops and locksmiths, they were almost all run by Hispanic businessmen too. Or at least they were. On this day, as on the previous many days, all of them were closed and most of them were boarded up.

Mike's white truck cruised lonely down the boulevard as if it were a movie set before filming began. He pulled into a small, two-story office building with a law firm's name on the marquee, Margolis, Ramirez, and Clarke. He drove around to the back. The building was locked, dark, and apparently vacant.

Marty had the rear entrance door open in about two minutes.

A tenant listing hung by the elevator. Marty ran his finger along the listing for Sanchez Investigations, Suite 2E. He led Mike to the stairs.

The second-floor corridor was windowless and dark. Marty had come prepared and switched on a flashlight. The law firm occupied most of the second floor. The last door on the end was 2E, and the nameplate declared "Emely Sanchez, Private Investigator." The door was, of course, locked. Marty had it open quickly.

They entered a reception room cramped by a desk and two easy chairs. The desk was cleaned off. Mike pulled open empty drawers as Marty picked the office lock. The door swung open. Sunlight flooded the reception room. Mike closed the last drawer and followed Marty.

That room, too, had been cleaned out. No computer equipment or phone. File cabinet drawers stood open and empty.

Marty began searching anyway.

"What are we looking for? Looks like she cleaned it out," Mike said.

"Maybe she didn't get everything. Emely's slick," Marty said. "I could find no home addresses for her anywhere. Every record I found came back to this office. I'm hoping she took her business files, but left something personal."

Mike tried the desk drawers while Marty went through the cabinets. None offered him anything. Mike searched a closet, and Marty dumped the trashcan on the desk.

The can had been pushed against the far corner from the desk and was filled with food wrappers, a broken pen, and several crumpled papers. Emely apparently was someone who liked to play trashcan basketball. He un-crumpled them one at a time, glanced and threw them back in the can. The fourth one he opened caught his attention just before he tossed it back.

"Ha!" he declared.

"What is it?"

"Looks like an old electric bill for a house!" Marty said. "And the address is on here!"

"The power company hasn't sent out bills for a couple of months," Mike said.

"Looks like Emely cleared out a while ago," Marty conceded. "She might be long gone, but let's go find out."

The address led them into a neighborhood not far away, to half of a duplex. The unit was closed-up, dark and empty-looking. They went around back. Marty fumbled with his lock pick; Mike leaped into the door shoulder first and sent it splintering open.

"I'm getting into the spirit of this," he said.

The house was as swept as Emely's office. They rummaged about, finding nothing. Mike suddenly grabbed Marty by the shoulders.

"What?"

"Shhhh!" Mike said.

They listened. They could hear someone in the unit next door.

Marty abandoned what he knew would be a fruitless search and led Mike back outside.

"Emely would have told someone where she was going. Someone needed to know."

They rounded to the front and knocked on the neighbor's door.

"¿Qué deseas?" a woman's voice demanded.

"Señora, somos la policía. Estamos buscando a Emely Sanchez y creo que nos puedes ayudar."

Marty put his badge up to the peephole.

"Larguense de aquí," she said.

"Por favor, señora. No es que tenga problemas con la ley, simplemente necesitamos su ayuda como ella es detective privada. ¿Son amigas ustedes? ¿Esta viva ella? ¿Sabes dónde podemos encontrarla?"

There was a moment of silence. And then the woman said, "Veinte dólares."

"¿Perdón?" Marty asked.

"Te va costará veinte dólares. Pasa el dinero debajo de la uerta."

"She wants twenty dollars cash to help us," Marty translated to Mike.

"I got that," he said. "I understand some. I just can't speak."

Marty and Mike looked at each other, then quickly withdrew their wallets. Cash was scarce. Cash was something you hoarded but rarely carried unless you knew you'd need it. Marty had twelve dollars in his wallet. Mike had four. Marty put the bills together, two fives and six ones, and spread them in front of the peephole.

"Tendrás que aceptar dieciséis dólares," Marty said. "Eso es todo. Tómalo o déjalo."

"Veinte," she said.

"Dieciséis!

"Veinte," she said.

"Just a minute," Mike said. "Um, Un momento, señora."

He ran off to his truck. He opened the driver's door and then dove under the seat. He came back with two Budweisers, still in the plastic ring.

"Sixteen dollars and two beers," he said to the peephole, holding them up. "Our best offer."

Beer also was scarce.

"Where'd you get those?" Marty asked. "Never mind."

"Dieciséis y dos cervezas," Marty repeated in Spanish.

"Sostenlas para que pueda ver que no están abiertas," she said.

Mike understood and turned the cans to show that they were still unopened.

"Eche el dinero debajo de la uerta y deja la cerveza alli al lado. Despues, vuelvense a su camioneta enseguida," she commanded. "Despues que agarre la cerveza, pasare la direccion nueva de Emely por debajo de la uerta."

They obeyed, sliding the bills under the door, placing the cans beside the door and then retreating to the truck. Once they were seated in the truck with the doors closed, the woman's door opened a crack. An old woman's hand popped out, snatched the plastic ring and pulled the treasure through to safety. The door slammed. Marty got out of the truck alone and walked back to the door as a piece of paper slid outside.

The address was not far from Marty's own neighborhood, but oh, so different. They found it in a posh lakeside enclave of very private, million-dollar homes.

The address was at the end of a street lined with mansions. They could not see the house from the road. The street ended in a small cul-de-sac, and Emely's address appeared on an eight-foot-high stone wall with a black metal gate topped by razor wire.

There was one other problem. They were not alone.

They passed a red sedan about a block back, and Marty saw a driver watching them as they passed. He did not like the look of the guy.

Mike reached out and pressed the intercom button. It made no sound, no response. However, as he pushed it a second and third time, Marty saw what he wanted to see: a video camera attached to the wall moved ever so slightly. Someone inside was taking a closer look. Marty got out of the truck and stood before the camera, holding his badge. He saw the camera move slightly again on its monopod.

But nothing else happened.

Except this distraction. The red sedan was rolling toward them. Marty scrambled into the truck. Marty felt his heart quicken and his arteries fill with pulsing adrenaline.

"Can you smash that gate?" Marty asked.

"With pleasure," Mike said.

He dropped the truck into first and locked the four-wheel drive. He stomped the brake and the gas. The tires spun and acrid, burning-rubber smoke poured out into the truck. Mike let off the brake and the truck lurched forward, ramming the gate.

But the gate held.

Marty's head bounced off the dashboard. He held it and stared at Mike.

"I disabled the airbags," Mike said. "Too many little-shit crashes."

The wheels dug, and the gate groaned. Rubber smoke clouded. They heard the metal screech with pain.

The red car stopped about thirty yards back. Marty turned and saw the driver, a young white man in tan-and-brown camouflage clothing, get out, holding a rifle.

"Go! Go!" Marty yelled as he unsnapped his gun.

Mike threw the truck into reverse and backed up ten feet.

The driver, running at them, fired a volley. A couple of the shots hit the back of the truck but did no one any harm. Marty stuck his gun out the passenger window—he was right-handed but forced to shoot left-handed—and fired back. One, two, three shots. The man dove to the pavement.

Mike threw the truck into first gear and floored it. This time it slammed hard into the gate, which hesitated just a little and then tore from its hinges. It fell flat in the driveway and the F-150 rattled over it.

Marty fired again as the man in the street tried to get up to follow. He dove again.

Mike pulled up to the portico of a tall, very-boxy-looking, two-story house. He turned the truck to cover and followed Marty out the passenger door. Marty took aim over the truck bed while Mike rang the doorbell.

"Go away!" a woman's voice shouted through the intercom.

"Emely Sanchez? My name is Dr. Mike Andrusek. I'm here with Lt. Marty Francisco. You know him. We have got to talk to you! And we're being shot at out here. Can you let us in, please?"

The man in the street fired several more shots in rapid succession. Who knew where the bullets went? None of them hit the truck, Marty or Mike. But now Mike crouched down.

Marty fired back as the man ran to hide behind the wall.

"No!" Emely replied. "Tell Francisco to kiss my ass."

The man in camouflage stuck his gun around the corner of the wall, where the gate once hung, and fired again. This time, some shots ricocheted off the truck. Marty fired back, and the man withdrew.

"Emely, we need your help," Mike said. "It's important. Maybe we can make a deal."

There was a pause. No rifle fire. No response. It might have been only a second, but it felt like a minute.

"Maybe we can make a deal," Emely agreed.

Mike heard the door lock buzz. He turned the knob and pushed. A very heavy door opened. He and Marty scrambled inside and shoved it shut. It closed with a clunk, followed by the snaps of several electric lock buzzes and clicks.

They had entered a foyer with high ceilings and tall paintings depicting very brutal, warlike scenes of bleeding men and crying women. Mike saw the paintings were not of the blood, but the anguish. They were masterful, powerful, boldly colored images of pain and suffering.

"I'm in here," Emely called out from around the corner. Come in with your hands up and guns pointed at the ceiling."

Marty and Mike exchanged glances and then did as commanded.

They entered a great room with even higher ceilings.

Two enormous windows, at least twelve feet high and six feet wide, filled most of the back wall, providing a view of a backyard pool and small courtyard, walled in and dropping downward away from the house. Beyond the far wall they could see the lake, blue and big enough for water skiing, ringed with equally impressive houses.

An enormous stone fireplace split the two windows, and it was roaring. In front of the fireplace sat a large papasan swivel chair. In the chair sat Emely Sanchez, looking like a queen in her throne, and pointing a hefty black and chrome revolver at them.

Emely was stunning, in a cobalt dress that cut a deep V across her breasts, framing a beautiful, heavy silver locket hanging from her neck. The dress also draped ruffles over her knees. Her hair was cut short and pixie, accenting a round face full of dark eyes and lips. Slender arms extended from the sleeveless gown; shapely legs dropped below the ruffles to bare feet, crossed at the ankles and pulled beneath the chair. A snake tattoo started at her left ankle and wrapped around and around her leg, with the head slithering a tongue, ending high on her thigh.

One hand held the gun high and the other lay daintily in her lap.

"Emely! So good to see you again. Glad to see you're well," Marty said.

She waved the gun.

"Put your weapons on that table behind you," she said.

Marty laid his gun down next to a lamp.

"You too," Emely said, waving the gun at Mike.

He withdrew his own magnum and placed it beside Marty's.

"The little one too, Marty," Emely said.

Marty retrieved a pocket-sized pistol from an ankle holster and set it down too.

Emely pointed hers toward the ceiling in a relaxed posture she could hold all day if necessary.

"So you gentlemen want to talk business? Come in. Sit down. Care for a drink?"

Mike and Marty sat on a big sofa with aqua cushions across from Emely.

"Nice place you got here," Marty said.

"Thanks. It belonged to a client. My client Samuel, Samuel Gutierrez, built this place. Know him?"

"Not as well as the DEA does," Marty replied.

"He built this as a safe house. And I do mean safe," she said.

"Where is he now?" Marty asked.

"Dead. So's his wife. And his bodyguards."

"You?"

"Heaven's no, detective. I found them. There." She pointed toward the kitchen on her left.

On the carpeting between the great room and the kitchen were several broad blood stains.

"I dragged them down and threw them into the lake. Such a pity. I liked Samuel. And Teresa. She had such good taste."

She smoothed a wrinkle in her skirt.

"Who?" Marty asked.

"Who knows?" she replied. "One of them got sick and started shooting, I imagine. They all were armed, all the time, so it would have turned into quite the shoot-out. There are bullet holes all over the place, over there. And over there. And over there. They were all dead when I got here. A few days dead, if you know what I mean. It was awful. I still haven't gotten rid of the smell. That's one reason I keep this fire burning."

There was a smell. It reminded Marty of dead rats, a smell his brain immediately recognized.

"And you came here...?" Marty invited.

"Looking for refuge, of course."

"Marty!" Mike snapped.

Marty looked up and saw Mike staring out the big window to the left. Outside was the man with the rifle. He saw them see him and raised the gun toward the window. Mike and Marty dove to the floor.

Emely stayed put.

The man fired. The window rattled and pocked but did not give.

"It's bulletproof," Emely said. "I have no idea how thick, but very. Like I said, Samuel made this a safe house."

The man fired again as Marty lifted his head and watched. He got up. Mike preferred the floor, just in case. More bullets rattled off the window like BBs.

"If he's bothering you, I can close the blinds," she said.

"No, no," Marty said.

"You sure?"

"I'd rather keep an eye on him."

Emely waved her gun around.

"The framing is rebar. All the outside walls are reinforced with plate steel. So's the roof."

The man fired again. More BBs scattered everywhere outside.

"All the glass is bulletproof. All the doors are solid oak. Very heavy."

"Samuel was careful," Marty said.

"He had enemies," she shrugged.

Mike finally made his way back to the sofa.

"You sure you don't want a drink, dear? You look a little jumpy," she said. "We haven't been introduced."

Mike watched as the man in camouflage finally gave up and wandered off.

"I'm Dr. Mike Andrusek," he said. "I'm a micro-neurologist."

He got up and approached her. Emely held out her empty hand. He took it and shook it.

"A brain scientist?" Emely said. "My, this should be interesting, no, Marty?"

"Dr. Andrusek is close to a breakthrough to fight this plague," Marty said. "We need to get some sick people to test. For that, we need a judge's order."

"And for that," she said, caressing her locket, "you need me?"

"Exactly," Marty said. "You told me your client, Veronica Van Zandt, had judges."

"She did."

"And I know you would have goods on them. That's how you protect your clients."

"I do."

"All we need is the goods on one of them. Just one," Marty said.

"And I get?"

"Name it. I'll see what we can do," Marty said.

She lifted a drink from a small round table beside her chair. She took a sip.

"Sure I can't get you anything?"

"It's morning," Marty said.

"I'm not going anywhere today," she said.

She sipped again. She crossed her legs at the thighs and leaned forward.

"I could use fifty-thousand dollars."

"Fifty? We're a little short right now. We gave our last sixteen dollars to your old neighbor to get your address," Marty said.

"And my last two beers."

"I don't need cash. A bank transfer will do. But I need it soon. Samuel is running out of food, and I have to get out of here."

"For fifty thousand, we could bribe our own judge," Marty said.

"Maybe. But bribery can be tricky to negotiate. And it never lasts. Blackmail is forever."

"You're asking for too much. Impossible."

"I," she said as if she was singing it. "Need fifty-thousand American dollars. You need me."

"Come on, Emely, there must be something else you want," Marty said.

"Oh, please. You could find it somewhere if you had to. And you have to. Call it a loan. I'll pay you back," she offered. "You know I'm good for it. I'm just in a liquidation bind. I transferred all my money offshore while I still had the chance. Now I want to transfer myself offshore, but the going rate for safe transport to Venezuela is fifty thousand dollars. And these guys want it in advance. I can't touch my money until I get home. Catch twenty-two, if you follow me."

They heard more rapid rifle fire coming from another side of the house.

"He's looking for a soft spot," Mike said.

"He won't find one," she said.

"There's no Achilles' heel to this place?"

"Not while there's a fire burning."

More gunfire rattled somewhere behind them.

"Didn't Venezuela declare war on the United States?" Mike asked.

"They did. So sad. Mi patria," she said.

"Didn't they promise to shoot down American planes entering their airspace?" Mike followed up.

"Not this one," she said.

"Look, we don't have fifty thousand," Marty said. "And even if we did, I wouldn't give it to you."

"Don't you trust me?"

"No."

He was smiling teasingly. She nodded. Point Marty.

"Bottom line. I need to get out of here now, Lieutenant. I cannot wait. You want what I have? You can have it all. But the asking price is the cost of getting me home."

The man in camouflage had appeared out back again. He was carrying a box now.

"What's he up to now?" Mike asked.

The man set the box down next to the window. He kneeled over it. And then he ran.

"It's a bomb!" Marty yelled.

He and Mike both flew over the back of the sofa, which toppled over on them as they dove.

The box exploded in a yellow fireball, followed by shattering and roaring of crumbling rock. The window burst inward. The massive stone chimney blew toward them. The fireball filled half the room, followed by a wall of smoke. Smoke and dust came from nowhere along with a rain of plexiglass shards, football-sized chimney rocks and other debris.

For Marty, the roar of the explosion and the cacophony of collapsing walls quickly gave way to silence, except for a high-pitched keening that cut through his consciousness. In a moment, he found he was on the floor and the sofa was on top of him.

Mike was not next to him.

Things continued to break and fall all over the room. The cloud of smoke and dust was too thick to see much. Marty coughed until he thought he would stop breathing, but finally caught some breath. His leg was hurt. But for the moment, he was alive. The avalanche had ended. He pulled himself out from beneath the sofa and the air was clearing just enough. The sofa was pushed up against an interior wall, ten feet away from where it and he had been seconds ago. He looked around. He saw Mike. He had been pushed or thrown all the way against the wall too, on the other side of the couch. Marty got up and ran to him. His leg was okay enough to run.

Mike, too, was coughing. He was still alive.

"You okay?" Marty asked, reaching out to him.

"Yeah, I think so." He got to his knees, and then to his feet. He tested his legs, feet, hands, arms, shoulders, waist, neck.

The room was half collapsed. Both windows shattered. The fireplace collapsed inward. The cloud was thinning; there no longer was any lake-side wall. The roof held, but much of the ceiling had fallen in. Chimney rock debris, pieces of plexiglass, pieces of wood, ceiling tile and metal plates were broken and bent, piled and scattered across the floor.

Some of it was on fire.

Where was Emely?

The two headed back to the middle of the room, where most of the debris had piled. Hanging out from a pile of chimney rock was a woman's arm, blinged with silver bracelets, and red with blood.

Marty tossed aside rocks, and Mike joined him. They dug her out, most of her. Her other arm was missing. Her head was smashed, her abdomen crushed. She was long gone.

Marty rolled her over as best he could. Her silver pendant fell with its broken chain. He reached down and snatched it.

"Poor, dear, Emely," Marty said.

Mike ran to the back and found his gun laying against the back wall.

He looked toward where the back wall had been, waiting for the man with the camouflage clothing to reappear. He did not.

Mike went through the opening to look for him.

"Mike, don't!" Marty called.

"It's okay, I got this."

There was a crater in the yard. Mike stepped around it, following his gun toward where the man had run.

Mike saw him.

The camouflage man had not gotten away in time. His body was balled up against the security wall to the left. Mike checked him. His neck clearly was broken. His back, too. His legs were wrapped around his shoulders and the clothing was gone from his back, baring oily, burned skin. The man's face was smashed.

The man's rifle looked okay though, laying nearby. Mike grabbed it and slung it over his shoulder.

When Mike stepped back into the great room, Marty was sitting on a rock next to Emely's body.

In his left hand, he dangled Emely's locket—open.

In his right hand, he held something up to his eyes.

"What's that?" Mike asked.

Marty turned toward Mike and grinned.

"A teeny little thumb drive."

CHAPTER 21

DAY 193: MONDAY, OCTOBER 21

The white, unmarked prisoner transport van pulled up in front of the office at the county jail shortly before four p.m.

The large white man with red hair, dressed in an Orlando Police Department uniform, drove. He carried a badge identifying him as Sergeant Trevor McKee but that name was not his. In the shotgun seat sat a tall, thin black man in a dark blue suit. He carried a U.S. Marshal Service badge identifying him as Rick Reese, but that was not his name, either. Any check of records would find that McKee was dead and Reese was white and missing, but that would be pointless. In the back sat Orlando Police Lt. Det. Marty Francisco in more casual clothes. His badge had his correct name.

Marty and Mike had handpicked five prisoners from about forty who were warrior gene candidates. The jail was more than happy to dump a few of its charges on anyone asking, and if the federal government wanted a few, the federal government could have them, too, with Orange County's blessing. So, after reviewing the order signed, perfectly willingly by U.S. District Judge Horace Crimley after only glancing at the identifications that Marty, Bubba, and Guy presented, the Orange County sheriff's deputies brought the prisoners out one by one and secured them in the van.

First was Daicey Rivera, age thirty-six, a short, heavyset woman who had just been incarcerated two days earlier for killing her own three children. Police caught her after she crashed her car into a light pole but failed to kill or even seriously injure herself in the collision. They jailed her on three counts of first-degree murder.

Tea Baker, twenty-two, a black college student, lean and mousy, was brought down by Taser after wandering into a mostly vacant student neighborhood, hoping to kill people with a knife. Finding no available and willing victims except the sheriff's deputy, she wounded him in the arm. They held her on a charge of assault with a deadly weapon.

Ira Levison, fifty-four, a white man who normally sported expensive clothes, perfect salt-and-pepper hair and a taut body sculpted by long, daily rides on an expensive bicycle, had imagined himself as a real-life chainsaw murderer. He attacked a food truck line with a three-horsepower Husqvarna, but could hurt no one with it as the crowd scattered. A National Guardsman shot him in the shoulder while he pathetically tried to chase people down wielding a twelve-pound power tool. They held him on attempted assault with a deadly weapon.

Chahna Patel, twenty-nine, an India-American woman engineer who worked at an airline's maintenance shop at Orlando International Airport, burned down a row of apartments and shot six people as they escaped the flames. They charged her with three counts of first-degree murder and many other crimes.

And last, biggest, and most problematic getting into the van was Antoine Lee, thirty-four, a black warehouse foreman who was an amateur body builder and ultimate fighter. He entered a squatter's camp and beat three people to death before someone clobbered him in the back of the head with a piece of wood and called the police, who gang beat him, and then hauled him away. He faced three counts of second-degree murder.

Subjects entered the van like chained, angry bears, screaming, kicking, wrestling and head-butting. Once in and restrained, they turned the van into a rolling, rocking, raucous scream-fest of rage spitting, bitching, and threats.

Thank God, Marty thought as he got in with them, carrying Emely's magnum in one hand and a Taser in the other, that these guys never cooperated to kill as teams. The more likely danger now would be that they tried to kill each other.

The drive was uneventful, but Marty doubted they would have such luck getting these five into the house and securely restrained. They had only three people to pull it off, as opposed to the half-dozen jail deputies who had handed them over. First out was the big guy, Antoine Lee. Last in, first out. He sat closest to the door. Guy pulled it open, and Bubba and Marty waited.

"Now whatcha gonna do, assholes?" Lee asked. "I'm going to break your—aww ow! Shit!"

Marty shot him with a Taser. After Lee shuddered, jerked and jerked again, he seemed to overcome it. He looked more annoyed than anything. So Bubba shot him too, and the second charge worked. The big man's bald head snapped backward. He convulsed.

Marty and Bubba worked quickly. They unlocked him from the car restraints and grabbed his shoulders while he seized. Guy slammed the van door and hobbled ahead. Marty and Bubba were having real trouble dragging him through the lawn and up the steps. Guy figured that on another day, the neighbors would have watched in scandalized wonder.

After breaking into the place the day before to scout, Marty had left the door unlocked. Guy pushed it open, entered and found a light switch.

That moment was when he heard the scream from behind him.

It was an unfamiliar voice and yet a familiar sound, and Guy's heart clanged like a cymbal.

Guy had left his crutches at home today because he had reached the point where he could hobble without. He still was not too swift on his feet. He turned around. He saw a man coming at him with a butcher knife. As Guy turned, his bad leg failed, and he collapsed.

The man ran, preparing to strike straight into Guy's chest. When Guy went straight down, the man stumbled himself and went down over Guy, who rolled his legs, tossing the attacker into a glass coffee table, which shattered under him.

The man sprang to his feet before Guy could get up. His face and left arm were bloodied, yet he still clutched the knife. He was a short, young, white man, balding and mustachioed. Wire-rim glasses, also broken, dangled sideways off his bony nose.

"Y-y-you are one of them," he stammered quietly, with a high, whiney voice.

"Maaa-arty!" Guy screamed.

The attacker turned toward the door just as Bubba's butt and back lurched through, dragging the top half of the big man. Guy rolled, scooted and got behind a couch.

"Bubba! Look out!" he screamed.

Bubba still was not in far enough to see the little man with the knife, who was torn between what was now a lost but easy victim in Guy, or the man known as Bubba, who was huge, but seemed to have his hands full at the moment.

Bubba got in far enough to see around the door just as the little man came at him. Bubba had his arms through the armpits of the big man, who still was convulsing, making him difficult to hold. Bubba dropped him with a thud. He swung around as the man was on him, slashing. He threw the attacker away, but took a slice across his forearm.

Marty finally dropped the big man's feet and ran across his chest into the living room, pulling his gun.

The little man ran at him screaming, "I'll k-kill you t-too!"

Marty threw a sidekick and his boot heel contacted the little man's knife hand, knocking away the knife. Then Marty continued around, following through with a punch that knocked the man flat.

"Geez," Marty said as he came around to prepare for a counterattack. "It's Father Biddle."

Behind him, Lee was coming to.

"Bubba! The prisoner!" Marty shouted.

Bubba was sitting on the floor holding his arm.

"Ow!" he said.

Marty scrambled over to get Lee, but the prisoner was already rolling over, getting to his knees. His hands were cuffed and his ankles were chained, but those restraints would matter little to the mixed-martial artist, who came up with his head into Marty's chest, butting him away, back into the house.

Father Biddle was getting up now, too. Guy scrambled over, grabbed him, and pulled him to the ground, laying on him.

Lee was on his feet now and came charging in like a bull. His head was not quite clear enough to recognize the full circumstances, and the chains denied his footing. He went down face first, rolled, kicked, and bucked.

"What did you do to me?" Lee screamed.

Marty was on him and stood unsteadily, preparing to drag Lee by the handcuffs. Lee bucked him off and spun on the floor.

Lee screamed.

So did Father Biddle.

Bubba managed a kick at Lee (though he missed any serious target, glancing off the big man's shoulder). Lee sprang at him, knocking Bubba into a chair, knocking it over. Marty got up again and fired his Taser. The shock went through Lee and right into Bubba, who screamed, spasmed, and collapsed.

Recognizing the real danger was Lee, not the priest, Guy released the bespectacled fellow and leaped onto Lee's back. Lee rolled and quickly pinned Guy. Marty grabbed Lee's legs.

The priest was up now and had found his knife. He ran at them. Marty let go of Lee's legs to stop Biddle from stabbing Lee, but Lee reacted first, swinging his chained legs around and knocking the priest down again.

Marty grabbed Lee's legs solidly and pulled. The man bucked, yet Marty had a firm grip this time and dragged him off Guy and Bubba and through the living room. He kept going, into the hallway. Marty kicked open the door of the first bedroom and wrenched the prisoner through the doorway. He swiftly clipped another pair of cuffs from the man's leg irons to the bed frame.

He emerged back into the living room to find Guy holding down the priest and Bubba up now, trying to tend to his wound, which did not look serious.

"You guys are worthless, geez, crap!" Marty shouted.

"Hey, I'm wounded here! And you zapped me!"

"You almost got us killed!"

"Marty, settle down," Guy said.

"And you!" Marty shouted at the priest. He gave him a square kick in the ribs. Marty then reached to pick him up, but Guy pulled him away.

"That's enough!" Guy shouted.

"Let him go, damn it," Marty said, cocking his gun.

"G-go to hell!" Biddle said. "I'll get you y-y-yet!"

He spit blood at him but missed by several feet.

"Why you…" Marty aimed his gun.

"Marty! I said that's enough!"

"You stay out of this Guy! You should have heard this hypocrite's eulogy! I could kill you just for that!"

Marty held his aim at the priest.

"Marty! Stop! Stop it!"

"Sh-Shoot me!" Biddle demanded. "You'll get yours! You all will! Ju-Just like that g-g-g-g-girl. Just like h-h-her friend will!"

Marty's gun arm stiffened.

"Marty! No!" Guy yelled and slipped in front of the priest.

"Get out of the way, Guy. So help me!"

In the other room, Lee let out a roar, and they heard him dragging the bed around. Marty raised the gun and thought for a moment.

"Bubba, are you all right?" Guy asked. "Can you hold this one down while I run out to the van?"

Bubba nodded and then climbed on top of the priest. Guy left for the van. When he returned, Lee was still howling, Biddle was laughing maniacally, and Marty was still holding his gun, pissed off, hoping he could shoot someone.

Guy pulled a syringe out of the bag. "That tranquilizer the doc gave us. We should give it to the others before we drag them in here."

He and Marty went into the bedroom. While Marty held down Lee, who was screaming and frothing, Guy gave him a double dose in the ass. A minute later, the struggle was over.

"Why the hell didn't you think of that before?" Marty asked.

"That's one," Guy replied, ignoring the indignation in Marty's voice. "Let's go get the others."

Again, Marty stood his ground for a moment. Finally, after Guy had left the room, Marty turned and followed. A small dose made the priest docile, and Guy tended Bubba's wound while Marty carried Biddle to another room and strapped him down.

By the time Mike, Dr. Crosby and Kanetha arrived with B.J. and the old man, Guy, Marty and Bubba had all the other prisoners sedated and secured in rooms.

With the two Mike had brought, they had eight, meaning every bedroom was taken.

Marty still was hot.

"I gotta go," he said. He stormed off.

Mike got up to go after him, but Guy grabbed his arm. "Don't. Let him calm down," he said. "Marty's always had a bit of an anger management issue. He'll walk it off."

"I'm going to my truck for supplies," Mike said.

Guy nodded.

Kanetha tended more to Bubba's wound, and then they all settled in quietly, pondering, but not talking much.

Mike returned with Stranger and a box.

Out of a box, he lifted a liter-sized soda bottle with a clear liquid.

"What's that?" Guy asked.

"Water," Mike replied. "Contaminated with Crosby's concoction of water-borne K38M, the antidote."

Mike poured the water into eight paper cups.

"Meds time for the patients," he announced.

CHAPTER 22

DAY 203: THURSDAY, OCTOBER 31

Over the next few days, taking care of the eight patients was an almost continuous chore. Mike and Kanetha stayed in the house full time while Marty, Guy, and Bubba came and went. Dr. Crosby hardly came around at all, but his indifference was okay with Mike because he knew now that his colleague would not cheat them out of any time. Dr. Crosby was obsessively working on the new virus strain back in the lab, while Mike had set up his own lab in the bed-and-breakfast.

The old man from the expressway on-ramp was the next to emerge. Quickly, two more, Daicey Rivera and Ira Levison, emerged, providing evidence for Mike's hope that regular oral doses would be powerfully effective.

They kept those three patients locked in their rooms.

The boy, B.J., became something of a trustee in this little lab-jail-vacation-home. He joined Kanetha on her rounds, helping administer doses, and spent time in the sitting room with her, sometimes sitting with her on a sofa. The vacation home had an extensive library of books and board games, and there was always something to occupy them. B.J. curled into Kanetha like a kitten.

B.J. also took to Mike's dog, and Stranger liked him too. When Kanetha was too busy, B.J. spent his time with Stranger.

He was a tall, thin, quiet, morose boy. He understood his mother and sister, and his whole relevant world, were gone. The only comfort he could find now was this motherly black woman he had met only a few days earlier. So he clung to her. B.J. had family in Missouri, aunts, uncles and cousins, assuming they were still alive. He did not know how to contact them. He had a favorite teacher and a pastor somewhere. He did not know how to find them, either. So for now his family was Kanetha, and maybe the odd group of conspirators who came and went.

He was eleven years old. Mike had originally figured him as older.

That evening, Guy and Marty dropped over with pizzas from a place that Marty knew about where such things still could be bought. It was the first time Kanetha had gotten pizza in months. B.J. too. He ravished a half a pie all by himself and then helped Kanetha pass out a few slices and dosed water to the other prisoners.

Daicey cried constantly. She was at it when Kanetha and B.J. entered her room with food. The old man from the freeway, his name turned out to be Ogden, said very little. Ira was full of indignant questions that no one would answer because, it appeared, even in his emerged state, he was a jerk.

The other prisoners were doped up and marginally responsive. When they came to, they would scream for a while, eat, drink, and scream some more. Mike would visit and give another dose of sedative and the screaming would stop.

When Kanetha and B.J. entered Antoine Lee's room, the big man was emerging.

"Where the hell am I?" he asked.

"You're in a medical lab. You're an involuntary subject in a medical research experiment," Kanetha said, reciting Mike's pat answer.

"I'm a what? Come again!? Bullshit! You can't hold me like this!"

"Oh yes, we can! We have a court order, signed by a federal judge. If you'd like to see it, I'll get it for you later."

Antoine looked around with small, probing eyes, suggesting curious intelligence. He was remarkably calm. Kanetha felt her shoulders and back ease with relief. A man this big and strong was hard to deal with, even when he was chained to a bed. Whenever he screamed and thrashed about, she was scared. She imagined that if anyone could break free and kill them all, it was him.

"Why?" he asked.

"You got the murder plague. The doctors here are trying to cure you."

"Seriously?"

"Feel like killing anyone now?"

Antoine did not answer. He looked around some more.

"This don't look like no lab."

"What? You'd rather be in a hospital bed in some cold-ass clinic somewhere?"

"Who's he?"

"He's a patient too. Only he's cured. So he's helping. You want some pizza or not?"

"Come here, kid," Antoine said.

B.J. looked at Kanetha. She nodded, and he inched a little closer to the bed.

"You're about the age my son was. He's dead now," Antoine said. "You kill anybody?"

B.J. blushed with shame. B.J.'s look broke Kanetha's heart (and, she suspected, Antoine's, but he did not say so). She knew no one had told him exactly what happened to his mother and sister. But he was a smart kid.

"You?" B.J. finally responded.

"I. I can't remember anything. Did I? No. Don't tell me. I don't want to know."

"Come on, B.J. We've got more dinner to deliver. Eat your pizza. Drink your water. You need to stay hydrated."

She took B.J.'s hand and led him away.

Out in the main sitting room, Mike had an announcement.

"It's time," he declared. "All the patients are coming out. It's time to expand our research to a few hundred thousand subjects."

"I disagree," Dr. Crosby said. "We need more time to observe them. We have no idea if this effect will last. We have no idea if there are adverse effects yet. What if they relapse? What if there are adverse effects? What if they start getting sick? What if they die off?"

"What if we get killed while we're waiting for them to get better? Time's something we don't have," Mike said. "Time is what the CDC and the other institutes are playing with. It'll be months. No. It's time now."

"What are you going to do with all the patients we have now?" Kanetha asked.

"We need to keep them here to observe them. They'll be our first warning signs of any future problems," Mike said. "With luck, if there are any bad long-term reactions, we can address them here first, then citywide."

"And then?" Kanetha asked.

"And then what?" Mike asked.

"At some point, you have to let them go," Kanetha said.

"They go back to jail," Marty said.

"No. They don't even know what they did."

"I'm sorry, Kanetha. They're all prisoners. But none of them have been convicted yet. If they have an insanity defense, a medical condition, they can make that plea at their trials."

"Bullshit," Kanetha said. "There aren't any trials anymore. They'll die in jail."

"What do you propose?" Mike asked.

"Let them go."

"They killed people," Marty said. "Or tried to."

"No. They did not," Kanetha snapped. "The disease killed people. This asshole's plague killed people. They're like Mae-Lu. They're victims too."

Kanetha still had not forgiven Dr. Crosby, and she still lashed at him every chance she got. He sat in a chair across from her and ignored the indignation. Again.

"We'll worry about that some other time," Mike said. "For now, they stay."

Mike was sitting on a sofa. Kanetha was beside him, and B.J. was beside her.

"When do you want to do this?" Guy asked. He had a chair in the corner, apart from the others.

"Tomorrow night," Mike said. "Every day we wait, we risk this thing coming apart."

"There's a lot I've got to do first. I can't just run a hose into the water supply. It doesn't work like that. It's got to be a timed release. We've got to use the clear wells. I've got to disable the chlorine supply. I've got to flush the systems. I've got to ..."

"You'll figure it out," Marty snapped. "You always do."

"You know the main plant doesn't serve everyone around here," Guy said.

"It'll serve enough," Mike said. "And it'll spread."

"So, you're just going to let this loose," Dr. Crosby said. "What if you kill hundreds? What if you kill thousands?"

"You mean like you?" Kanetha said.

"That's out of line," Dr. Crosby said, finally defending himself.

"It doesn't matter. All that matters is it stops as soon as possible," Guy said. "You know my wife, Pam, was not even supposed to be at the mall the day she died. She went there because a friend did not have time to buy a present for another friend. She did not even know this other woman. She asked Pam if she could stop there and grab something. Pam just did it.

"And when she died, when that dude opened fire, her body was on top of two little kids. She was trying to protect them. With her own body, only the bullets went right through. Those kids. Pam. All those people. They died. They're dying while everyone sticks their fingers in their ears and says, 'Oh, but nothing can be done.'

"I don't even blame that dude anymore. I agree with Kanetha. His flesh held the gun. But he did not control his flesh. The virus pulled the trigger."

Guy had brought his crutches. He realized the day they delivered the prisoners, it had been a mistake to abandon them. He could handle the physical without them. But he could not handle the emotional. The crutches were Pam's oars. They were Pam. The day he left them at home, he realized that, so now he kept them close. He practically hugged them.

"I know she speaks to me. You guys'll think I'm crazy. But she does. What she wants. What they all would want," Guy said and then paused, checking everyone's faces. "Is for it to stop. We can do that. Mike, Dr. Crosby, we've seen this stuff work. We gotta do whatever we can. I know what my Pam would say. 'Too many have died already. Too many. Too many. Jesus, Lord, help us, help us, Lord, do whatever we can.'"

Guy choked up and stopped. A sigh turned into a sob he could not stop. No one moved. He picked up the oars, stood up and then hobbled away, down the corridor, vanishing around a corner into the reading room, which was his room.

"What's the matter?" B.J. asked.

"He'll never get over losing her," Marty said. "Whenever he feels stressed, he goes off to be with her for a bit. He'll be all right."

"We've all lost people," Dr. Crosby said. "He'll get over it."

"Who? Who have you lost?" replied Marty, suddenly angry. "Co-workers? Friends? Your fucking house maid? You have no idea."

"I'm just saying," Dr. Crosby said.

"I lost my son," Marty said. "You don't get over it. You get past it, maybe, but you don't get over it."

"Don't make it sound like I'm not hurt by all of this, too."

"Guy's whole life was Pam. I only hope you never, ever find out what that is like. I lost Eddie, but for me, it's different. I…"

"You what?" Kanetha asked softly.

"I never made him my life. Not like Guy did. And now that's my hell. That's my hell. Knowing that I never gave him what Guy gave Pam."

"I'm just saying," Dr. Crosby said.

"To hell with you!" Marty yelled. He kicked over the small end table beside Tim's chair. Marty's face looked like a raging bull. Crosby shuddered but sat still.

"Marty, settle down!" Mike said. He stood to block the detective from doing any more damage. Marty stopped.

"Go to hell," Marty said. "You all can go screw yourselves."

Then he followed Guy down the hall and disappeared.

That exit left Dr. Crosby, Mike, Kanetha and the boy.

"Are you really going to do this?" Dr. Crosby asked.

"We, Tim. Yes, we are," Mike said. "Are you ready?"

"I've got enough L38 cultured, but I'm not convinced. I really would like another week to run more tests."

Angry shouts between Guy and Marty echoed down the hall, interrupting him. "You just don't get it Guy! You never will!" Marty shouted.

Then he stormed back through the sitting room and out of the house again. They heard his car fire up and his wheels squeal.

"What was all that about?" Kanetha asked.

"We all should melt down. But none of us has seen as much shit as Marty," Mike said. "That's why we've got to do this now. Enough sitting around in lab coats with our thumbs up our asses. Gotta do it."

Silence fell on the room. Suddenly, Mike felt his own doubt and fear creep in.

Crosby could be right. Huge, awful consequences could arise from this rash rush.

He reached out and squeezed Kanetha's hand, because he knew she was feeling pain too. It surprised her. It was the first time he had touched her with such caring. She squeezed it back and her face and body melted a little.

The boy noticed.

"So I didn't know you two were a thing," B.J. said.

Dr. Crosby's head raised in surprise at the child's observation.

"We're not," Kanetha said. "We're only human."

Yet she and Mike were still holding hands.

Dr. Crosby took the hint and stood.

"So, we're going to need to have the truck ready to go tomorrow night," Dr. Crosby said.

"It'll be there," Kanetha replied. "Clean enough to haul milk."

Dr. Crosby nodded and left.

"Time for you to go to bed, kid," Mike said.

"But it's early. And I'm not tired."

"Go to bed."

In the past six months Kanetha had given few thoughts to her own needs and comforts, except for late at night, alone in her apartment, when she would drift away into a cloud of remorse for all that was lost and going away. At times like that, she sometimes indulged in a little self-pity, mixing thoughts of macro and micro horrors with more personal concerns that otherwise struck her as trivial.

She usually succumbed to the slide for a few minutes and then fought her way back out to a hardened reality. Mae-Lu was first, but she certainly was not the last loss in Kanetha's heart. They had mostly vanished. During the first few months, Kanetha would get calls and texts. At least one cousin and several friends all had been killed fairly early in the plague. Others, her aunts and Margaret and Danielle, had disappeared too, though Danielle at least had told her she intended to go home to Tennessee. Now her father was gone. Thinking about them, thinking about the images she saw every day on TV, or around town, hardened Kanetha. If her burden was to go down as a rock while the world drowned, it was a small price. Kanetha Wilson doubted that there was anything in any of this caper for herself, so she had abandoned that aspiration. Just walked away. Pity her not or fuck you for trying.

So much death. So much terror. So much pain. Families wiped out. Friends vanished. Horror, grief and fear everywhere. From the beginning, Kanetha was an outsider to it all, choosing, because she had to, an alternate world view and response, of feeling sympathy for the perpetrators of violence. From that start, her course through the pandemic of terror had set her in defiant isolation, not because of fear of the plague but because of her own personal rejection of the greater public reaction. Even when society finally caught up with her, she still felt like a hardened outsider. She still felt it was Kanetha against the world. Never mind, Mike and the others who had joined her early and in united purpose. Kanetha kept her rebellious mindset, seeking her own way. Others be damned.

Mike and the others had decided to poison the city's water supply with a virus strain that could, should it work, create a counterattack on the pandemic. But whether that wave happened or whether it went unexpectedly badly, was Mike missing the point?

There were reasons germ warfare was on par with nuclear warfare. Scientific and pharmaceutical research protocols were horrendously involved and painstaking for good reason. Kanetha knew she had little information on those rules and should not guess at those reasons. She was not a scientist, but they seemed to her intuitive, obvious. Don't mess with this stuff. Don't subject people unwittingly to biological agents that could make them sick or kill them—or change them in ways neither they nor anyone else could grasp in advance—or change their unborn babies. It was as wrong as any human decision Kanetha could grasp.

Her thoughts went to B.J., an innocent, a victim in so many ways. She saw him as a little boy on the cusp of adolescence, still lacking in the education and understanding but beginning to explore reasoned thinking. His thoughts had to rely on the idealism and hopefulness of children, up against the adult-like need to figure out what was going on. Yet he was still, as children are, under the power and mercy of adults who may or may not know any more than he about what they were doing. Was that blind, totalitarian power where the true tragedy lay? Were we all cast to fates controlled by people capable of missing or disregarding universal human good to drive our own unmoored good intentions? Was she alone in doubting whatever means to the hopeful ends?

At the worst of times, at the quietest moments, like this one, Kanetha felt small, just a single woman split off from the world. She felt so alone, lonely.

And then Mike reaches over and takes her hand on the couch and it felt like her father enveloping her in a hug that held her safe from her mother so many years ago.

But who was this man? Kanetha had concluded the only loves in Mike's life were himself and his dog. His self-confidence bordered on egomania and his humor had a mean edge. He was a man used to pleasing and amusing only himself, and who counted on no one else to please or amuse him. But it also released him from all the social and professional restrictions that had held back so many other men Kanetha had known. It amazed her at how much he could compensate for his lack of camaraderie with a singular, focused purpose.

And yet, as she thought about it now while they sat there in silence, she wondered why he had taken her hand, and why she had responded with an internal meltdown of all her hard edges.

It was a forbidden thought, because she never expected those edges to be met by anything but disappointment or death.

Still, he had a way of reaching out with genuine compassion, backed by commitment, once he saw someone was worthy. He had done that for her in the institute's lobby, and since. Mike had kept his distance, and she hers for these months that they had worked together because they shared that ability to be singularly focused. But she saw now that he also had been doing what she had been doing, staying just close enough. This response was not professional, this was activity watching over each another. This trial was for the two of them.

As B.J. made his way up the stairs to his room, Kanetha felt, as she had told him, human. At last.

She gave Mike's hand a squeeze and then released it.

* * *

Somewhere in the night, Kanetha's shadow of doubt, fear and loneliness lifted. She had never talked about it, let no one else see it in her eyes. But it had kept Kanetha Wilson's self out of the way of Kanetha Wilson's earthly presence. Awake, she thought more of Mike and hoped—the way someone who has none does—they would have a future together. An end would come to all of this madness. They would re-emerge. On the other side there might be a new life, and it would include them together. It gave her something new to drive herself toward. The prospect of something better on the other side. For the first time since she had received that message in Africa, she felt herself seeing something ahead for herself, a new dream. She was going to accept falling in love with this man and pursue that path. When they got through all of this craziness. The rest, suddenly, was just the horrible journey. At last, she slept.

She dreamed of her childhood.

Her father was there, and her mother was there too, along with her cousins and uncles and aunts. It was Thanksgiving or some similar family get-together. Her father and her two uncles were frying turkeys on the back porch, drinking beer and watching football on a small TV. Her mother and Kanetha's aunts were in the crowded kitchen making food. Her mother was out of place in this setting in her dream. Kanetha sensed she was too old to coexist with her living mother. That realization entered her dream with wonder. But her mother looked good, well, and happy. That relief brought Kanetha great joy. She and Kanetha's aunts had their glasses of wine and were drinking, yapping, and laughing. Kanetha wandered and found her cousins Marla and Chris on the front porch, smoking cigarettes and listening to music while keeping their eyes on her younger cousins and some neighbor kids out front. The younger kids were chasing each other with squirt guns in the front yards. A car drove by slowly, with a sub-woofer pounding, and with young men staring menacingly out open windows, checking out the scene. In the shotgun seat was Leonard Fuller, and he literally had a shotgun in his lap. He nodded to Kanetha as the car crept by and continued down the street. She sat down beside her cousin Marla and took her cigarette. She sucked the smoke in deep, full of all its life-shortening chemicals and life-affirming choices to be bad. Then as she coughed until she choked, Marla and Chris laughed at Kanetha, two years younger than either of them, until they fell off the stairs.

CHAPTER 23

DAY 204: FRIDAY, NOVEMBER 1

Marty was having a tough day. A full moon appeared this morning, and he had always associated full moons with loony crime. He had seen enough to know it was true, thank you very much. And boy was the moon hard at work today.

Marty was supposed to meet with Guy and the others at the vacation rental home at seven p.m., but that prospect was looking unlikely as he motored toward a call: shooter in downtown Orlando. It was his fourth call of the day, though he never got to the third.

This time, Marty was not the first to the scene. A high-rise condo was on fire. Fire trucks stopped three blocks away, waiting, because a sniper was shooting a rifle from a shorter tower, a bank across the street. He had hit at least four people who, presumably, had run from the front of the condo building. They lay in the street. Sirens, sirens, sirens, all types of sirens wailed through downtown.

The condo was thirty-six stories of glass and balconies overlooking Orlando's signature downtown green space, Lake Eola Park. The living units began on the second floor and a bunch of them, randomly, on the lower few floors were on fire. Flames played out where glass walls used to be. A few puddles of fire flickered among the bushes, sidewalk and streets running past the building. Marty did not know how fire-secure the tower might be, but he figured that if the fire department waited long enough, fire would engulf it.

Marty knew the routine. Most of the fire department would not proceed forward until the police cleared the shooting scene. And that hesitation meant that as long as the guy was atop the bank, the building would burn. They were gathering in big red traffic jams a few blocks away to the south and north.

This incident was a big one, even by current standards. The police set up a command center on a side street a block away. While Marty was getting briefed there, not much was stopping the sniper. Cops and some fire department specialists were in the condo, leading whatever residents they could out the back, into the condo's parking garage, rather than into the street. A SWAT team was in the bank, currently stymied because he had set still more fires in that unoccupied building, in the stairwells. He had somehow disabled the elevators. Helicopters were circling, gunmen in them, awaiting instructions. The police were setting up their own sniper positions in the condo's higher units. They, too, were not yet ready for action.

The killer, who had quickly scared off all his easy targets, must have packed plenty of ammo. He was taking more desperate shots, shooting randomly through the condo windows facing the garage, hoping to hit someone he could not even see. He had more than one hundred units to harass with high-powered rifle rounds.

The commander wanted Marty to lead a team to the corner of the park, across from the parking garage, and set up a perimeter there. That assignment was like telling him, "Stay out of the way. We'll let you know if we need you."

Commander Cody and Marty had a history. Ten years earlier they had worked together, and the moment Cody got promoted to run homicide, he had tried to transfer Marty out of the bureau. Marty figured he was a potential rival, to be sent to Siberia. Marty fought and won. Cody punished him every chance he got ever since. Cody, the mindless climber, was promoted again and again and now commanded all special operations. At least he was away from homicide. But in cases like this one, he commanded, while Marty got commanded.

Cody was tall, thin and nasally, with a self-styled Vulcan-like conversational style, full of himself, dismissive of others, a superficially cool temperament that simply waited for his charges to agree with him.

"Damn it, Steve, you know I'm more useful here, or over there," Marty said, pointing up the street to the frontline units hidden behind armored vehicles on the side street across from the garage.

"I need someone I can trust keeping the park clear," Cody said. "We may be staging from there."

"This won't last long enough," Marty said. "You'll—"

They both turned toward the sound of a Ffffffffffffffffffooooosh! They watched a flaming rocket arc from the bank roof, cross the street and then crash through another condo window. It exploded inside, blowing out colorful sparks and flames.

It was a flaming arrow. The sniper had some fancy fireworks.

A moment later, a second Ffffffffffffffffffooooosh! Sounded but this missile arced toward the police frontline unit down the block. It crossed above the barricade of armored trucks. Cops behind it ran for their lives. When it hit and exploded, several officers rolled.

Marty checked his watch. It was getting late.

"I'll take the park, Steve, thanks," he said.

•   •   •

Kanetha stole a truck from her former employer.

Borrowed it, actually. Either way, it was no longer being used by the dairy, which was running at only about twenty-five percent capacity. At any rate, the dairy was almost only producing powdered milk.

The company she had worked for had wisely, and now conveniently, cross-trained its human resource workers so that they had a keen idea of the jobs they were filling and monitoring.

She knew where the disinfected trucks were. Though she never actually got to drive one, she had watched, and she knew how to operate them. She had a good enough idea about how to drive one that she could take one unnoticed. She intended to return it.

She and Bubba filled it from his apartment building's fire hose and then headed for the medical institute so that Dr. Crosby could contaminate the water with a huge batch of cultured virus.

• • •

Marty set up his ops among the courtyard tables beside a little outdoor café in the park, just across the parking lot from the bank building. The trees and the sheer angle of drop from the bank gave them cover. Still, they had a pretty good view of the scene in the street and the park behind them.

The park was five blocks long and four blocks deep, mostly covered by a lake. A huge, intricate, green fiberglass-enclosed fountain made the lake iconic, occupying a spot slightly offset from the center, to the far side from Marty's post. The park featured an amphitheater, a Japanese garden, picnic areas, a playground and a mile-long jogging path around the lake. Office and condo towers lined the perimeter streets. The park was central to almost every civic celebration. The fountain was the city's symbol. As far as Marty knew, it was the only fountain in town still operating. The city fathers did not have the heart to shut it off, so it ran its show of timed, choreographed blasts of shimmering water continuously. At night, the water danced under a multi-colored light show.

The park was secure. Not that anyone was out and about today anyway, but no one was in the park except cops. No one was getting in, had there been anyone thinking about coming to the park. Marty had one officer with him, a young patrolman, big and strong, eager but scared, named John Padilla. Marty's job was done for now, except to watch the scene and await developments.

The shooter had launched a couple more rockets into the condo building. Cody had the SWAT team in place in the stairwell, ready to rush the rooftop. First, the helicopters would attack. A police helicopter buzzed over the bank and a police sniper got off a couple of shots. The man on the roof shot back, pointlessly. But the second time the chopper came by, with a second chopper waiting to the east, the man was ready with a rocket. Marty could not see the man, but he saw the rocket zoom toward the helicopter. The pilot swerved and the blade wash blew it off course. During that maneuver, the man popped off some rifle shots and got a direct hit. The helicopter rotated and smoke appeared. The pilot put it into a dive, heading away from the bank. Marty could not see, but presumed the pilot was putting down safely.

Marty watched the second chopper circle the building as the pilot mulled things over. It pulled back farther, a block or more away, and hovered in the distance. Marty figured the SWAT unit was next. Suddenly, the man appeared on the edge of the roof, facing Marty. He stepped back out of view, and then the leading point of a huge, yellow kite emerge over the roof edge.

Not exactly a kite; more of a hang-glider.

The man appeared again, under it, and jumped. The glider lofted then turned toward the park. The shooter did not look very good at this exploit. Rather than go anywhere out of reach, the glider was headed straight and downward at a steep enough angle that it veered unavoidably toward the middle of the lake.

"Let's go!" Marty shouted at the officer with him.

Marty led him straight to the water's edge, where there was a boat dock filled mostly with swan-shaped paddle boats for tourists. They also found a couple of small, powered dinghies and a party boat. Marty glanced, realized they required keys, and he did not have any time to find them. Rather than figure out how to jumpstart a boat, he climbed into a swan. Padilla stopped for a moment of disbelief, but then cast off the rope and joined him.

Marty had picked this officer well. He was in great shape and provided plenty of leg strength to paddle this monster swan.

The shooter splashed down into the lake's dead-center, about fifty yards from the fountain. He emerged from the kite wearing a life jacket. Marty realized for the first time his black clothing was not some sort of Ninja outfit, but a wetsuit, now covered with an orange lifejacket and a black backpack. He swam toward the fountain.

Marty and the officer peddled their swan as fast as they could.

"This guy's not sick," Marty said.

"Lieutenant? Padilla responded.

"This guy's thought through everything, even an elaborate escape," Marty said. "This took weeks of planning and preparation. These sick killers don't do that. They usually don't last for two hours. They just go out and kill, helter-skelter."

The officers paddled. The shooter swam.

"This guy's a damn copycat," Marty said. "By God, we got ourselves a genuine mass murderer."

"Aren't they all?"

"Nah. They're sick. People who just shoot or set things on fire or crash cars into crowds because they're enraged, they don't think about hang-gliders and, and, wetsuits, and life preservers, and shit. Hell, they don't think about escape. This guy did. He's real. Smart. And he ain't done. See his backpack?"

Padilla peddled in silence. The killer swam. The second police helicopter arrived and hovered above the lake, awaiting orders. Sirens screamed. Police cars moved into place along the park shore. No one was dressed for a swim, so it looked as if Marty and Padilla were the first line of offense, at least until Cody came up with a better idea. That prospect could take all day.

The chase proceeded in what appeared to be in slow motion. Padilla and Marty peddled the swan smoothly across the lake. The man swam. The sun shone.

Except for those damn sirens, and the fires and smoke and shooting, and the fire victims lying around behind them, this setting could be a pleasant day in the park.

"Got any family?" Marty asked.

"Wife and two kids, three and two," Padilla said.

"Are they safe?"

"Hope so. They went back home to Maria's family in Puerto Rico. They live in San Sebastian. It's just a small town, and there's not much trouble there. I haven't heard from them in a while, though."

"Good for you," Marty said. "Are you from Puerto Rico?"

"Born in Kissimmee. I got family there too, though."

"Me too."

It was becoming clear that the shooter would reach the fountain before they reached him. The swan was scooting along, but it had four times as much lake to cross.

They peddled. The shooter swam.

•   •   •

Guy Phillips and Mike Andrusek were having a very busy day, too.

The water plant was heavily secured by National Guard troops who manned the gate and walked the fence line. No one got in without high clearance. Guy, who drove despite his bad leg because his car had the sticker, convinced the captain that the scientist was there on a critical public health research mission. True. Guy got him through.

One thing they could not get through, though, and did not bother trying: weapons. The plant was a strict no-weapons zone. Even though Guy worked there and came and went regularly, a munitions-sniffing dog thoroughly swept his car before they could pass.

Inside the operations center Guy checked in at the plant manager's office, where assistant plant manager, Herb Cartier, now ran things, even though he had never gotten the official promotion.

A round, white man in his late forties with no hair, a long, shaggy mustache, and a fondness for bluesy country music, Herb maintained a salty demeanor that kept most of the workers just scared enough to keep doing their jobs. He was not crazy about the idea of a scientist making an unannounced, semi-official visit to the plant, but he and Guy had worked together for a lot of years. He instinctively deferred to whatever Guy wanted. He would just as soon let the plant run itself and do nothing if he had the chance. Herb was going home for the weekend in a few minutes anyway, so he was happy to dismiss this visit as not-his-problem.

Herb had ZZ Top playing in his office—not the eighties crap, but Tres Hombres, from back when they still were one of the hottest Texas blues bands around.

"Great album," Mike said.

"Got that right," Herb said.

Instantly, Herb was good with Mike.

When they left the office, in the eyes of everyone else in the control center, they had Herb's blessing for whatever the hell they were doing. Guy gathered two of the technicians and set them to work. They had to manually shut down the chlorinators, he told them. He did not explain why. The techs were fine with not knowing why. They entered the disinfection facility and wrenched valves closed. They had to bypass the disinfection wells, which took more valve openings and closings. The ozonation tanks and wells also needed to be bypassed, switching the flow. More manual labor. Nothing to think about. Mike took samples from lines and tanks here and there, a completely pointless exercise he performed entirely for show.

The only person Guy feared was his assistant, deputy engineer Darcy McKnight, a young woman with a Purdue engineering degree, an overly developed professional ambition, and a nose for everyone else's business. If they crossed paths, she would want to know exactly what they were doing and exactly why—because she would want to be a part of it—her two cents, anyway. Unfortunately, she was smart enough and experienced enough at this plant that she would see through any story Guy offered except flat-out truth. And she would never go for that strategy.

Darcy had been running engineering mostly since Guy got shot, though he had been coming in all this week, if for no other reason than to reassert himself. He had to wrestle back control from her, even though she had been in charge for just a couple of weeks. She might not come in today. He had told her to take the rest of the week off, but that option was not likely. When Darcy was around, she mostly stayed in the control center. If she was here, lurking, anytime now she would see the flows had been redirected, and the chlorinators shut down. She had come running to find out what was up. Guy had warned Mike.

Sure enough, as they left the ozone wells, Guy saw Darcy striding their way. Guy stood still on his crutches, waiting for her frontal attack. She wore a blue dress suit that would be way-overdressed for any ordinary engineer at any municipal plant.

"Darcy!"

"What the hell's going on, Guy?"

"Darcy McKnight, this is Dr. Michael Andrusek, a scientist from the Nona institute, who's taking samples looking for the virus. Mike, this is my deputy."

"Why the hell are you shutting down and bypassing the disinfectants? You know that's insane. It's dangerous."

"Ma'am," Mike said. "We're running an experiment on the effectiveness of the systems on the virus."

"You're what?"

"We need to collect samples of water supply with and without the disinfectants to see if there is any water-borne virus."

"That's insane," Darcy said. "Who authorized this?"

Guy knew they were in trouble. If he said Herb, she would storm his office and find out he did not know what they were doing. If he said the orders had come from downtown, she had to go make the call.

Mike saw the look on Guy's face. Loss. Near panic. He had not known Guy long, but he could tell he was not very good at lying. Mike knew he had to take over this matter. Now.

"Can we go somewhere private and secure to talk?" Mike said. "I don't want to alarm anyone. And this is on a need-to-know basis."

Darcy studied his eyes, which looked frighteningly serious. She turned to Guy's, which looked stumped.

"There's a small office in the depot there," Guy said, pointing to the building closest to them. Let's go in there."

Guy excused the technicians, then led the way on his crutches. Mike followed a couple of steps behind them, steeling himself for what was next.

•   •   •

The condo shooter climbed out of the lake onto the fountain. Immediately, he stepped through cascades, turning into a shimmering phantom somewhere behind the falling water. He stepped his way around until he disappeared on the other side.

Marty had taken two calls from Cody, who wanted Padilla and him to stand down. Cody wanted to handle this episode with the helicopters and snipers who were already taking new positions. Marty did not trust Cody. The idiot could not even find someone to turn off the fountain. This scenario called for just-do-it. So Marty ignored him. He and Padilla pushed the swan onward. They reached the fountain a couple of minutes after the shooter. Padilla got a handhold on the fountain. Marty climbed from the Swan's neck onto the ledge. He then pulled Padilla up. They stepped through the water. The young officer went clockwise; Marty, counterclockwise. When Marty saw the shooter on the other side, he was standing without a weapon, both hands in his backpack straps, as if he were contemplating his next move. The man was white, in his mid-sixties, with a full, salt and pepper beard and streaking, soaked gray hair. He looked as if he once were a substantial man. His back, shoulders and chest still were formidable, but he also had a belly stretching an extra-large red lifejacket. He saw Marty and turned with a start.

"Get away!" he screamed at Marty.

"I'm comin' in," Marty said. Marty had his gun out. This meeting was, at the moment, clearly one-sided.

"I've got a bomb in here," the shooter screamed.

One-sided, all right.

The man had a desperate, terrified look on his face, like a cornered, angry dog. No, he was not sick. But he might be suicidal.

"Why are you doing this? Just tell me why," Marty demanded.

"You know why!"

"Bullshit. You're not infected," Marty said, his voice dripping with judgment. "People with the plague don't plan these things out like you do. They don't bring hang-gliders and lifejackets. Hell, they don't even try very hard to escape."

"I'm infected, I tell you!"

"Bullshit. You're just a stupid, evil killer."

"You want me to pull this ripcord?"

That is the instant when Marty saw the man had a yellow nylon cord coming out of the backpack, wrapped around his right hand.

"No. No. Don't do that. But I don't think you want to do it either. Tell me why."

"They killed everyone!"

"Who? Those people you shot in the street? Those people in the apartment building?"

"My daughter. My granddaughter. My grandson. He was just a baby. Amy's husband. Sally, my wife. They killed them all."

"So you want to go out like this?"

Padilla had made his way up behind the man. Marty signaled with just a glance and Padilla stopped, about ten feet back.

Water cascaded down, sprayed up, and misted all around them, blurring the rest of the world.

"What's your name?" Marty said.

"Why?"

"So I can tell the families of those poor people in the street who their bastard is. That's what you want, isn't it? I'm Police Lt. Francisco. You can call me Marty."

The man looked around as if he were contemplating jumping.

"What's the matter? You didn't think through your next step after hang-gliding into the lake and swimming to the fountain?" Marty asked. "You didn't think we'd come after you?"

"I was supposed to land closer to the shore."

"So you screwed up. What's your name? What'll it hurt now to tell me?"

"Paul. Paul Davis."

"Why don't you let go of that cord and unstrap that backpack, Paul? You know, they took people from all of us. But we're still here. Take off the backpack and we'll talk about it."

"You'll kill me!"

"If I was going to do that, you'd already be dead. I had a clear shot at you from the swan. I should have shot you when I first came around the corner here. But I didn't. I'm taking you in, Paul. But we can talk on the way."

"You ever kill anybody, Marty? Huh? Huh?" Paul asked, almost spitting out the words. "Because I just killed a bunch."

"Four. But who's counting?"

"What?"

"They tell me four dead."

"Four?"

"For all your planning, you really suck at all this, Paul. I've seen people with the plague kill more than you did with just a damn box cutter. You come armed with rockets and a high-powered rifle and who knows what-all, and you manage four? Then you crash your escape into the middle of the lake?"

"You want me to pull this ripcord? Just keep at it, Lieutenant."

"Yeah, I've killed people. Just a few days ago, I killed a guy. He deserved it, though. Those people in the street, they didn't."

"I swear I'll pull this cord if you don't shut up."

Marty eased a step closer.

"Oh, shit, go ahead. I'm betting it works about as well as your other plans. Nothing happens, then the officer behind you and I can take you down with no more hassle. Go ahead. Pull it. I'll wait."

Paul looked around. One thing was obvious to Marty. He did not want to pull that ripcord. Marty thought he might jump. If he did, Padilla would be on him. Paul must have reached the same conclusion, because he turned to Marty. He was indeed cornered.

"You want me to pull it?"

"No, no, no. I changed my mind. Look, Paul, we've figured this thing out. We can stop this plague. We can stop the killing. But I need you to stop first. You're just getting in the way of the solution. Stop now, and we can stop the rest."

"You're lying."

"I swear. I know some scientists that have developed an antivirus. They're preparing to release it. It'll stop the plague."

"It's too late."

"It's never too late. You're alive. I'm alive. Officer Padilla behind you there is still alive. His wife and kids are still alive. Most of those people you shot at are still alive. We can make this a good world again, Paul."

"It's too late. Everybody I love is dead."

"Is that why you did it? Revenge? Justice? To piss at God? Because it did nothing, Paul. Nothing! But stopping this plague, that'll do something."

"I just needed to fight back."

"And now your fight is over. And we're going to win this war against the bastards. Don't you want to see that happen? Don't you want to be alive to see that happen? Let go of the cord, Paul."

He did. He dramatically opened his left fist and moved it outward. The cord tightened just enough to unwind from his palm until the end slipped over his hand, swung back and dangled. Paul looked back at Marty with eyes of a scared child needing a hug. He removed his left shoulder strap from his shoulder.

That movement brought the bullet. Marty would never know who shot it, but it was a damn good shot. It knocked Paul down onto the fountain's walk. Paul was not dead, though. He rolled over and Marty saw his left hand groping for something.

"Dive, Padilla!" Marty yelled.

Marty dove. Just as he hit the lake's surface, the thunder of the bomb followed. Marty felt the percussion shove him over and downward. Underwater, he tumbled and slammed further through the lake, toward the bottom, which was suddenly illuminated by the bright blast of fire unfolding above. The concussion, together with the cold, cold water, also blew all the air out of Marty's lungs. He needed to come up immediately. He needed to find the surface. He just was not sure which way was up.

Finally, with a struggle and a gulp of water that left him hacking, then gulping more water, he splashed through to air. The lake surface roiled. The last of debris just splashing down. Marty coughed and hacked and choked until finally he could gasp air and his eyes cleared. Half the fountain was gone, but the waterworks continued, spraying undirected into the darkening dusk. Almost nothing was on fire, but smoke clouded the area.

Marty looked for Padilla, but saw no one else splashing around.

"John! John!" he yelled at the sky, as white-capped waves, curious on Lake Eola, rolled over him.

Marty spotted the officer, who floated face down in the water. He swam over and turned him by the shoulder. That arm was missing. So were both legs, making the torso and head easy to flip. The other arm was shredded. So was his face. These remains were only part of what just seconds ago was Officer John Padilla, Orlando's finest, and a devoted husband and father.

Marty splashed the water with his fist. That bastard Cody ordered the shot, showing no faith in Marty. Now everything was fucked.

"Damn you, Cody!" he screamed with his full lungs. And then he coughed and hacked against the water in his lungs.

• • •

Darcy, Guy, and Mike entered a small equipment tool storehouse full of cutting benches, drill presses, stacks of pipe and crates. The place was vacant. Halfway back, a small manager's office had been walled off, looking for all the world like a half-finished room of unpainted sheetrock, with a door. Guy fumbled with a big ring of keys and opened the lock and switched on a bright, overhead, florescent light.

The small, windowless room was a riot of hanging clipboards and pinned up water plant schematics. A cheap metal desk and two visitors' chairs crowded a tight floor.

"Sit down, Miss McKnight. I want to take a look at you," Mike said.

"Excuse me?" she replied.

"Out there, I thought I saw... In your retinas. I didn't want to alarm the technicians. I didn't want to alarm you."

"What about my retinas?"

"It's okay, Miss McKnight. I'm a doctor. A neurologist, actually. Please, sit down a moment."

She sat.

Mike gently lifted her right eyelid.

"Look up."

She did.

"What?"

He examined her left eye. Guy stood back and watched.

"Miss McKnight," Mike said. "Please be calm. You might have the plague."

She pushed his arm away from her and stood.

"I do not! What's going on here? What are you two up to?"

"Miss McKnight! Sit!" Mike ordered.

She sat again.

Mike had a fanny pack, and from it he withdrew a syringe and a vial.

"What are you doing? Oh, no, you're not!"

"Miss McKnight. You might have the plague. The CDC is testing a newly developed treatment, and I have some. You can fight with us here and get angry and maybe become homicidal, or you can sit there and let me give you this and see if you survive. It's your only hope."

She looked at Mike. She darted her eyes to Guy. Back to Mike.

"I think I can see it too," Guy said. "Her eyes have red rims."

"Uh huh," Mike said. "First telltale symptom. That and her apparent paranoia."

Mike filled the syringe from the vial.

"I am not paranoid! You are up to something!" Darcy said.

"Sit still, miss. If you don't have the plague, this serum will do you no harm. You might have a few minor side effects, but they'll pass. If you do have the plague, this may well be your only hope."

"What sort of side effects?"

Mike wiped a spot on her shoulder.

"Drowsiness, a bit of confusion, mild loss of coordination, need for extra sleep," Mike said. He injected her shoulder. "You shouldn't drive tonight. Don't operate any heavy machinery for the next couple of days. Don't take on any complex tasks, even if you're feeling better.

"Oh, and you might feel some powerful sexual urges. Be careful with that."

Darcy batted her eyes. She smiled. She closed her eyes and curled a bit. And then she slept.

"What was that?" Guy asked.

"A powerful sedative. You said she might be a problem. I came prepared."

Guy checked his watch. It was almost seven. Marty was supposed to join them a half-hour earlier, but never showed and never called. Guy had tried to call Marty, but there was no answer. He was not worried. Marty was often called away. On the whole, he was pretty unreliable, unless his duty called. Then there was nothing anyone could do. Guy and Mike went forward without him, because they had to, and because Guy knew Marty was resourceful enough to catch up with them as soon as he could.

•   •   •

Marty was furious, sore, wet, and cold. By the time they fished him out of the lake, he was ready to kill Cody, but he had more important matters first. His gun was at the bottom of the lake. His cell phone, car key fob and watch were destroyed. He headed on foot straight for the vacation rental, which was in a trendy old neighborhood of brick streets only a couple of blocks away.

Paul was right. The bastards win. They always win. A block from the park, Marty passed a Toyota parked on the street, still in unmolested condition. That luck was about to change. Marty's eyes rolled back and for a moment, he was lost in anger at everything and everyone. The anger swelled. He could think of nothing but lashing out, smashing, crashing, bashing. Marty wriggled a loose brick from the street and pounded it on the car's hood. He heaved it at the windshield, which shattered into spiderweb cracks but did not give. The brick rolled onto the street, and Marty picked it up. Now his walk was a mission, the brick clutched as his only tool, his only weapon.

The vacation rental home was locked. Marty smashed the lock with the brick, over and over, and then shouldered the door. He had secured this door and he damn-well could unsecure it. He smashed the lock a couple more times and crashed the door with his shoulder again. It gave, popping inward.

Several of the kitchen cabinets had heavy-duty hardware and locks on them. Those cupboards were where Andrusek stored his drugs and supplies. In most of them. One cabinet was where Marty stored guns and ammunition. This cabinet needed a key, and the lake did nothing to damage the small piece of cut steel. Marty opened the cabinet and withdrew two guns and ammunition. He loaded the guns. He cocked the revolver, aimed and fired at the wall. It blasted a hole, working just fine.

Marty all along had harbored reservations about this plan, and he had damn little faith in a new, untested, unknown antidote. He had not spoken opposition because he did not have a better plan. And he knew they would not listen. That damned Andrusek would not allow it, and Kanetha had lost her bearings. They were crazy. Dangerous. And they now were out of control.

Andrusek needed to be stopped. Anyone like him needed to be stopped. They were the bastards that had started this whole damn thing. They were the bastards. It was all their fault, when you think about it. Slicing and dicing the origins of life. They did that black magic for a living, for Christ's sake.

Marty knew the stopping had to begin here.

He went upstairs, where there were four bedrooms with captive patients. He kicked open the first door. The Episcopalian priest lay on the bed with one wrist and one ankle tethered to the bed frame with nylon rope. They had melted the knots into mangled plastic, thick, secure, and unbreakable.

"You!" Marty shouted at him. "You go to hell first!"

The priest looked at him in terror. He had apparently emerged from his plague rage.

"N-no! Please! I b-beg of you!"

He squirmed away screaming, but he could not get far. Marty shot him in the temple. The bullet passed all the way through the skull, exiting from the back of his head and splashing blood, bone, and brain on the pillow. His body heaved and then settled.

Downstairs, B.J. was in the bathroom when he heard Marty break the front door open and he sat there in total silence and fear. When he heard Marty go upstairs, B.J. stepped out, cautiously, hopefully.

Then he heard the screaming upstairs, stopped by a gunshot. At that moment, B.J. was standing outside the bedroom of Antoine Lee, who had emerged a couple days earlier, but who, unlike B.J., was still bound, because they needed him to stay against his wishes. B.J. had visited with Antoine a few times and had gotten to like him. He rushed in.

"Antoine! Someone broke in and he's upstairs shooting people!"

"Get me out of here, little guy!"

B.J. looked around. He did not know what to do. He heard a woman screaming upstairs, and then another gunshot. Two. And then silence.

Other prisoners upstairs screamed for help.

B.J. ran to the kitchen. The sharpest thing he could find was a steak knife. It would have to do. He got it into Antoine's free hand and the man began sawing powerfully at the rope attached to his right wrist.

"Run, little guy! Get out now!"

"No! We have to help the others," B.J. pleaded.

"It's too late for them. I'll try. You. Get outta here! Do you hear me? Run!"

But B.J. did not run.

They heard another gunshot upstairs, then quickly a follow-up shot. The knife sawed through the cord and Antoine turned to the one at his ankle.

Another shot boomed. And another.

The ankle rope snapped under the blade. Antoine sprang from the bed. B.J. ran into the hall. Antoine was right behind him. Marty appeared at the top of the stairs.

"Marty!" B.J. called out, confused, thinking for a moment the policeman was here to save them.

But Marty raised his gun toward B.J. Antoine leaped, tackling the little boy just as the shot zipped past. Marty fired again and hit a rolling Antoine in the butt. The prisoner popped to his feet, lifting B.J. with one arm around him as if he were a stuffed animal. Marty fired again as Antoine dove for the doorway, hitting the frame, splintering it. A moment later they were gone, running down the street in Antoine's best, hobbling sprint.

Marty did not care. He still had two more prisoners, and two escapees would make no difference. He stood on the stairs and reloaded.

•   •   •

Kanetha ground through the gears plenty, but she got the tanker truck to the water plant. Bubba rode beside her in the cab with Dr. Crosby in the shotgun seat. Behind them rode five-thousand gallons of water highly contaminated with Tim's latest batch. This truck and its shiny stainless-steel tank were clean of logos, though if anyone had bothered to check the DOT placard, they would have concluded it was full of milk. It was dark out though, and the National Guardsmen had little or no training in DOT shipping codes, nor were checking placards among their duties.

The trio were on the list, thanks to Guy. They stepped out; the guards wanded them; the dog searched the truck, and they could pass.

The trio were too nervous about setting off any alarms with the guards to worry about anything else. So none of them noticed that a white pickup truck, which looked exactly like Mike's, had pulled up in the drive and stopped about fifty yards behind them, waiting to be next. The truck would have looked familiar because it was, in fact, Mike's.

•   •   •

Behind the wheel was one Detective Lt. Martin Francisco of the Orlando Police Department.

He, too, was on the list and got a nod from the guard at the gate when he identified himself.

But when the guard motioned Marty to get out so that they could search the truck and he for firearms, Marty refused.

"I'm a police officer and I'm here on official business. I'm not surrendering my weapons," Marty said.

"I'm sorry, sir, but orders are orders. No weapons are allowed inside the plant. Please step out of your vehicle."

The guard stepped aside, and a second guardsman came up to join him. Marty looked around. He did not see a third. So he opened the driver's side door and then stepped to the ground. He spun, his gun in his hand, and shot them both.

And he screamed. "Goddamn you. Goddamn! Why didn't you just let me pass?" He kicked one body in the side. He climbed into the truck, dropped the transmission into first, stomped the brake, spun the rear tires, then bolted the vehicle into the chain-link fence gate. It gave just like Emely's gate, easier. With a pop, the gates pulled from their hinges and heaved downward. The truck ran over them.

· · ·

Mike and Guy heard all of this noise, of course, from about two hundred yards away, deep inside the plant, as they waited to greet Kanetha and direct her to the well. She pulled up and stopped, keeping the motor running. Mike climbed up on the running board. Dr. Crosby got out and Guy climbed in next to him to direct her.

"You okay?" Mike asked her.

"Yeah, why?"

"You didn't hear that?"

"Hear what?"

"Never mind."

"Where's Marty?"

"We haven't heard from him."

Mike climbed down. Kanetha put the truck back in gear with a grind and a groan, and the tanker moved on. Crosby and Mike walked out of the way, headed over to the pad by foot.

As soon as they cleared the roadway, a white pickup pulled across where they were standing and followed the truck. Mike and Guy watched it from the shadows, looked at each other, and then quickened their pace to a jog.

Kanetha parked beside some ten-foot-high pipe stacks coming out of the ground beside some huge reservoir tanks. The trio climbed out and Guy directed Bubba to a large fill hose that he and Kanetha dragged over to the tanker. Kanetha hooked it up to the truck and threw switches to dump the water through the hose.

"This is a clean reservoir. It'll mix gradually with the main stream coming through over the next few days," Guy said.

He then leaned his crutch-oars beside the truck and directed Bubba to a valve at the stack. He and Bubba reached to turn the valve wheel. A gunshot roared and echoed, and Bubba went down.

He had been hit in the side. He crashed face-first into the low concrete bunker wall around the stacks and fell silently in a smear of blood.

Marty emerged from a shadow behind the reservoir tank.

"Marty!" Kanetha called.

"Shut up, bitch," Marty answered.

He used the gun to wave Kanetha over beside Guy and Bubba, who had come-to, groaning. Blood soaked the side of his white Guns N' Roses concert shirt.

"Ow," Bubba moaned.

"Sit down! Both of you!"

They sat next to Bubba.

"Marty, listen to me," Guy said. "You'll be OK. You have the virus. You just need the antidote."

Marty turned the gun toward Guy.

"You! You should have died a long time ago," Marty said.

"Marty, no! You know we can fix you!" Guy said. "We can fix everything!"

"It's too late! Don't you get it? Pam is dead! Dead! Just like Eddie! You've got nothing now. You stupid fool. You're pathetic!"

"I know," Guy said. "But…"

"But nothing! I am so sick of everyone saying it's going to be okay! It's not! What a joke! You're so sad, Guy. I'm sick of it? Don't you get it? To hell with you!"

"Marty," Kanetha offered. "Marty, I know you're in there. Somewhere inside. Marty?"

"Where are the others? Marty demanded.

"What others?"

"Andrusek. And that other guy."

"They're not here," Kanetha said.

Marty moved in close and put the gun to her throat.

"Don't lie to me, bitch!"

Then Marty yelled. "Andrusek? Andrusek! Come out now or so help me. I will shoot this girl in the throat right now! Andrusek?"

Kanetha gasped as he dug the barrel into her throat.

"I'm here!" Mike called out.

Marty stepped back from Kanetha and looked around. Andrusek was stepping out from behind the truck, walking towards them with his hands up.

"I'm here, Marty. Don't shoot them."

"Get over here!" Marty commanded.

Mike came over slowly as Marty kept flipping the gun back and forth between Mike, Kanetha, Guy, and Bubba, who was curled on the ground. Marty motioned for Mike to sit, but he did not.

"Sit down!"

"Marty, if you'll just let me, I can make you feel better."

"Sit down! It's gone too far. You bastards started it. I'm going to end it! I'm just sick of this! I'm sick of ya'll pretending you can make a difference. You make me sick."

"Marty, I'm not going to sit."

"If you don't sit, I'm going to shoot Guy right now!"

Marty stepped toward Guy and put the gun to his head. Guy heaved a deep, shaking breath.

"Marty, please," Guy said. "I don't mind dying. I believe Pam is waiting for me. It's the only thing I believe anymore. But let us turn this wheel first. Then kill us all if you have to."

"Shut up!" Marty ordered.

"Marty, what have you got to lose if we turn this wheel? Marty? Remember," Guy pleaded. "Remember who you are. What we're doing!"

"Guy!" Marty said. "You are such a stupid, pathetic fool. Don't you get it? It's over! You just won't let go. You never will let go. You are. You make me sick."

"Marty. I love you, man. This is our adventure."

"That's what I'm talking about, you stupid, pathetic fool. You just don't get it. Everything is over. Now!"

And then off in the distance someone yelled, "Heyyyyyyy!"

"Heyyyyyyy!"

Somewhere behind them and to the side, Darcy appeared, staggering toward them, waving. She walked three steps forward, wobbled a little, walked to her left a couple of steps, stopped, walked forward a couple more steps, staggered, stumbled to her right a couple of steps, and then continued forward.

"Heyyyyyyy!" she called out again.

Marty had no time for this nonsense. He aimed his gun at Darcy and fired. He missed.

She stood still, put her hands on her hips and looked indignant.

"Are you shooting at meeeee?" she said.

Marty fired again. She was a good thirty yards away, and he missed again.

"What? Whyyyyyy?" she demanded. She held her arms out, down, her palms up, open. "I didn't do nothin' to you!"

Marty aimed again, this time carefully.

And then an oar came out of nowhere and slammed into the side of Marty's head.

Dr. Crosby stood behind him, holding Pam's oar, which came in flat. The end of the way-too-long bolt that held rubber onto the bottom of the blade slammed and jammed into Marty's temple. The policeman fell to his knees with the modified oar bolted to his skull. His fall wrenched the handle from Dr. Crosby's hands. Marty went down on his face, then turned as the oar clattered to the ground, wrenched free sideways from his brain. Dr. Crosby stood still with his hands shaking in front of him, as if he could not believe what he had just done and needed a moment to process it.

Guy and Kanetha both leaped up. Kanetha grabbed Marty's gun. Guy grabbed his wrist.

"He's not dead!" Dr. Crosby screamed. "Tell me he's not dead!"

Guy gave him a half nod.

"I didn't mean to. I. I just wanted to hit him. I just wanted to stop him. I. I didn't know that was sticking out of the board."

Dr. Crosby went down on his knees. "Oh, God."

Darcy, standing in the distance, raised her arms and called out again. No one had bothered to answer her question.

"Heyyyyyyy!"

And then she stumbled on her impractical heel and hit the ground.

CHAPTER 24

DAY 205: SATURDAY, NOVEMBER 2

They dropped Bubba and Darcy at a hospital. Dr. Crosby headed for his home. Back at the vacation rental home, they found the six bodies. Marty died; his body came back in the bed of Mike's truck.

They agreed to bury him tonight, in the same cemetery with Mae Lou. They needed to remember Marty as he was before he got sick, Kanetha insisted. That was not Marty, she insisted. Guy nodded. Otherwise, he said almost nothing.

They were not sure what to do with the other six bodies, but they supposed they should bury them too, as best they could. Or they could just call them in. The county would landfill them.

In a week, if all went as expected, the murder plague should drop off in Orlando, Mike predicted. He and Crosby would announce to the world, through the CDC and scientific channels, what they had done. They would face immediate and long-term repercussions. Outrage. Shock. Maybe arrests. But as the new virus spread and the murder rate continued to plummet in Orlando—as they could only hope with some confidence—the efficacy of their virus variant would be undeniable. Ultimately, it would be backed and adopted, first by any other maverick authorities, then nationally, then internationally.

Nothing to do now but wait and see.

For now, they rested. It was all but over. Mike was absolutely sure of it. He and Kanetha leaned against each other on the couch for a long, quiet moment.

Kanetha did not know what to feel. A sense of horror at what they just unleashed on the world? A sense of victory that they may have beaten back the murder plague? Accomplishment for avenging Mae-Lu and restoring her good name? Anger at what the disease did to Marty? Sadness? Fear of what lay in store for them? Worry for Guy and Bubba? Guy, if he were here, would tell her to reach for amusement. Marty would too.

Amusement.

Kanetha reached out and put an air mic in Mike's face.

"Dr. Andrusek, you may just have saved humanity. What are you going to do next?"

He looked at her with eyes that seemed to travel through the same elixir of emotions she just swam. The smile came to him slowly.

"I'm going to Disney World!" he replied. Then he took the air mic from her and turned to her. "Kanetha Wilson, you may have just saved your friend's reputation. What are you going to do next?"

Kanetha smiled the happiest smile she had felt in about six months. "I'm going to dance in the goddamn street at Disney World."

He kissed her. She felt the whole swirl of emotions warm and settle within her, stilling, as if on command.

Antoine and B.J. stepped through the broken door. The big man was leaning on the boy for support. Once B.J. saw Kanetha, he slipped away from Antoine and ran to her. She took him into her arms. They both sobbed laughs. Stranger came in behind them and leaned against Mike's legs, hoping for a good back scratching.

Antoine, with his bloody ass, hobbled over and took a chair, sitting awkwardly.

"I got no place to go," he said.

"Welcome home," Mike said. "We could use your help tonight."

• • •

An exhausted Crosby saw lights on in his house as he pulled into his driveway. That situation troubled him because it was so late, and Nadine and the girls never were up anywhere close to this hour. The garage door went up. He drove in. It came down. He exited his Lexus and entered the house through the laundry room. The kitchen light was on.

As he turned the corner, he saw Nadine's arm on the tile, stretched out around the cooking island. His heart hammered so hard he felt it in his head. He almost collapsed.

"Nadine?"

He raced around the corner to see his wife lying in a pool of blood. She wore her blue and white striped top and off-white shorts and they were soaked red. Blood matted her dark hair.

"Oh, God!"

He lifted and turned her. She was clearly dead.

"Oh, God!" he cried. He sat in her blood and tried to cradle her in his arms. It was a heavy load. His arms waved like they were blowing in the wind. "Oh, God! Oh God, oh God!"

Then he recalled the girls.

"Kelli! Cindi!" he screamed, crying. "Kelli? Cindi?" He rocked with his wife's body laying across his lap. "Kelli? Cindi?"

There was no answer.

He gently lifted his wife's body off his lap, laid her carefully on the granite tile, got up and ran into the living room.

His older daughter sprawled across the bottom stairs. Blood soaked the carpet there and below.

"Argh!" he cried in anguish. He rolled Kelli over, but her wounds were more than he could bear. He felt all his own muscles going limp. He fell to his knees and his insides heaved. He vomited bile onto the stairs. And then he forced himself up from his older daughter's body.

"Oh my God! Oh my God! Oh my God!"

He left her.

"Cindi? Cindi?"

He rushed up the stairs to her room. He pounded on the door.

"Cindi?"

"Daddy?" a terrified voice responded.

He pushed open the door. She huddled in the far corner of the room, holding his revolver, pointed at the door. She looked as if she was unharmed, but terrified beyond words. She managed a smile when she saw him and tipped the gun toward the floor.

"Cindi!" he declared. "Cindi, thank God you're safe. Oh, God! Oh God! Oh God!"

She was crying hysterically.

"Daddy?"

"It's okay, baby. It's over. Oh, God!"

Dr. Crosby watched his daughter's face lighten for just a moment, and then tighten into a cringe. He saw the gun barrel rise.

Lastly, he saw the muzzle flash.

THE END

ABOUT THE AUTHOR

Scott Michael Powers is an author of thrillers inspired and directed by aspects of science fiction or other speculative fictions. His published works include the UFO-hunt novel *The Roswell Swatch* and the short stories *The Brazilian Millionaire's Butler* and *The Thirteenth Floor*. Powers was born in Ohio and grew up all over the country, eventually in Texas. After studying both journalism and creative writing at Ohio University, he pursued a journalism career for decades while keeping his ink wet for his creative writing. He and his wife Connie Powers now live in Orlando, Florida. He roams the region in study of The Florida Man, seeking ways to include him in stories.

NOTE FROM SCOTT MICHAEL POWERS

Word-of-mouth is crucial for any author to succeed. If you enjoyed *The Murder Plague*, please leave a review online—anywhere you are able. Even if it's just a sentence or two. It would make all the difference and would be very much appreciated.

Thanks!
Scott Michael Powers